FLYING HOME

a novel

by

R. D. KARDON

Flying Home
First Edition
Copyright © 2022 R. D. Kardon
All rights reserved. Printed in the United States of America.
For information, address Acorn Publishing, LLC,
3943 Irvine Blvd. Ste. 218, Irvine, CA 92602.

This story is a work of fiction. References to real people, events, establishments, organizations, or locales are intended only to provide a sense of authenticity and are used fictitiously. All other characters, and all incidents and dialogue, are drawn from the author's imagination and are not to be construed as real.

Cover design by Damonza.com

Interior formatted by Debra Cranfield Kennedy

ISBN—Hardcover 979-8-88528-045-7
ISBN—Paperback 979-8-88528-044-0
Library of Congress Control Number: 2022922148

To the 2,977

Also by R. D. Kardon

Flygirl

Angel Flight

To laugh often and much;

*To win the respect of intelligent people
    and the affection of children;*

*To earn the approbation of honest critics
    and endure the betrayal of false friends;*

To appreciate beauty;

To find the best in others;

To give of one's self;

*. . . To know even one life has breathed easier
    because you have lived—*

This is to have succeeded.

—Ralph Waldo Emerson

July 12, 2001
Denver, Colorado

THICK CURLS OF SMOKE snaked around the cockpit. Tris squinted at the navigation instruments, her hands and feet engaged in constant coordinated movement as the heavy jet slowed for landing. The autopilot was inoperable. An engine fire raged out of control. Unconscious in the right seat, her co-pilot offered no support. Only the most rudimentary instruments remained to guide her. At least the gear was down. The best thing she had going for her were those three wheels.

The airplane rested, hard, on the pavement, its nose wheel plumb with the runway centerline. Tris stood on the brakes to force the aircraft to a quick stop, careful not to engage reverse thrust on the burning engine. The airplane's aural warning system bleated "FIRE, FIRE, FIRE," over the sound of crash trucks racing closer with sirens blaring.

The signature sounds of an aircraft emergency. How well she knew them.

Tris keyed the mike. "Legacy One, requesting immediate medical assistance for my unconscious crew mate." She glanced over at her co-pilot, slumped in his seat, secured from flopping over on the controls by his safety harness.

Suddenly, the scene before her went dark, the noise stopped, and her co-pilot popped up. A long whistle came from the "God Seat," where the Legacy Airlines simulator evaluator sat in front of rows of buttons which caused the havoc she'd just managed.

"All right," he said, resetting the simulator for the next applicant. "That's all, Miss Miles."

Tris let her lips curl slightly. She eyed the two Legacy Airlines training captains assigned to evaluate her skills as part of the pilot interview process at the largest airline in the world. The one who'd played her incapacitated co-pilot to perfection stuck out his hand. He lowered his chin and nodded slightly, the universal sign of respect among pilots.

These were the moments that built a career.

The simulator evaluator thrust his hand toward her. "Well done, ma'am. Sorry about the multiple failures. It was just for fun, you know."

And a way to see what she could do, how much she could take.

"Is that the standard interview profile?" she asked, smiling. Multiple failures in the simulator were taboo—unless someone was trying to make a point.

He backed up slightly at the question, then recovered. "You were killing the standard profile, so I wanted to see what you had." He flashed a wide grin. "You've got skills."

Opening the door and pointing down the hall to an Exit sign, he said, "Out that way. HR will let you know. Nice meeting you."

Tris hurried down the hallway, its air ripe with the stink of desperation mixed with despair and a faint dash of hope—the unholy blend of sweat, anxiety, and prayers from fifteen applicants, each vying for a coveted pilot position at Legacy Airlines. The holy grail of flying jobs was at stake; the dream itself.

She was familiar with the scents, sights, and sounds of pilot simulator interviews. The suspended white capsules reproduced flight scenarios that were all too real and could level the best fliers. The steady swish of hydraulic fluid kept those white airplane replicas moving in step with applicant inputs.

Most job seekers eyed them with terror. For Tris, the sixteenth applicant, it was yet another thirty minutes of simulator time, flying maneuvers she could master in her sleep, followed by the instructor piling on emergencies to see if she cried "uncle."

She didn't. She couldn't.

Not in a simulator. Not in an aircraft.

You fly like you train, and you train like you fly.

Tris strode toward the exit to make her escape. It had been a long day.

Eight hours ago, she'd aced the oral interview, mostly answering questions about her background, and the well-known "tell me about a time" behavioral questions that she herself used when hiring pilots. Her simulator evaluation was delayed because an overly nervous candidate threw up on one of the seats, which took the cruel machine out of service for over two hours.

Tris couldn't wait to get out, get home, get this whole ridiculous exercise over with. Anxiety over being out of the office on a personal mission propelled her past the framed photographs of airline glitterati from the bygone days that hung on the corridor walls.

She threw her weight into the heavy glass door's exit bar, stepped into the sun, and inhaled deeply. Something about the Colorado sky seemed bigger, less constrained, than any she'd ever seen. The air smelled of open space and wildness.

Or maybe the altitude was getting to her.

What am I even doing here?

Danny. This was for Danny. Tris flipped open her phone, and found that he'd already left four voice mails, undoubtedly excited to hear how her day went.

Since Emily had sued him for divorce, Danny was pulling everyone else in his life closer. Tris was his best friend. She met him while flying for a small commuter airline years ago. She'd ended up at Westin Charter Company, and he flew for Legacy. He'd begged her to apply, trying to entice her with the promise of more money, bigger airplanes, more exotic destinations. None of that was persuasive. His final plea—"at least we'll work for the same company again"—revealed his true motivation. So, she applied. Whether it was to make him happy or to get him to stop nagging, she couldn't say.

Tris didn't have the time to invest in trying to leave a job she loved. But she couldn't say no to Danny.

As the Chief Pilot of Westin—where she'd hired and trained nine pilots in the last year—she'd done dozens of candidate interviews. She'd helped owner Woodrow "Woody" Westin grow the business from a one-turboprop to a four-aircraft operation, the busiest charter company at Exeter International Airport. Tris bore responsibility for the careers of all ten Westin aviators, including herself. Her biggest point of pride: six of them were women. Every day, she led them by example, provided advice, let them see that the final authority over pilot scheduling, training, and advancement was someone who looked like them.

She looked around for the cab she'd called to take her back to the airport. A black Mercedes pulled up. A familiar woman exited the rear passenger side door wearing a full Legacy Airlines captain's uniform, with a scarf in airline colors tied around her neck. Her hat was perched over feathered shoulder-length salt-and-pepper hair.

Tris was sure she'd seen the woman somewhere before. At a conference? On the ramp? She was probably another Legacy training captain heading into work. But why would she arrive in a chauffeured luxury car?

The woman walked up to Tris.

"Captain Miles?" She stood eye-level with Tris.

"Yes. I'm Tris Miles."

"I'm Jenn Prince from Legacy Airlines. Sorry to ambush you like this, but I wanted to catch you before you flew home." She held out her hand. Tris grasped it, eyes wide.

Jennifer Prince. In person.

Jennifer Prince oversaw all flight operations at Legacy. A former Air Force fighter pilot and the first woman to publicly challenge discriminatory hiring practices at a major airline, Prince was renowned as one of the few women in aviation who didn't "go along to get along." She was also the first woman put entirely in charge of the 10,000 pilots at the world's largest airline, and every single one of its thousands of daily flights all over the globe.

"Captain Prince? How can I help you, ma'am?"

"You know who I am?"

Tris felt her cheeks redden. "Of course. Everyone knows."

"I saw you on our interview list and asked your simulator evaluator to call me as soon as you were done. Just got off the phone with him. You nailed the profile, and all the little extras he threw in. I chided him for that, by the way, but I understand you handled the multiple emergency scenario expertly. I didn't doubt it for a second. Congratulations, Tris. I'd like to officially invite you to join Legacy Airlines."

Airline job offers came from Human Resources, weeks after interviews. Exclusively.

"Captain Prince," she stammered, "I only finished five minutes ago. How . . .?" Tris had a million questions and wasn't sure which to ask first. This made no sense.

A beat passed. Then another. After one more, the most recognized, decorated female pilot in the world spoke, her voice steady, businesslike, but unmistakably insistent.

"You'll accept, of course. Let's go inside and personally schedule your new hire class date right now." Prince took Tris by the elbow and guided her back toward the training center, retracing the steps Tris had used to escape.

Ambushed and confused, Tris couldn't think of any way to extricate herself from this legendary woman's presence.

"Tris, the opportunity we can offer you here at Legacy is unique to say the least. It's taken years, decades in fact, but *I've* made it a place female aviators *want* to be. Join us, and I'll personally make sure you're considered for a training position."

There was no more coveted assignment at a major airline. Training pilots had the best schedules, and priority bidding for vacation. Not to mention higher pay and bonus opportunities. It was the aviation jackpot.

Prince led Tris to a paneled office, where they sat in rich brown cracked-leather chairs, with a fully appointed buffet behind them. Important people sat in this room.

"I see from your application that flying is your second career," Prince said. "You were a teacher. Then a flight instructor. Did you enjoy that work?"

"Of course. It's the best part of my job." Tris didn't hesitate. As Westin's Chief Pilot, some of her most rewarding moments were spent training and mentoring her team of aviators.

"How many pilots on your team?"

Tris tried not to blush. "Ten. But we'll be adding more next year."

Prince nodded slightly, her smile curt and her eyes sharp, as though she were giving orders to a subordinate. "Well, imagine impacting the careers of the *thousands* of pilots that come through this training center every year."

The hook hung suspended between the two women.

Tris settled on a response. "I'm flattered, Captain Prince. But I don't understand. Why are you doing this? Why me?"

"Because I know who *you* are."

PART I:
COUNTDOWN

September 6–8, 2001

One

ALONE IN THE MAIN conference room at Westin Charter headquarters, Tris's index finger glided absent-mindedly along the beveled edge of an oblong glass table. Her eyes moved between floor-to-ceiling windows and the mullion walls, most decorated with framed feature articles about Westin Charter, many sporting her photo.

The angel flight. The trip that made possible everything that followed—the growth of Westin Charter, her promotion to Chief Pilot, the meeting with Jennifer Prince.

Heroine Pilot Lands Plane During Gunfire.

The story had been picked up by national news. For days, her face was everywhere. She'd always believed that news was transient, that there truly was no more than fifteen minutes of fame. Yet, over a year later, people still stopped her on the street. "Are you that pilot?" they'd ask. Once, a shopper at the local Jewel store even paid for her groceries.

It wasn't the way she'd ever hoped to be noticed. Yet there she was, posing along with Woody in front of the aircraft, having microphones shoved in front of her as she received the key to the City of Exeter. In one candid shot, taken in Bangor, Maine, after the harrowing landing that started it all, she looked like a stereotypical pilot-gazing-wistfully-into-the-distance, chin up, contemplating the sky. Anyone who bothered to examine the photo closely would see the pain in her eyes. Tears always threatened when she remembered the moment that photo was snapped: the man she loved being removed from the cabin on a gurney, shot twice by their passenger, a terminally ill woman who then put a bullet in her own head.

Only one of the thin mullion walls featured something other than Tris. It sported a framed motivational quote that implored her to, "Go Confidently In the Direction of Your Dreams."

Which way is that, exactly?

The sentiment dragged Tris back to the thick binder in front of her. Its padded leather cover, embossed with "Patricia F. 'Tris' Miles, Chief Pilot" in gold letters across the front, compressed against her fingers' tight squeeze. Inside were clipped piles of papers, organized in order of consequence. The top stack was by far the most important, and the last one she wanted to deal with.

Westin's new offices at Exeter International provided a comfortable backdrop to avoid them. Their digs on the airport's private jet ramp were the envy of every operator on the field. The space's seven private offices curved around that private ramp. At the far end, Woody occupied one that seemed as large as their old airplane hangar.

In charge of flight operations at Westin, Tris enjoyed higher pay, a bigger staff, and larger, more plush surroundings than she'd ever worked in before.

Outside the glass conference room door moved a mesmerizing parade of colleagues—her charges, her people—each engaged in their own private reverie over schedules, weather, passenger manifests, coffee, and catering; everyone an individual part of the sum which made up a greater whole.

I did this. I made this. I scratched and clawed and fought for this. Almost died for this.

Why isn't it enough?

The disturbing stack of papers should have elated her. It was her boarding pass to the next level, yet she'd ignored it adroitly for days. Every time it caught her eye, she'd grab a snack, engage a co-worker in conversation, or go check on one of the airplanes in the hangar.

Today was the day. Tris dug the heel of her palm into the stack and tapped it with her hand. She forced herself to focus on the complication in front of her, which she could no longer blame on Danny. Captain Prince had laid it out for her.

The *coup de grace*, the irresistible pull, was Tris's passion for teaching. After ten years as a high school teacher, Tris gave up the classroom to fly. The satisfaction of reaching someone with knowledge, of seeing the light go on, was a high that never faded.

Prince offered the chance to pass on the skills and experience she'd honed during thousands of hours of delays, bad weather, mechanical breakdowns and professional obstacles to other pilots; all while teaching them to fly the largest, most sophisticated aircraft in the world.

"Build the expertise, then pass it on," Bron had often reminded her. "It's the critical piece of flight safety no one talks about. Teaching. That's why I became a training Captain."

The two had shared many kinds of devotion. A love of teaching, the whole learning process, was one of them. Here, four years after his death, the job at Legacy presented a unique opportunity to honor his life.

She took a deep breath, expanding her lungs until her chest strained against the buttons of her white pilot shirt, then let it out, to the beat of airplanes taking off only thirty yards away, the whine of engines whose increasing power pushed them to break their leashes and rise.

Her first day at Legacy was October 8th, six weeks away.

The job offer was technically conditional. There remained one hurdle: the company's pre-hire background check, complete with authorization forms permitting Legacy to dig into every corner of her personal and professional life. The troublesome stack of papers that peeked out of the folder.

A new law required prospective employers to probe more deeply into pilot flying backgrounds than ever before. Born of seven preventable fatal accidents in the U.S., all caused by pilots who hid their training failures during job interviews, every airline now had to obtain five years of training records for each pilot they hired.

These weren't simply forms. They were a shovel that would dig into her past.

No. They were advancement. Forward motion.

Today, she was the boss. At Legacy, she'd be an FNG.

A move ahead. A step backward.

Woody needed to sign the Westin form. Woody. After all he'd done for her, she'd have to look him in the eye and say she was leaving.

More than the conversation she had to have with Woody, she dreaded the single sheet of paper on top of the stack. A form requesting training records from Tetrix, Inc., where she'd spent the worst year of her flying career.

She pushed the forms away, again, as the conference room door whooshed open.

"Hey Tris?" Ip Niblick, Westin's junior dispatcher, popped his mop-haired head through the door. The din of commotion behind him filtered in.

"What's up, Ip?"

Ip shook his head in mock disdain.

"Is it possible, I mean when the queen's not around, to call me Phillip? You know, use my, like, actual *name*?"

Westin's lead dispatcher Phyllida, who Ip idolized, was always called Phyll. When they hired Ip, whenever someone called him Phil, both answered. Another pilot suggested the new moniker, saying that since they called Phyll by the beginning of her name, they might as well use the end of his. It was ridiculous, even childish. Much to Ip's chagrin, it stuck.

Tris smiled broadly. "Nope. What do you need?"

The inner workings of a busy charter operation are like the process of making sausage; no one wants to know the details before biting into their bratwurst or boarding their flight. Pilots strut through the hallways, each jostling for any opportunity, however small, to display their prowess over the others. They act contrite with the bosses and arrogant with their peers. Tris was accustomed to the bravado—it was how pilots hid, a time-honored procedure to push the outside world away and exist, unencumbered, in the flying world.

It wasn't uncommon for Tris to be greeted by that special look from Ip, the one that warned her that some pilot with a complaint might be hovering near her office door.

Ip referred to Westin's pilot team collectively as the "savages," which was a fair nickname. Always haunting the company flying schedule, waiting to see who got assigned to sit for a week in Key West, and who got dumped in Sioux Falls one day and Detroit the next.

The lucky ones made sure to plan their down time in full earshot of those going to less exotic locations. Such conversations revolved around whether to bring golf clubs, roller blades, tennis rackets—or all three—and mentioned favorite restaurants from past visits.

Tris couldn't blame them. Pilots lived a major part of their days on the road, away from their real lives. All Tris could do was try to divvy up the plum trips fairly, hoping to keep the savages away from each other's throats.

Ip sighed dramatically. "Today's critical flight dispute is between Jean and Sam. They're arguing over which trip our maintenance crew should staff."

"Sure they can't work it out themselves?"

Ip shook his head. "Not this time. They need input from a higher pay grade."

Tris donned her uniform jacket and followed Ip into the pilot bullpen. Two of Westin's most reliable and least compatible captains stood nose to nose. No matter how often Tris implored them to keep the peace, they argued about everything. Sometimes, their tiffs were about critical flight safety issues. Sometimes they were about passenger snacks.

Judging from their body language—Jean's arms were crossed tightly, and Sam stood with hands on hips—Tris assessed that this dispute fell in the middle of the importance scale.

"So, what is it this time? Who gets the last package of Oreos?"

Both pilots laughed, their shoulders visibly relaxing, arms at their sides at the sound of their boss's voice. They respected Tris, and more importantly, wanted her to respect them.

The two warring factions nodded to each other.

Jean explained. "Sam's jet is *technically* scheduled out before mine tonight, but my passengers have a much tighter deadline. They need to get to LaGuardia before the curfew. If you can delay Sam's departure a few minutes, so our maintenance crew can launch us . . ."

Tris knew that blowing curfew meant they'd end up in Newark or Kennedy. Then their passengers would be put on a bus. That was not what they paid charter rates for.

Tris nodded, and looked over at Sam.

"Boss," he began, "my passengers are exhausted. They arrived here this morning at 6:00 a.m., have spent all day in meetings downtown, and are anxious to get home. If we launch on time, she'll still make her curfew easily."

Tris considered his plea. "Sam, have you heard from your folks? Are they on time?"

He looked at his feet. "That's . . . well . . . not . . . they're trying to be."

One thing you could count on about charter passengers was that there was nothing you could count on. On-time departures were rare. Their customers took the phrase "on demand" seriously. That's why they spent the extra money to charter—to move when they were ready.

Tris was sympathetic to both positions.

"I'll have maintenance pull out both aircraft and authorize overtime for an extra mechanic to hang around, so if you both want to leave at the same time, we'll have the ground crew to do it." It was an extra cost but warranted in this rare case—an opportunity to make everyone's passengers happy.

Tris smiled and headed back to the conference room to a chorus of thanks. Ip fell in behind her, nervously thumbing the corner of a piece of paper atop the stack on his ever-present clipboard. He closed the door behind them.

"What else?" Tris turned to him, hands on hips, face in the semi-permanent expression of frustration she'd learned to wear when talking about crew member issues.

"A rumor's getting around." Ip whispered to his clipboard.

"What rumor?"

His eyes teared and lips quivered. "That you're leaving."

In the practiced way aviators had of maintaining the majestic calm, Tris forced herself not to change her expression at all, and to move with minimal effort.

"That I'm leaving," she repeated quietly. She glanced over at the manila folder. This was aviation, where gossip about who got hired where tended to travel faster than the speed of light. Ip was steadfastly loyal to her, one of the rare people she'd met who could keep a secret. She needed him to stop the spread. Woody had to hear the news from her.

"Does Woody know?"

Ip startled. "No. No no no. No one *here* is going to stir that boiling cauldron."

Ip's love of Broadway shows was frequently reflected in his over-dramatic expressions. In this case, Tris wished he were being too intense. Woody'd blow for sure if he heard the news from anyone but her. Heck, he'd implode regardless.

"He'll be happy for me," she murmured.

Ip wasn't convinced. "You think so? Because, you know how he is . . ."

"Huh? What did you say?" Tris was already having an imaginary conversation with Woody, where the man shook his head and with a tear in his eye, wished her well.

"I sure hope I'm not here when that conversation takes place. Who do you like for your replacement? Someone internal, right? Someone, I don't know," Ip feigned lack of comprehension and rolled his eyes toward the heavens, "someone like *you?*" He thumbed toward a petite woman in a captain's uniform, who happened to be walking by, getting ready for a trip.

"Chuck's next in line."

Ip shrugged. "Everyone knows she's your favorite."

"Chuck's been here longer. He's my Assistant Chief."

Ip shook his head. "He's so . . . dull. Anyway, you don't do things in the traditional fashion. Right? That's your managerial signature." Where in the world did Ip get this stuff from? "She's perfect for it. We both know it."

"She" was Captain Jannat Madden, the least senior and arguably most talented pilot at Westin.

"I haven't told anyone that I'm leaving. I'll decide when it's time."

Ip ran his pinched thumb and forefinger across closed lips. "They're zipped, Boss."

"Thanks *Phillip*."

A big smile revealed Ip's perfectly straight teeth at the sound of his full name.

"I'll tell Woody when I get back from Edinburgh next week. In the meantime, please try and keep the gossip from spreading if you can."

His expression became dire. "I'll do what I can, but you've got to—"

"I know. The industry is a petri dish for rumors. You told Jannat I wanted to see her before her trip, right?"

"Yes, of course."

"That it?"

"One more thing. I have a fax for you. It's on FAA letterhead." Ip's eyes widened at the mention of the federal agency that oversaw all of Westin Charter's operations, the Federal Aviation Administration.

"Another interview request for their PR newsletter?"

Ip shook his head. "I don't think so. It's addressed to you, specifically." He walked toward her, holding the shiny curling fax paper out in front of him. Westin's offices may have been updated, but Woody insisted that they "keep humble" and continue to use their original equipment: fax machine, HP desktop with its enormous monitor, and prehistoric Bunn-O-Matic coffeemaker.

Unfurled, the slick document turned out to be a letter from Richard "Rex" Parker, the FAA official who oversaw all of Westin's operations. Apparently, Westin was voted "Charter Operation of the Year," for 2001 at Exeter Airport. Tris skimmed the letter that outlined the "heroism" on the angel flight, talked about a feature story in their newsletter, and invited them to a ceremony. The event was scheduled for Wednesday September 12th.

Bummer. One day earlier and I'd be in Edinburgh and could skip it entirely.

Tris smiled at Rex's signature on the bottom of the page, amused but not annoyed, although she could well have been. Rex hadn't mentioned this earlier when he'd kissed Tris goodbye at Starbucks.

Two

THE FULL LIGHT of the sun peeked through the vertical blinds in her office, momentarily blinding Tris. Chuck "Cliché" Monroe, her second-in-command, had flown out early that morning on an overnight trip, or she'd have him in the room along with the subject of the note. She shielded her face with the slim piece of paper, which bore his familiar scrawl and trademark butchering of the English language:

"Boss . . . your new girl really scrwed the pooch this time. I was talking to our pax about a weather delay and she counterdicted me in front of them. I told them we couldn't launch because of thunderstorms, and she gave them a weather lecture. Bad call. Freaked them out. Talk to her. C-man."

Cliché might not be the best quickest thinker or best communicator—his reliance on overused statements had earned him the nickname—but he was a rock-solid aviator and loyal to a fault. Cliché expected to be promoted if—when—she left Westin. She tapped his goofy note against her desk.

Jannat Madden rose from her seat opposite Tris at the small round table in the Chief Pilot's office and closed the shades on the floor-to-ceiling picture window. Tris gazed at the young woman as she sat back down. At only sixty-one inches tall and 105 pounds according to her medical certificate, she was dwarfed by the leather office chair she sat in. But her gravitas easily filled the space around her.

"Guess the sun is coming out after all," Tris muttered. She scanned the brief memo again.

Exeter had been blazing hot that summer, with temperatures reaching the 90s every day since June, and the humidity hadn't quit. Still, Jannat sat across from her in full uniform, jacket buttoned. Tris had turned the office air-conditioning down to 68, but Jannat had to be roasting. Posture erect, gaze fixed, Jannat sat with her hands folded neatly in her lap. Her full head of black-brown hair was pulled back tight, the clip with the red flower at the end that she always wore tightly fastened. Her smooth caramel-colored skin was a signature of her Iranian descent. She wore little makeup, but by contrast, Tris, with her pale complexion and lank straight hair looked quite pedestrian.

Sitting across from her boss on the complaint of a senior pilot, Madden's expression was calm, her countenance still; she had no tells. Anyone else on the pilot staff would be sweating and blathering by now. That kind of composure was a gift, something that couldn't be taught. Calm in a crisis saved lives. It was a compulsory character trait of a Chief Pilot.

Jannat's challenges were of another sort. "Difficult," was the judgment that wafted through the infamous pilot grapevine when Tris first considered Jannat for a position at Westin. The aviation rumor mill frequently took tiny mounds of gossip and whipped them into insurmountable peaks.

The people Jannat listed on her reference sheet gave glowing testimonials, as voluntary referrals were wont to do. They used all the right buzzwords. "Loyal," "competent," "hard-working," "respectful." It was difficult for women in the industry to garner any respect, so those accolades must have been even harder to come by.

Jannat was strong in many ways that Tris recognized in herself. Still, Tris was white. By definition, that meant no matter how hard it had been for her, Jannat's road was more difficult.

Curiosity drove Tris to call Jannat's former boss at the company she'd resigned from, who wasn't listed as a reference. To her surprise, he'd said Jannat was a "natural leader," and that she was the future of his company if she'd stayed. Tris pushed him on negatives, and after deflecting question after question, he cracked. "That girl don't get along," he'd said, voice laced with frustration. "She knows how. She chooses not to. It's the damndest thing I ever seen."

Tris hired Jannat immediately after that call. Six months into her job at Westin, she'd emerged as a superstar aviator. Yet, Jannat and Chuck had clashed consistently. They were similar in so many important ways, it was no wonder.

Chuck's note was unsettling. Jannat had challenged him in front of passengers, a huge no-no in the charter business. In the open, cooperative environment Tris fostered, Jannat was not only permitted but encouraged to speak her mind, and to disagree with any other crew member, including Tris, on issues affecting passengers and/or flight safety; but in private, and never in a way that might erode the perception of a single-minded crew in front of passengers.

Way more expensive than airline travel, private charter offered customers seafood trays instead of peanuts, toys for their designer dogs and a firm promise not to scratch their Louis Vuitton luggage. The wealthy expected not only safe and seamless transportation, but happy pilots who were excellent hosts.

This wasn't the first time Chuck had complained about the new hire.

"Jannat, tell me what happened. I want to hear your side," Tris began solicitously, as she'd been taught in the expensive management training seminars that Woody insisted she attend.

Jannat's eyes narrowed. "When?"

"Chuck told you why I wanted to see you, correct?"

"No."

She'd specifically asked Cliché to tell his fellow captain why she'd been summoned; he'd chickened out. Or perhaps he wanted to make her sweat. Nah. *Avoiding* conflict was a classic pilot trait.

"The other day, on the trip to Aspen, there was a discussion in front of the passengers about the weather, correct? Chuck, who was the pilot-in-command on the trip, was explaining why takeoff would be delayed. Do I have that right?"

"Yes."

"You contradicted him?"

"Yes."

"Tell me what happened."

Jannat rolled her shoulders back before she spoke.

"Certainly. Chuck told the passengers that the weather system over the airport—with heavy rain, thunder, and lightning—was, what did he say?" She looked away for a second. "Nonconsequential. Yes. That's what he called it. 'Nonconsequential to our flight.' I simply told our passengers that it was indeed consequential, but that we'd wait for the worst of it to pass before we took off." She enunciated her words precisely, with a hint of an English accent.

Tris suppressed a smile. She could hear Jannat, with her explicit prose, challenging the words of someone whose college education had been fashioned to avoid anything that smacked of the English language.

"Don't you think that's what he meant?"

"Perhaps. But it gave the wrong impression. The passengers were frightened. I meant to put them at ease, which he decidedly did not do. I do believe he said something like, 'Patience is valuable, or virtuous,' or some such thing."

Again, Tris swallowed a smile, leaned forward, and donned the sternest expression she could muster. "This isn't about right and wrong. The senior pilot on your flight made a point, and it sounded like you were arguing with him. The passengers were already afraid of the storm. Then they saw their pilots disagree about what was safe. Your intentions, and dare I say your instincts, were correct. Your actions weren't. Do you understand?"

Jannat's eyes closed as she nodded slightly.

"Good. Okay. That's it." Tris got up and stepped toward her desk, a sure invitation for Jannat to leave.

The expressionless woman remained seated.

"Ma'am? May I hear what you would have done?"

Tris savored those times when her team recognized a teaching moment and invited her expertise. Often, she resisted initiating minor corrections, preferring to encourage confidence in her crews to problem solve for themselves.

Yet here was her chance to give advice to the woman who might well succeed her.

Ip was right. Jannat was *her first choice.*

"In a situation like this, let it go. If the passengers have questions for Chuck after his explanation, let them ask. You don't need to assume their concerns, then argue on their supposed behalf. He's the Assistant Chief here at Westin. He earned the role. I trust him. I'd like you to." Tris struggled to be diplomatic. Jannat was one of the hardest workers at the company. Her confidence had to be nurtured, not shattered.

Tris took a long breath and exhaled slowly. "Jannat, you know your stuff, and you're smarter than every other line pilot here. It's okay to know that, and not smack your co-workers in the face with it."

"That's not what I was doing, and—"

Tris held up her hand. "I think it was. And I understand. You and I, we work in a world where how things look is more important than how they are."

"Right. Of course. I was taught differently, I suppose. My parents are scientists. I was brought up to expect that there are right and wrong answers."

"In this case, Chuck gave the right answer, only not how you would have given it."

The two women sat in the uncomfortable silence of feedback given but not completely accepted. "Change the subject," is what those executive seminar leaders advised in moments like this.

So, Tris did. "Tell me about your last job."

Jannat's eyes widened. Tris didn't think they could look any bigger. "We talked about that at my interview."

"Not interview-speak. What was it like? *Really* like?" Tris decided to swing the door open wide. If she truly was considering Jannat to replace her, she needed to know what she'd been through. The sum of a pilot's good and bad experiences, their accomplishments and failures, their joy and pain, all added up to a steady, compassionate Chief.

Tris offered a glimpse into her own past to coax the self-possessed woman across from her to speak. "I was in a very difficult position at my last job, the one before Westin. I was not welcome, and the other pilots reminded me of that every day, on every flight. I know a little about the place you were flying by reputation. Please. Tell me about it."

Tris had lived the nightmare of the unintentional trailblazer, the first woman to integrate an all-male pilot group. The constant exhaustion, relentless struggle, and never-ending obstacles built up a kind of emotional muscle.

Jannat leaned forward. "The worst part wasn't the incessant harping on every little mistake, or even being ignored, not advised about staff meetings—'we forgot, so sorry,' my boss would say. It wasn't the snide remarks—'hey do you need a step stool for that?' It was the wall. It was being excluded. Laughter at a joke I might have been the butt of. 'Private' conversations spoken loud enough for me to hear about 'those people,' or 'short pilots,' or how tightly another female pilot's uniform fit. The kinds of things you can't complain about, that you must swallow." The dark-haired young woman's back was ramrod straight as she spoke, even when she took a few seconds to collect herself. "Not being part of things. That was the worst."

Tris nodded slightly. Jannat wore a faint thin smile. In that brief review of what she'd faced, the younger pilot and her superior established a bond forged by survival.

"Jannat, you made it. So many give up."

"I was lucky," Jannat said, her hands moving along with her words, animated for the first time since their meeting started. "I had my fiancé, Randy, who's a Legacy Airlines pilot. My best friend, and my parents—especially my father, who could tell me about his horrible experiences when he first came to this country, how he was treated. Yes, very lucky. So many have no one."

Tris had lost her father long ago. How he'd have loved that she was Chief Pilot of the most successful charter operation at one of the biggest airports in the country. Somehow, Tris believed he could see her success.

Jannat looked around the room. Her gaze stopped at a large plaque which displayed one of the full spreads the *Exeter Tribune* published about the angel flight.

"May I ask you about that flight?"

Tris had just chastised the junior captain, so she didn't feel like she could thumb off the request, much as she'd like to.

"Of course."

Jannat nodded slightly toward the placard. "I've read everything about it. That moment in the air . . . the shooter. That woman . . ."

"Christine," Tris whispered, as though their long-deceased angel flight passenger might hear. Everyone asked the same question. Why? Why would Christine shoot herself on a flight meant to save her life?

"She had ALS, Lou Gehrig's disease. I believe she was also very sad. Bad things had happened in her past. Not sure we'll ever truly know the extent of her desperation." Except Tris did know. Christine's terminal illness was simply the match that lit her internal detonator. She'd run to the wilds of Canada from a terrifying marriage to her obsessive ex-husband; the same man Tris had been about to move in with.

You can't make this stuff up.

Ip rapped insistently on her office door. The conversation with Jannat was over.

"Tris, time to go," Ip said.

"All right. Jannat, thanks. Take it easy on Cliché, okay? You two have to work together."

One of you will soon be reporting to the other.

"Yes, ma'am."

Jannat shook Tris's outstretched hand firmly, turned with head held high, and strode toward the pilot bullpen. Truth was, she'd irritated everyone at Westin a little, even Tris, with her self-assurance. Like any good Chief Pilot might.

Tris tried to imagine Jannat in the role. It was a close fit, but Tris sensed that something might be missing. She couldn't put her finger on what.

Ip lurked outside Tris's office, shifting his feet. He pointed toward the ramp, then his watch, and mouthed the word "go."

Exhausted by the delicate dance of giving feedback while ensuring the subject maintained their dignity, she was off to her respite, her challenge, her sanctuary; to exercise the privilege for which she'd given up so much yet gotten way more in return.

It was time for her to fly.

Three

OUTSIDE, the private jet ramp sang its full-throated melody. Airplane engines whined at start-up. A fuel truck pumped; its continuous *whir* labored but efficient. The leaves of the airport's single oak clicked under a warm sun.

As the symphony entered its second movement, Tris caught her own personal grace notes: cloudless sky, light winds, another opportunity to cheat gravity.

The sight of an El-Al 747 on final approach caught her eye. Exeter International Airport, host to jets from all over the world. A universe in itself, its square footage of asphalt, corrugated steel and travelers in transition as large as the town she grew up in.

"Captain?" The fueler called to Tris, clipboard extended, waiting for her to scrawl her initials on the fuel order so he could move on to the next airplane.

It was hard to tear herself away from the orchestral wonder of airplanes and the equipment that serviced them on an airport ramp. It never, ever got old.

"Coming."

The young man wiped both hands on his greasy uniform before he absent-mindedly handed her the clipboard. He held the fuel hose with his right hand, while trying to separate it from its seat underneath the wing with his left.

Suddenly, the hose jumped from his hands, twisting like an airborne serpent. Leftover fuel sprayed all over Tris.

He yelped and grasped at the air, trying in vain to hold the hose and catch the droplets.

"Hey! Stop!" Tris commanded, but the flying fuel didn't obey; it landed on her uniform shirt and tie. Tris now modeled the signature scent of aviation, *Eau de AvGas*.

"Damn it." This from the fueler.

"Ugh." Tris shuddered.

"Captain, I'm so sorry. Damn it. Damn it," he muttered, gaining control of the hose. "Oh man, I am so sorry," the flustered fueler continued tripping over his words as the color in his cheeks deepened. "Oh . . . no . . . not man. Fuck. Wait. That's ma'am. Oh, I'm so sorry,"

Tris squeezed her eyes closed against the fumes and flapped her hands in a useless attempt to shed the scent. "Don't worry. Look, I've gotta go change. It's okay. Really. Just don't light a match."

Her attempt at levity fell flat, as the horror-stricken fueler skulked away. Her trip was scheduled to launch in an hour. She had to wash her face, grab a clean shirt from her overnight bag. *How many shirts did I pack? Do I have enough?* Her co-pilot could finish pre-flight items, and—

"You don't smell so good, Captain Miles."

Tris stood stock still. That voice. That deep, scratchy, just-woke-up voice.

She no longer smelled fuel, but sulfur, smoke, blood. The scent of gunshots, of death, of lies—and the rotten-fruit aroma of another failed relationship.

Mike.

She didn't turn around. "What are you doing here?"

"Tris. Look at me."

"No. What are you *doing* here?"

Lightly, he touched her shoulder. The odor of death vanished. Now, the only scent was the familiar smell of his aftershave. Black cherries.

"I've been back for a few months now. Since my recovery . . ."

"From the angel flight," Tris said. The flight that made her famous, that almost got them both killed.

The Exeter ramp, right before a trip, was no place to relive her last memory of him, watching as EMT's carried him from her airplane, covered in blood and barely breathing.

No. Not here. Not now.

"Please go away, Mike, or whatever name you use these days." A jab at the deception that had ripped the two apart a year before.

He lifted his hand and stepped back. "We need to talk, Tris. We have unfinished business."

Whirling around so suddenly she almost made herself dizzy, Tris faced him. His red hair was shorter, going grey, and the full beard he'd had was now close cropped. He still held himself with the shoulders back, chest out bearing of arrogance endemic to pilots. Yet there was something, a hitch of some kind in his stance as he pawed the ground with one foot like a nervous quarter horse.

"Oh, we do not. We've been finished for some time." Mike wore a pilot uniform. How else could he have access to this secured area? "You aren't flying, are you? After what you *did*? How in the world . . . You can't be here. What the hell are you doing here?"

"I'm crew on a Citation at WhisperJet Aviation." He pointed off in the distance to the rival charter company's hangar. "Been there three months."

Surely, his boss at WhisperJet had heard the story behind his final flight as her predecessor. She'd taken over for him as Chief Pilot of Westin Charter. It had been all over the news. Still, other than lie to her, the woman he'd said he loved, the person who he was about to move in with, what, really had he done wrong? *He* was a gunshot victim.

Her expression hardened. "You have no right to be here."

A slight sneer crossed his lips, surprising her more than his actual presence. The man she'd loved—a man named Mike—wasn't like that.

Tragedy changed people, and not always for the better.

"I do. Flying's my profession, like it is yours." Unfairness, the *yang* that vastly outweighed the *yin*, was a staple of aviation. But this?

"How could anyone hire you after . . ."

He shrugged. "Yet here I am. And I know you want to talk to me."

She balled both hands into tight fists. "I *did*—after the accident. You ignored every one of my calls. You had your *mother* leave me a message in that syrupy-sweet 'bless your heart' Southern accent of hers, telling me to stop calling. You couldn't even come to the phone to tell me . . . that . . . you . . . were okay." She looked away as the final, strangled words passed through quivering lips. If she didn't get away from him—and fast—she'd lose it for sure.

When she faced him again, tears streamed down his cheeks.

He wiped his face, pinched his nose, sniffed, and reached into an inside pocket of his flight jacket. Out came a plain white envelope, with her name written in his blocky print. His hand extended, the offering floating between them.

"For you."

Her mouth must have been open, because she felt it close, lips dry as sandpaper. Brows furrowed, her head shook slowly.

"I can't take that," she said softly.

He dropped it on the ground.

The white rectangle lay on sparkling asphalt, framed by the glow of the Midwestern sun.

"Let me back in, Tris."

"Why? Why should I do that?"

The smile he wore was guileless. "Because I know you."

She snapped back, needing to hurt him. "But I didn't really know you, did I?"

Mike's shoulders fell. "You'll want to read it." He pointed at the envelope.

"No."

"Call me when you've read it. No matter what time."

They stood silently for a few moments, the pain of the past a shatterproof invisible barrier between them.

"No chance."

The tall man nodded; his characteristic thoughtfulness returned as he absent-mindedly stroked the chin that was no longer covered by a long beard. Habit.

"You sure got a lot of attention after that trip. Lots of accolades. You deserved them. Reporters stopped calling me once they learned I wasn't going to be crippled for life. When I could have used the attention, during rehab, to, you know, lift my spirits, it was all gone."

"Bummer for you."

"Read the letter, then call me. Please."

His last words to her lingered on an answering machine message he'd left on the day of that fateful flight, begging her to let him explain. She would have, back then. She'd have let him tell her all the reasons he'd kept his secrets, betrayed her, and why he'd lied, and lied again.

She'd loved him.

As Mike limped away, the now-putrid scent of jet fuel filled her nostrils, strong enough to make her gag. Viscous poison seeped through her soiled clothes, burning her skin.

Four

DANNY AND EMILY were engaged in yet another unwinnable marital dispute.

She wanted a divorce.

He didn't.

The yellow manila envelope arrived via FedEx from Emily's lawyer. Like she didn't think he'd accept it directly from her.

Danny couldn't bring himself to open the delivery, so he threw it against the wall. That way, he reasoned, the papers inside would miraculously pop out, fully reviewed, without ever having to touch them.

It slid to the floor. Undaunted, he picked it up, walked a few steps away and hurled it again. It came to rest in about the same spot it had landed the first time, still sealed. There it lay, like a dead rodent. He pinched the flap of the parasitic packet between his thumb and forefinger and stepped back as he lifted it so no part would touch him.

Third time's the charm.

The couple's marital possessions were strewn about, waiting to be packed. The corner of his wedding photo peeked out below a pile of books, which they frequently dusted but neither had ever opened. They were decorations. Emily wanted to portray the couple as people who read.

The outlines of family photographs removed from their hooks and buried in bubble wrap haunted the walls. How quickly this place went from their home to an empty house.

Emily had moved out. The plan was that she'd leave until he could find a place. He was deep in the process, but his reserve schedule at Legacy Airlines made looking for an apartment difficult. Worst-case scenario, he could always ensconce himself at the crew crash pad at his base in Boston until he found an apartment. His nose twitched at the thought of spending any extra time in that hovel, one-eighty-out from this beautiful two-bedroom house.

Danny raised his middle finger to the mustard-yellow nemesis and checked his watch again. Tris would arrive any minute. She'd only be there a short time—it was dangerous to have Tris and Emily in the same room together. It would take Emily at least an hour to get here after her class. Tris would be long gone.

Then maybe he could bring Emily to her senses. There was no reason for them to divorce.

The couple had wrestled with Emily's jealousy over his friendships with women—one in particular—from the beginning. Danny had known Tris for years: they'd bonded in the cockpit and mourned Bron's death long before he'd even met Emily.

"We've never been anything other than friends," Danny assured Emily.

It was true. Yes, he'd been in love with Tris. When Bron died, Tris lost her lover and Danny lost his best friend, which tied the two together in grief. Time passed, the pain dulled, and while Tris held a private corner of his heart, he knew he wasn't her choice. They stayed friends. Danny moved on: met and married Emily and saw less and less of Tris. That was that.

Emily's insecurities began to fade as the two of them established the routines of a married couple. They even started trying to get pregnant. Tris got serious about Mike, and Danny thought any marital tension over his friendship with Tris was over.

Then came the angel flight. That damned flight. So many people well beyond those aboard were affected, but the spotlight shone on Tris. Hailed as a heroine, her name and photo appeared on television and in the papers every day for weeks.

She was an apparition constantly floating in front of Emily's face. One night, Danny was commuting back to Exeter from Boston and his flight didn't arrive until 3:00 a.m. Due at the airport later that day for training at 7:00 a.m., he crashed on Tris's couch. Her couch, he assured Emily—and, really, did she want him driving all the way home in the middle of the night, only to turn right around and head back to work? That didn't persuade Emily. She'd snapped, and her rant caused the too-full cup of her suspicions to finally spill over the rim.

Emily's jealousy was ridiculous.

Nervous, but sick of pacing around the living room, Danny opened the refrigerator door, and was almost knocked down by the fetid smell. He searched in vain for something to eat, slamming the door at the sound of tires crunching on the gravel drive.

Outside the curtain-less living room window, Tris was wrestling with some large boxes she'd broken down. They had "Miles/Living Room," "Miles/Bedroom," Miles Miles Miles all over them. He'd have to make sure to have her name face the wall before Emily arrived.

Danny flew out the front door.

"Got it, Flygirl?" He asked as she lined the clumsy cardboard bodies up next to her old Corolla. Tris flinched. She'd asked him repeatedly to please stop using that nickname.

"You ever gonna get a new car?" Danny chided her. For some reason, even though she could well afford one, Tris was determined to keep her ten-year-old Toyota running.

"Hey, I'm helping you out here. Talk about something else." She smiled at him the way she always did—with affection and concern. He'd long ago stopped expecting passion.

After the two old friends awkwardly deposited the empty boxes on the living room floor, Tris stopped and looked around.

"Wow. It's real, isn't it?"

He could only nod.

"I'd offer you something, but I got nothing. The fridge is empty. Em's almost completely moved out and I—" He choked on the last words. Tris moved toward him and placed a warm hand on his back. The two stood there as tears silently fell down Danny's cheeks.

The silence was broken by the front door's squeaky hinge that Danny never seemed to remember to oil.

Emily strode into the living room like she still lived there, like she hadn't moved out in a storm of accusations and tears, throwing clothes and toiletries indiscriminately into a green garbage bag. He picked up the scent of sunscreen; she must have spent another day out by the pool at her parents 'club.

His wife looked at the two old friends, shook her head, huffed sarcastically, and headed directly to the bedroom without a word.

"I'd better go," Tris said softly.

"Right. Thanks." Danny used both sleeves to wipe his face.

The front door squealed again before it shut behind Tris, and soon Emily re-appeared. She perched on a counter-high stool at the kitchen island.

"Em, look . . ." He started.

"Nope. We're done. *Obviously*." She motioned to Tris's car backing out of the driveway. "We should never have gotten married. Let's finish this."

The anger and frustration with which she hurled those words were like a punch to a fighter already sprawled on the mat. He'd desperately wanted this life: a wife, kids, a home. The pull of the two-car garage was strong. Pretty and smart, Emily had truly cared for him. Together, they'd been building the foundation of his nirvana brick by brick, a little at a time.

A framed cross-stitched motto declaring this a "House Full of Love," caught his eye. It lay in the middle of a sea of bubble-wrapped wedding crystal.

I am a good husband. I love my wife.

Danny broke the silence. "She was helping us out, Em. She's a friend. She brought *boxes*."

Emily raised her hands in that business-like manner that always silenced him. "We need to sell the house. Right away. I need the cash and staying with my parents is a tight fit." Emily's parents' house was already crowded before she left Danny. Her sister and brother-in-law, Heather and Bruce, claimed the basement with her eighteen-month-old nephew Jacob. Emily ensconced herself in her old room, still decorated with pink lace, hearts, cheerleading ribbons, old photos and stuffed animals.

"Em, why don't your parents buy me out, if you're dead set on this. Then you can live here." There was so little equity in their home, the cost would barely make a dent in his in-laws' substantial savings.

Emily quashed that idea right away. "I don't want to live with the memories."

Danny grappled for something to derail this train. "I'm still on reserve in Boston. I don't have time to get it sale-ready. And we can still talk, right? About, you know, staying together."

Emily absent-mindedly rubbed the tips of her fingers together and didn't answer right away, which made Danny more nervous. Something was on her mind, something she hadn't shared.

"I'm going to need the money, Danny."

This was nuts. They had to give their marriage another chance.

"Emily. Please. Listen to me. Please. Look, if you need some time, want to be with your family for a bit, I totally get it. Do it. There's no rush to make anything final. I mean, come on. Our problems are small when you compare them to what Heather and Bruce—"

Emily flipped. "We are *nothing* like Bruce and Heather. Bruce has never even looked at another woman since they've been married." Sobs shook her. They would be followed by coughing, then steady crying. Danny knew the motions, and the emotions, by heart.

Danny stepped slowly toward his wife. His hand touched her cheek, softly brushed away her tears. The woman he'd promised to love and honor "until death" closed her eyes and leaned into him. Her hand grazed his. He lifted it to his lips and kissed her palm, then pressed it to his heart.

If he couldn't hold on to Emily, couldn't persuade her to stop this crazy divorce talk, he'd lose his best chance to have a family of his own. How would he ever find another woman who'd love him this much?

Lost in tender thought, Danny startled when Emily said, "Have you read it?" She straightened in her seat, broke the tenuous physical contact between them, and motioned toward the envelope.

After a heavy sigh, Danny folded up the wings of the metal clasp and slid out the documents. The stack was thick, thicker than he'd thought. Titled "Separation Agreement," there had to be at least 50 pages. What the fuck did they have that required 50 pages?

Thumbing through them, he saw all the subparts he'd expected.

Finances. Personal items. The tiny savings account, the house. Even their cars.

At the very end of the document, after it seemed there could be no more attention paid to money, possessions, and legal status, there was one additional section that had been left blank.

He froze. "What's this? What's missing?" he asked his wife.

Emily looked out the picture window. "Danny, there's something I haven't told you."

"What? What is it, baby?"

Her eyes widened for a split second, then she choked back a sob. "Not now. Four o'clock. At the lawyers."

She slid off the bar stool and was out the front door before he could respond.

Five

THE OFFICE OF The Wright Lawyers LLC, in a small strip mall near the airport, was flanked on one side by a sex toy shop and on the other by a 7-Eleven. Danny parked his Jeep beside a familiar luxury sedan and pictured Emily in the waiting room, sitting between her parents.

She brought her arsenal.

Danny was exhausted by the mere thought of them; he didn't want to fight anymore. Why go ten rounds over photos, his-and-hers potholders, or the decorative plastic fruit bowl? Emily would keep her car. He'd keep his. They'd sell the house.

Her sister wouldn't be there. Heather had a soft spot for Danny. Her parents shot lasers at him, but Heather would smile, touch Danny's hand, talk about how the pain would pass, how he'd move on. Heather should know. After the angel flight put an end to her husband Bruce's flying career, a toughness and grit surfaced that Danny would never have guessed at. She got a job, sublet their house, and moved Bruce and their son into her parents' basement.

Before the angel flight, Bruce was set to interview for a job with Legacy Airlines. Now he was Mr. Mom, home with his son while Heather worked at an accounting firm. She also attended a local community college part-time at night, vying for an associate degree.

Half the time when Danny called to talk to Emily, Bruce answered the phone. "Give me a minute, gotta grab a diaper," Bruce had said in the middle of their last conversation. The harried happiness and pure contentment in Bruce's voice was something Danny had never heard while Bruce was flying—that's what he wanted for himself.

This mental image made it even harder to walk in, say a casual hello to the three of them and sit down. He glanced over at Emily. She looked great.

Maybe she'd been with someone else. Wait, *Emily*? Well, why not? If Danny were being totally honest, he'd lugged the vestiges of unrequited love for another woman into his marriage. Didn't everyone have a first love in their past?

Danny struggled under the weight of the guilt that came with those feelings. Every now and then, the memory of his love for Tris still overcame him without warning, as it did right in that moment, so strongly that he had to bend over and stick his head between his legs.

"You gonna puke?" His father-in-law, Andy.

"Huh? What?" Danny popped up like he'd been startled out of a sound sleep.

"You gonna hurl? 'Cuz if you are, here's a trash can."

Emily didn't look at him. Her eyes focused straight ahead, in that phony way they did when people forced themselves to look away, look anywhere except at the elephant in the room. Her lips pursed so hard, they turned white.

"I'm fine, Andy. But, hey, thanks anyway. Thanks for *caring*."

He didn't so much speak the words as toss them at Emily.

A Jim Brickman piano solo spilled out from a speaker somewhere on the wall. After years of hotel elevators, airplane boarding music, and the ever-present TV at every crash pad, Danny could block out any sound. Today the music made his skin itch. He repeatedly laced his fingers together to keep from scratching; they entwined in time with the lilting piano.

A woman stepped from behind a door. Dressed in a flowing skirt with a tie-dyed headband that kept long stringy black hair away from her overly made-up face, she led them all to a small conference room. A chipped particle board table with eight chairs—three on a side and one at each end—sat empty but for a thick folder. Probably full of the same paperwork Danny had heaved against his living room wall.

Moments later, a short, skinny guy who hardly looked old enough to be called a man walked into the room, wiping his nose on a handkerchief. He coughed behind his hand and sat down at the head of the table.

"Folks, hello. I'm Reggie Wright. I'll be handling this case for, uh . . ." He opened the file in front of him, "Uh . . . Terry?" He looked over at Emily. "Are you Terry?"

Danny suppressed a grin. *So, this was their high-powered divorce lawyer.*

"I'm Emily Terry. Emily Gustafson, actually." Her maiden name already? Danny tried not to panic.

"Ahem . . . excuse me." The baby-faced attorney made guttural sounds as something fluid and thick crackled in his throat. "So sorry, Mrs. Terry. Uh, Ms. Gustafson," he stumbled again, but didn't look up or seem bothered. Emily's parents didn't move at all. Andy's eyes were closed.

Danny focused on a scuff mark meandering across the wall.

"So, is this everyone?"

"Yes. Yes." Andy used his most impatient voice.

"Great. Good. So, everyone's here that needs to be here. Let me begin by asking you . . ." Baby-face droned on while Danny considered his options.

I don't want a divorce. I'm not getting a divorce.

"Mr. Terry? You are Mr. Terry?"

Danny snapped to attention. "I'm Danny Terry."

"Okay, Mr. Terry and, uh, Ms. Gustafson, I'm told you two wish to speak privately. Follow me." When did this get decided? Did she ask for this? Danny must have missed something important while Little Man was talking.

The lawyer walked them to yet another conference room, then left them alone. "I'll be in my office if you need me." The married couple settled on opposite sides of a rectangular table in chairs that were far more plush than the ones they'd left.

This was the perfect place to persuade Emily to stop this foolishness. He didn't want to push too hard, so he'd let her say what she needed to say first. Then he'd make his pitch.

"Em, please, start. Okay?" He looked into the eyes of his wife. Was it possible he saw hope there? Tenderness? Concern?

Please, please let it be doubt.

"This isn't ideal, the timing—I'm pregnant, Danny."

"What?"

"We're having a baby."

"Are you sure?"

"I went to the clinic, saw the doctor. I'm sure."

Emily let her hand rest next to his for a moment. Then she pulled it back, hugged herself, and looked away.

"You're pregnant? That stuff the papers left out, I thought that was . . . You're pregnant? Really? Oh wow. How long have you known? Oh wow!"

"I'd been having some second thoughts about having a child, Danny."

"Huh?"

"The doctor, the clinic I went to was at Planned Parenthood. We talked about options. It'd be easy to, you know, take care of it. We can't have a child now, Danny."

He finally caught up. His son. His daughter. His. And no one, *no one* would take it away from him.

"Take care of it? Oh no, no Em. No. This is our child. We've waited so long for this. This is the perfect time to have a baby. Don't you see, Em? We'll stay together. We'll have our family exactly the way we'd planned."

Emily hesitated. "There are things that I . . ."

"Oh baby, I know. So many things. But now we'll handle them together. I'm so glad, Em."

She shook her head. "Danny, please let me finish. If I have it, I've got to stay on your insurance. Can I do that if we're divorced?"

"Em, we're not getting divorced now. Of course not."

"I don't have insurance at my new job, and I won't be there long enough to qualify for maternity leave. We may have to stay married. For the baby's medical expenses. Or . . . there's always that other option."

Other option? That was craziness. "No. I mean, yes, of course, we'll stay married. I want to be with you. For you to have my child. *Our* child. I want to raise him—or her—together." He waited a beat. "Don't you love me?"

"I always have. Your . . . attention. Your . . . affections. They haven't always been mine."

He cut her off. "Not true. I love you. I *married you.* Emily, there is no other *option.*"

She looked at her feet. "Please," he begged.

Emily began to cry quietly and wiped her eyes with the long sleeve of the Heart t-shirt she wore, the one they'd gotten at a concert when they were dating. "You don't love me. Well, maybe you do, in some way. Admit it—there's always been three people in our marriage."

"Huh?" Danny had no idea what she was talking about.

"You know what I mean. Me. You. And . . . her. I have never had all of you, Danny. That's why—well, maybe it's best to let it go." Emily sniffed again and straightened up in her chair.

His own wife had never trusted his love.

"You're wrong. That's not true." Then he added softly, "Don't you want our baby, Em?"

"I don't want to be a single mom."

"You won't be. I'll be there. Let's stop all of this. Come home."

It was so quiet that Danny heard the squeal and puff of an air brake. Outside, a bus let off passengers. His wife nodded, as if she'd settled an internal argument. "If we get back together, Danny, she's got to be gone."

There it was. The "she" who he'd carefully tucked away in a corner of his heart, in a place his own wife couldn't enter.

"Gone?"

"Out of your life. Our baby's life. *Our* lives."

Danny couldn't remember a time when he wasn't a pilot, when he wasn't required to exercise judgment, and make quick but solid decisions. Sometimes a call had to be made, do or die, unplanned, right there in your face. This was one of those times.

He had to choose. So, he did.

"You're asking me to end my friendship with Tris."

Emily moved around the table, sat on his lap, and held him tightly. She was crying and nodding. He lightly touched her belly. There was no choice.

"Okay."

He sobbed along with her—for their future, for their child, and for the love that had flickered for years in his heart, and in this antiseptic place, had finally died.

Emily smiled. "Oh, Danny. Thank you."

Danny's heart pounded in relief and despair as tears ran down his cheeks. He tightened his hold on Emily and dug his fingers into her back, grateful he could hide the face of his joy and his agony.

Six

JANNAT HAD TO PULL herself together. She had been called out by the company's Chief Pilot. Now she had to fly with a "preemie" co-pilot—someone with minimal flight time who needed a strong captain to train him up. Perhaps the greenest first officer at Westin, Sean, was sitting next to her in the cockpit on a round trip to Pittsburgh. His nickname was "BTDT," for "Been There Done That." His constant suggestions, unnecessary reminders and announcements of his aviation prowess during trips were exhausting.

Jannat had plenty of experience with the type. She felt the envious eyes of more senior company pilots on her when Tris assigned her to one of these flights. It signified the boss's confidence in her, and signaled Jannat's rapid rise to the head of the line at Westin.

Some disgruntled male pilots thought she'd jumped to the top only because she was female, and the women assumed it was because of her brown skin.

Jannat knew better. She had more total flight and pilot-in-command time, facts often overlooked by other pilots, especially the two women she'd eclipsed. She only hoped the recent rift with Cliché didn't knock her out of favor. After all, she'd heard the new rumor, too. And she wanted Tris's job.

From where she stood at the reception desk, thumbing through trip paperwork, she caught the familiar sight of Tris in her office, bent over her desk, a lamp glowing despite the bright sunshine outside. At first, Jannat figured that perhaps her boss's close vision wasn't that good. Phyll set her straight: Tris liked to get in before the sun rose, to catch up on paperwork before the phone began to ring, and pilots lined up at her door. She'd switch the lamp on, and as day broke, she'd simply forget to shut it off.

I will work even harder.

Jannat and Sean were flying a King Air 90. The aircraft only required one pilot, so Sean was regulatory window dressing for their passenger. She'd let him read checklists and talk to ATC for as long as he proved up to those tasks.

He walked toward her with his usual smug expression. "So, Janette. That's your name, right?" The first few times he'd mispronounced it, she'd corrected him. "Jan-NAT. You know, like Nat King Cole?" Offering the name of Maman's favorite singer was her best effort. When that didn't work, she gave up.

Sean pointed at the weather radar on the computer screen. The monitor sat on a long silver table surrounded by discarded Styrofoam cups with various levels of leftover coffee in them. "So, instead of, you know, waiting to take off, we can fly around the cell, right? You see that, right?" What Jannat saw was a line of thunderstorms with a thin break that an airborne arrow couldn't slide through.

Save me from first officers who think they are smarter than I.

Jannat's command muscles were well-defined. Stretched and torn by her previous employer over the last five years, they always grew back stronger. Jannat had developed the vaunted neutral countenance required of people who operate complex machinery with lives at stake. She felt no need to defend her route strategy to someone like Sean.

"I'll take a look at the radar when we get closer to launch. Now how about putting coffee and water on the airplane, *Shane.*" Her co-pilot huffed, then slunk away at his captain's mocking tone.

The trip's flight-planning documents were thicker than usual, owing surely to the ominous weather along their flight path. Jannat thumbed through them, quickly digesting the complex information they provided. The route was navigable, but the challenge of safely flying around the storms would alarm most pilots. Thankfully, Jannat wasn't most pilots.

Sean walked by with refreshments for their passenger, and finally addressed her in respectful tones. However, while doing so, he stood particularly close to her and made sure to straighten his posture, as if his over-six-foot frame didn't already cast a shadow which engulfed her completely. It was funny, really, the way he tried to intimidate her.

Sporting four stripes on her slender shoulders, someone so petite often startled people in this business at first glance. Each stripe she wore came with its own price, measured in the torrent of slights, insults, and dismissals that accompanied being a woman in this decidedly male world. Every time her two-year-old cousin said she wanted to be like Aunt Jannat, her heart skipped, and her internal voice screamed, "Never. I'll never let you be treated like this."

Jannat accepted the occasional sexist remark from significantly more senior pilots; the uneducated ones, who were neither trained nor raised to respect women. They didn't know any better and would never change, no matter how many sexual harassment courses the FAA mandated that they take. She'd force a smile at their bigoted jokes and pretend not to hear their rude remarks. Jannat could handle it, but resolved that no one she loved would be subjected to this treatment, not if she could help it.

So very often in those moments, when she stood impotent against offensive talk, the voice in her head was Maman's.

"Such are the consequences of your choice, Jannat joon."

Baba and Maman tried unsuccessfully to hide their disappointment over the career choice of their only child, their cherished daughter, who'd elected to become "just a pilot." Just a pilot. A Muslim woman born to over-achieving—because they had to be—immigrant parents, flying an airplane in the United States?

They didn't realize that wasn't "just a pilot." That was a revolution.

Still, they didn't want their daughter to be an innovator. Rather, they would have been more than content—proud even—for her to show an interest in their professions and pursue a career as a surgeon or research chemist.

Jannat spent her youth looking up at the sky. Her childhood home, where her parents still lived, was in the approach flight path of Exeter International, where airplanes arrived and departed in a line that curved high above. That elegant queue of aircraft was called a "string of pearls," a phrase she'd learned from an air traffic controller she'd dated a few times.

Jannat resolved to fly, with or without her parents' blessing. Over time, their staunch opposition mellowed into tacit acceptance. Her upcoming marriage to Randy, the huge wedding, the spectacle meshing American and Persian cultures, was Jannat's olive branch.

"So, *Jean*-ette." Sean couldn't even get it wrong consistently. "Our passenger is here. Should I put him on?"

"No. Please make sure the rampers got the barf bag our last passenger used off the airplane. If they didn't, you do it. There might be some spillover splashed on the seat. Clean that up, will you? I'll get our passenger."

Sean grimaced. "Why can't we let, uh, someone else do it?" There was absolutely no one else around, other than Jannat herself.

"Welcome to charter operations, Sean. This airplane burns jet fuel, unlike that tiny Piper you used to fly. You want to take this step? You want to build that turbine-time to get to Legacy Airlines, right? Well, this is part of it.

"Those big airplanes? All that money you see in your future? It doesn't come without effort. It is not something that you are *entitled to.* You are certainly not going to slide by and shirk your duties as long as my name is listed as pilot-in-command. Now, please go and take some ownership of this flight, some pride in your airplane, and clean up the mess."

His mouth agape, a resigned slouch preceded Sean's slow march to the airplane to liberate the nasty container and clean its spattered remains. He'd be no more trouble for this trip.

There were others like him on the pilot team at Westin. Jannat tolerated them because she chose to be here. She'd had multiple offers, but she wanted to work for Tris Miles, someone who might understand the extra challenges she faced.

Tris had exceeded her expectations. Jannat had never worked for a Chief Pilot as even-handed and honest. If Tris was truly off to Legacy Airlines, Jannat was ready to take her place, to be the Chief Pilot, to carry on and expand the work environment Tris created. The best way to show that she was ready was to conduct herself as if she already had the job. If that meant flying with less than stellar aviators, showing them by example and training what was expected of them, so be it.

Mostly, though, her job at Westin offered her the chance to engage deeply, to thrust her personal life to the side and concentrate on her career. With all of Westin's different aircraft and complex schedules, she could easily avoid what she faced at home, immersing herself in the world of mechanical systems, engines, wings, air, and sky, far away from the less predictable, less navigable world made of flesh and bone and heart.

Jannat used the same key she'd carried since she was a little girl to unlock the front door of her parents' home in the upscale suburb of Avon. Once over the threshold, she was transported to a country whose images Jannat could only conjure from the stories they told. The daughter of Iranian refugees, she let her gaze touch the few mementos they'd carried with them until they rested on her favorite: a replica of the Cyrus Cylinder, considered to be the first written human rights declaration. King Cyrus was revered in Persian culture for having abolished slavery when he conquered and freed the Jewish prisoners of Babylon.

Her fingers caressed the lines of cuneiform text. This copy of the famous artifact had been passed down through the generations in her father's family.

After five years in aviation, Jannat had learned that her commitment to honor her Persian culture had best remain private. She deflected any questions about her background with a smile, saying she attended Avon High. The Cyrus Cylinder, this old white tube with unreadable characters, a time-honored symbol of strength and justice, and its presence in this house, reminded Jannat to be exactly who she wanted to be, free of constraints. Most constraints.

The smell of stew coming from the kitchen made her stomach growl. She hadn't eaten yet that day. Flying with Sean gave her a headache, and she'd ignored her catered meal. The aromas of her mother's cooking sparked her appetite.

"Maman, it's me. How long until dinner?"

Her mother, an older version of Jannat, entered the library in an apron, holding a spatula.

"Oh, Maman. Can't you let Aria do the cooking? Isn't that what you hired her for, so you don't have to stand on your feet after a long day at the lab?"

Maman's nose crinkled at the mention of their long-time housekeeper.

"*Azizam*," the older woman kissed her only child on the forehead. "You know she cannot cook!"

"Her barbari is delicious." Jannat, now ravenous, pointed to the flat loaf.

Maman smiled. "Go grab the scissors and cut a piece."

There was an extraordinary amount of work to be done in the coming weeks to pull off the wedding, and Maman insisted on being involved in every detail. Yet she found time each night to make the evening meal for Baba, who was still hours away from returning home, likely hunched over a PET scan, or holding the hand of a recovering patient he'd operated on.

Jannat would defer to her mother on most wedding decisions. She trusted Maman's understated elegance and impeccable taste.

Randy's mother favored opulence—a white horse-drawn carriage, the path from the country club entrance to the wedding hub lined in lace and roses. Baba and Maman would spare no expense for their daughter's wedding. What Maman didn't know was that her greatest gift to the couple was keeping Jannat's future mother-in-law's excesses at bay.

Maman was steadfast about introducing as many items reflecting Jannat's Persian upbringing as possible, such as the *sofreh aghd,* the table that displayed a collection of items meant to symbolize the couple's loving future. More than a memory table, it was a staple of Persian weddings, laden with symbolic items meant to thrust the happy couple forward in married life. Hers would be a bit different, reflecting both the world she came from and the one she'd chosen.

The Cyrus Cylinder would be on it, of course, to symbolize their independence. Some traditional items—a dessert to ensure the sweetness of their union, for example—would adorn the table. Photos of grandparents from both sides would represent her history. She and Randy had chosen a photo they'd taken of the two of them in uniform, posing on the Exeter ramp to signify their professional futures.

The couple naturally invited the Ellers to contribute. Randy had asked his mother for something from their family that went back generations. Mrs. Eller offered a confederate flag.

"That is preposterous. I will not have it!" Maman was horrified. To punctuate her disapproval, some kitchen implement got smacked on the stove to the resounding sound of metal on metal. A lifetime of hypersensitivity gave Jannat the useful skill of correctly gauging the feelings and reactions of people from small inputs—a glance, a scant movement, a twitch. With Maman, those skills were not necessary. Her opinions were always sharp and sure.

The couple had both been on trips and contributed by speaker phone, Randy apologizing profusely for his mother's insensitivity.

"The *sof-reh,*" Maman enunciated both syllables with her best Persian accent, "is a time-honored tradition, Randy. This is the place where the bride and groom look at depictions of their *lives together.* My Jannat likely would have been considered a *slave* during the confederacy. That is what your mother wants to celebrate? Under no circumstances. No no. Absolutely not." Another crash in the kitchen.

Sadly, this was not the last moment of conflict over wedding details.

The tantalizing smell of Maman's cooking erased the memory.

"The stew has just begun to simmer. It will be some time yet. I have more information from the florist. Let me get it." Maman bustled away, untying the apron fastened around her slim waist. Jannat inherited her dark wavy hair from her mother, whose bun was now streaked with grey. Maman returned shortly with a stack of photographs. "Come, let us see what they sent me."

"Maman, please. May I have one moment to relax without wedding nonsense?" She was exhausted.

"*Azizam*, there is so much to do. The wedding is so soon. We got our 250th RSVP today—232 people plan to attend. This is going to be a huge event, dear."

"Well, maybe if you and Baba had not invited the entire neurology and physics departments, it would be a bit more informal."

"It is not only us, darling. The Ellers invited more than half of the attendees. Their lineage goes back 100 years!" Maman wagged her finger, mimicking the mother-of-the-groom.

Both women laughed. They frequently made fun of the way Mrs. Eller had of turning every conversation into a lecture. The thought of all those lily-white Southerners at her wedding made Jannat shiver. It was supposed to be *the bride's* day, and she wanted her own people around her. Which is probably why her parents had invited so many colleagues.

Laleh and Ali Madini had no family in the United States when they arrived. They fled the Ayatollah's oppression of 1970s Iran. Their families were wealthy and counted many friends in the Ayatollah's government, yet Laleh and Ali publicly opposed the Ayatollah. All four of Jannat's grandparents were executed by the Ayatollah's men in a gruesome attempt to scare their offspring. It worked. Petrified, and filled with guilt over their parents' deaths, Laleh and Ali feared they'd be next if they remained.

Laleh was the first to get into medical school in the U.S. It wasn't traditional for the wife to be educated first; still, she attended full-time while Ali worked to support her. Ali did all kinds of odd jobs, from driving a taxi to stocking shelves at a hardware store while Laleh studied. Despite the long work hours, Laleh told her daughter stories of waking in the morning to fresh flowers in a vase placed there in the dead of night by Ali who lay snoring beside her. Jannat so admired her father's devotion.

The Madinis' dream for their only child included marriage, a family, and a career that inspired her. Instead, Jannat changed her name to Madden, eschewed the matchmaking of her parents, and insisted on forging her path as a pilot. It disappointed the two doctors at their core. As a form of amends, and to honor her parents who had sacrificed so much, she felt obligated to give them the wedding they never had.

She'd met Randy Eller at a gas station. He was having trouble stretching the nozzle to the gas tank on his car. Without saying a word, she yanked the hose to give him more room. She rubbed her hands together with a sharp clap, commemorating a job well done, and started to walk away.

"Hey." The first word he'd ever spoken to her. "*Hey*. Young man," he called again when she didn't stop.

Jannat wore sweatpants and a baseball cap, her long dark hair barely peeking out from the sides. She turned toward him with a smile, and removed her cap. Her thick wavy hair tumbled down her back.

"I'm so sorry, ma'am. I'm so sorry," he drawled, which he only did when he was nervous. "I . . . I didn't . . . Well . . . Aw, can I buy you a cup of coffee? You know, for helping me here?"

He was tall, well-built, blonde, and very attractive, but Jannat was eager to be on her way. After a brief conversation she'd learned that they were both pilots flying out of Exeter. It was too much of a coincidence not to at least stop for a beverage with him.

As coffee turned to dinner, then multiple dinners, and dinners turned into long, comfortable nights on her couch falling asleep to old World War II movies, the two young aviators learned how very much they had in common. Jannat listened quietly as Randy spoke of his old-line Southern family, and their furniture business that had given him a comfortable childhood. He talked often of the importance his family placed on his settling down, another thing he had in common with Jannat.

Randy proved to be intelligent, easy-going, and reliable. He had so little guile that the first time he told Jannat that he loved her, a mere two weeks after they'd met, she didn't question it. Their relationship wasn't the continuous courtship her parents had, fueled by a passion that still existed. Jannat was more of a partner, invited into all his decision-making from the beginning. He relied on her advice and checked in frequently when he was on the road. Randy also wanted to be involved in the wedding planning.

By far his most important attribute was that Maman and Baba adored him. To maintain their respect, Randy honored their wish that the couple forego intimacy until they were married. Jannat understood that she'd have to fully become his wife after the wedding and often wondered what type of intimacy he enjoyed. Randy was a gentleman, but a man, nonetheless. She looked forward to experimenting with him.

Maman had finished closely reviewing all the florist's latest arrangements.

"Jannat, should we ask Suzette her opinion? After all, she is your maid-of-honor."

Jannat stifled a grin. Suzette took the timeless position as Jannat's "second in command," as she called it, mostly to keep an eye on her. She probably wouldn't notice if her bouquet was dead as long as the ceremony finished quickly.

"Maman, let me see your favorites and I'll run them by Suzette."

Breathing deeply, Jannat continued mentally drafting the blueprint of her future while she discussed wedding flowers with her mother. Her plans were tricky, to be sure. The mention of Suzette's name shifted her focus away from flowers. Between Randy's schedule and her own, it had been many days—too many—since the two women had been together.

Randy would be home in an hour or so. Luckily, he'd only be in town for one night.

Jannat closed her eyes and imagined the moment she'd kiss him goodbye and welcome Suzette back into her bed.

Seven

A HONKING HORN got Tris's attention. Her right hand lifted in apology and her foot pressed the gas pedal. She peered through drops of fine mist on the windshield. There was enough rain to obscure her vision, but if she turned the wipers on, they'd only smear accumulated dirt. It was way past time for a visit to the car wash.

Tris twisted her wrist to check the time on her brand-new watch. She hadn't worn one in ages. Trying to establish a habit, she forced herself to look at its gold- and silver-toned face at least once or twice an hour. Thoughtful and generous Rex bought it for her after two dates. It was a Fossil, the upscale watch manufacturer with a shop in the mall. Still, she'd had to force a gratitude she didn't feel when she'd opened the box.

Rex was slowly chipping away at her carefully constructed plan to keep their liaison casual. Tonight's dinner at his place was another tap of the ice pick.

She'd told Rex about her previous relationship with Mike.

Saying that it had ended badly seemed to satisfy Rex, who, thankfully, didn't ask many questions. The wounds Mike had inflicted were scabbed over, but if rubbed the wrong way they would bleed all over again.

Almost. The whole fiasco was almost behind her. Then Mike reappeared.

Shaking her head to dislodge any curiosity about the letter she hadn't read, Tris focused on the top-notch mechanics of the inappropriately lavish gift. It had a button she could press that would illuminate the watch face in the dark.

Great for checking the time during those boring sci-fi movies Rex likes, or in one of Woody's deadly staff meetings.

Traffic moved forward by the inch. It was one of those sloppy evenings, where the cars in front of her kicked up muck. It wasn't cold, but the combination of dark skies, precipitation and sunset caused her to tug her jacket closed across her chest.

Rex had ordered takeout at the Italian place near the airport, and she promised to pick it up. The longer it took her to get to the restaurant, the less time she'd have to spend, famished, smelling garlic and tomato sauce while she sat in the chairs for waiting carry out customers. She tapped the steering wheel along with the Beatles' "I've Just Seen a Face," the first song on the mix tape she'd put together a few weeks ago.

"You still make mix tapes?" Rex pursed his lips as if he'd found a dirty tool in a spotless drawer. Rex, so organized, so *linear.* "Why combine songs from different people, different albums? I play the whole album. You start something, you finish it." His favorite expression.

Rex's passion for organization led to comments about her less-than-spotless housekeeping. "Your bathroom sink is dirty," he'd announce. Or he'd pick up a towel she'd thrown on the floor after a shower, pinching it between his thumb and forefinger, holding it away from him like a dead skunk and ask, "Why not just hang this up?"

Her lack of homemaking skills mostly amused him—his long, thin fingers covered his mouth as he chuckled over spilled cat litter, trying not to get caught in a moment of levity. His lips had a natural downward curl, and his posture was always ramrod straight; his rusty laughter came out more like cackling. He seemed to find Tris hilarious, often giggling in response to comments she made.

She let his barbs about her messy habits and lack of concern about putting things away float by. Tris wasn't interested enough in his opinions to let them hurt her.

"That's what you get when you're seeing a charter pilot," she'd reply, an off-hand reference to the unpredictability of the on-demand type of flying she did. The irony of the comment wasn't lost on Rex. As Chief, Tris was way more than a charter pilot. She controlled every one of Westin's pilot schedules, including her own.

No, Tris and Rex weren't suited for the long term. Rex was a fine fit for right now.

Another honk jolted her into action. The song had changed to the Eagles "Desperado," and the little strip mall where the restaurant was tucked between a florist and a hardware store came into view.

She popped the tape out of the old Corolla's cassette deck and wondered, not for the first time, when she'd get around to buying a CD player. She'd have to replace all her albums and cassettes with CDs. That all seemed overwhelming, so best to keep rewinding.

As the restaurant door swung open, the gold Christmas bells hung with a red ribbon clattered.

Isn't it a little early for those?

The racket obscured the first ring of her mobile phone. She picked up on the second.

"Hi Rex."

"Got the food yet?" He never said hello.

"I'm here now. Hold on," she said and requested her order from the owner's wife, who was always at the cash register no matter what day or time Tris stopped by.

"Can whatever you want to talk about wait?"

Rex coughed, his only nervous tic. "I guess. Yeah, of course." But Tris could sense it couldn't.

"What is it? What's up?"

"Had a visit today from a friend of yours."

Tris scowled. "Our order is coming up. I'll see you soon. Bye."

"Your past came calling at our office today," Rex said the moment he opened the door, even before he leaned in to kiss her hello.

"Uh, hi. Can I please come inside?" That was Rex. When there was something on his mind, it had to come out immediately. It made her wonder how he could have had so much success in a place as political as the FAA.

"Is this about that award? You know, the one you didn't mention?" Her voice dripped with sarcasm.

"Tris, come on. I apologized already. I didn't tell you about it because—"

"Because you wanted to *surprise* me. Right?" Rex loved surprises and imposed them on her even though she'd told him she didn't like being caught unaware.

Rex looked chagrined. "It's a big deal for us, Tris. It's great press. Our very own icon."

He kissed her neck.

Tris moved away. "Can you please put the food out? I'm starved."

As much as she loved the symbolism of her uniform, it always made her feel like a little boy dressing in his father's pants, and she couldn't wait to shed it at the end of the day. One by one, off came her Captain's jacket, tie, and epaulets. Tris exhaled deeply as she unbuttoned her collar.

"Why in the world is every pilot uniform for women cut and sewn as if it is going to be worn by a man?" she mused, as she hung the jacket on an empty chair. Rex, busy in the kitchen, grunted.

Naturally slender through the hips, as she neared forty, Tris's body had begun to show some additional curves. She liked them, but they made her uniform a bit snugger.

Rex lay a Mepra ladle in the spoon rest. "Why Miss Miles," he said with a slight Texas twang left over from growing up in Dallas, "aren't you aware that pilot jobs are for *men*, and you should be in the kitchen, barefoot and pregnant, and not wearing some ol' boy's pants?" He put his arms around her and nuzzled her hair.

She turned to him and stuck her tongue out.

"Uh, don't pull that tool out unless you intend to use it."

"I think I might."

Laughing, Rex continued removing reflective paper tops from round aluminum containers of penne marinara, garlic bread with melted cheese, and meatballs. He'd ordered and paid, so Rex got his favorite meal tonight.

He reached behind the stained glass fronting his kitchen cabinets to bring out two pieces of fine cut Wedgewood Osborne China that he got to keep after his divorce. It seemed oddly formal for takeout Italian, but that was Rex.

Rex twisted out the cork from a bottle of red wine and poured generously into two Baccarat crystal glasses. Also from his divorce, so he said. Rex came from money but was circumspect about the details of his family background, and she didn't care. Maybe he'd tell her someday. Maybe not. Either way, she loved eating on plates and drinking from glasses that were valued at a thousand times the cost of their meal.

Rex talked and served. "It's extremely important to me that we include Jannat Madden in the award ceremony. Well, it's important to you, too." If it was important to *him* then it must be critical to everyone in his perceived sphere of influence.

"Is that so?" Tris munched on a piece of garlic bread, then stabbed some pasta with a Chrysanthemum fork and slid it into her mouth with a murmur of appreciation.

He pushed himself back in his chair. "Yes, that is so. You should make her the next Chief Pilot. It should be important to you. You remember the investigation that took place after that angel flight?"

Now Rex had her complete attention. "I do. It was a cluster." Woody had taken some heat for hiring Mike as Chief Pilot without conducting a criminal background check, or any background checks at all. Turns out, Mike had a past he didn't disclose—and Woody never asked. That was a mistake the FAA would stalk Westin to make sure they wouldn't repeat.

"Westin paid a fine and agreed to be on probation. Woody and I completely revamped our criteria and process of hiring. For six months, you personally reviewed every hire we made. But it wasn't all bad." She smiled and briefly touched his hand. "Here we are."

"Yes, yes, yes. But the FAA wants to see more diversity in your pilot group."

"More? I have six women out of ten total pilots. That's way more than any other charter operation at Exeter." Tris took pride in hiring the best of the best—and it thrilled her that so many of them were women.

"Right. But Tris . . . I don't know how to say this . . ."

"Say it, Rex."

He coughed again. "That's not the kind of diversity I'm talking about. Madden, well . . . The optics would be very good. She's from a very prominent Muslim family. She's a bit of a black sheep—" He abruptly stopped himself. "I have got to learn to stop saying that. Anyway, she's . . . unusual in her, uh, you know, *culture*."

Tris enjoyed Rex's discomfort. Diversity hiring was serious business to her. And, after all, she wasn't serious about Rex.

"And what culture is that, exactly? The culture of the professional aviator?" She pushed back, and immediately felt bad about it.

Rex's eyelids drooped and his lips parted slightly. "Hey, I'm not trying to insult her," he bleated. "It's just that, she's, um, different. In many ways." Rex nodded slightly, satisfied with his response.

She swallowed and shrugged. "I am always looking for diverse candidates of every type. Look, if I'd had one, even one, resume from an Asian, African American, Latino, or any other underrepresented group, don't you think I'd have jumped on it? Everywhere I look to actively recruit pilots, I have to wade through resumes from at least thirty white males before I see one from a qualified woman. What more can I do?"

"Let me make Madden a big focus of our spotlight. You won't be sorry."

"Do whatever you want. I'm curious, though—what's your angle with her?"

Rex answered in the next breath. "I told you. Diversity."

Tris took a sip of red wine. This conversation was going in circles. As she munched a mouthful of meatball, she caught a glimpse of herself. Across from the long kitchen island where they ate was a full-length antique mirror bordered in Fleur De Lis with a green patina.

"Do you have some personal stake in this, Rex? You seem obsessed with her."

A fleeting look of confusion passed over his face. "I don't have a *stake,* per se. I know her maid of honor casually. You know Madden's getting married right? Interesting choice for her, given her lifestyle."

The implications of that statement vexed Tris. A man trying to make sense of a female pilot's choices. As if Madden had to choose between marriage or being a pilot.

"Lifestyle? You realize she can be a married pilot, right?"

Rex grinned and shook his head. Tris had the feeling they were talking at cross purposes.

"*I* believe she can do anything, and everything, she wants. This is a tough business, Tris. You know that. A woman like Madden . . ." His voice trailed off.

"Well, thanks for your input." With that, Tris leaned over her plate, almost toppled her wine glass, and kissed Rex full on the lips. He pushed his lips against hers, then pulled away and vigorously wiped his mouth.

Tris went back to her meal. "I had to have a come-to-Jesus meeting with her. She's not a fan favorite in our hangar. Not sure how a big focus on her would get you what you want, whatever it is."

But Rex had already moved on. "So, as I mentioned, an old friend of yours stopped by today. To talk about you, as it happens."

Tris held her fork suspended in mid-air, tubes of pasta pierced on the ends. Aviation was incestuous, and pilots gossiped way more than any other group of professionals she'd worked with.

"What did Mike have to say?"

"Marshall? No, Ed Deter came by."

Tris's fork bounced against her plate, chipping the fine porcelain before landing on the floor. Sauce spattered her sleeve.

"Deter? Me? About what?"

Rex ran his finger over the damaged China and clucked his tongue. "I'll toss it," he muttered, then cleared his throat. "It was nothing big. He asked about your training records, you know, what documents to send to Legacy. He runs a corporate flight department, Tris, not an airline. He doesn't get many record requests, and he's not familiar with them."

She spoke slowly, trying desperately not to reveal that her pulse was racing. "What exactly . . . what *exactly* did he ask, Rex?"

Rex chewed a mouthful of meatball and swallowed before responding. "Not much. He wanted to know what should be included in the package he sent to Legacy."

"And you told him . . . what?"

Finally, he seemed to notice her discomfort. "Tris, calm down. It was nothing. He said he had lots of paperwork and was trying to parse it. That was all."

"Paperwork? What kind? Paperwork about *me*? Rex, be specific. What did he *say?*"

"You know, training records. That's all. He wanted to know if that's what he had to send. I told him yes. He said thanks and walked away. Tris, what happened was years ago. Your career survived—it thrived. Look where you are."

"And where I'm headed, right?"

Rex took a moment to wipe his mouth, and make sure his knife and fork were perfectly crossed on the plate. He shot an annoyed glance at the ruined China, then straightened up in his chair.

"You're crazy to leave Westin. Why go? It's a great company— you made it great—and you know Woody will never be able to hire anyone better. I don't understand it."

"But to work with her—Jennifer *Prince*, my god—the impact that woman has made on the lives of so many pilots, so many female pilots. How can I not want to be part of that?"

Rex closed his eyes and shook his head slightly, a cue that he was about to say something she wouldn't like.

"You're kidding yourself, Tris. I hate to say it, but you can't possibly have more impact there than where you are now. This fantasy about being able to affect the lives of female pilots by the thousands. It'll never happen. Flying is a narcissistic enterprise. Pilots think only of themselves, their careers, their incomes. I'm not saying you won't be a dedicated teacher. I know you love it. I'm saying those pilots won't care about what they can learn from you. You're a box they must check on their way to wherever they think their career is going. Beyond that, they won't give a damn."

"I have to try," she whispered. "Otherwise, what am I doing this for?" She gestured to her captain's jacket.

Rex was nothing if not perceptive. He didn't fully know what was motivating her, but he could tell there was something.

"Is there another reason?"

Bron's influence pervaded her entire professional life. The topic wasn't anything she could discuss with Rex.

"So, I should say screw it, right? Not accept the challenge. Maybe you're right about what I'll be able to achieve. But what if you're wrong?"

"More wine?" Rex winked. "Maybe take the bottle into the bedroom?" Like a typical pilot, when the conversation got difficult, he changed the subject.

Tris pretended to weigh her options. It was easy to be flippant with someone she didn't love. "Why Rex? What could we possibly do in there?" Of Rex's numerous talents, Tris most valued his skills and experience in bed.

He laughed heartily for the first time that night, a real laugh from deep down inside, picked up the glasses, and inclined his head toward the bedroom. Smiling, she followed him, grabbing the bottle on her way.

The two undressed themselves, neither aroused by the ritual.

When they lay down together on top of his down comforter, Rex ran his index finger along her lips, then down to her chin, then her collarbone, slowly working his way around to her breasts.

When he touched them, he let a quick gasp escape before lightly kissing each one. Tris took his head in both hands as he worked his way down her body, stopping to graze each part until he arrived at the place that would bring her the most pleasure.

The two writhed and twisted, stopping only briefly to look at each other and smile. Their acrobatics brought them both to the brink.

When their bodies could resist no longer, they let go together, and Rex took her hand in his and placed it on his heart, his unspoken language for how lucky he felt to be with her.

Eight

IT WAS EASIER to walk to the Boston crash pad some nights than to take a cab. Plus, the early September evening was crisp and clear, and Danny needed some fresh air. So much shit had happened today he could barely make sense of it all.

It didn't help that every few seconds, he checked his mobile phone for a call from Tris. Each time, the screen showed only the date and time. No voice mail. No missed calls. He'd left three messages but was still at a loss about what he'd say when she called him back. How do you tell your best friend that you can't ever talk to her anymore?

Danny's foot twisted in a hole made by someone working on the Big Dig near the airport. He yelped, but there was no one to hear him—construction workers had long ago gone home for the day. Local lore told the story of this gargantuan project that would likely never finish. Even at twilight, the shapes of backhoes and diggers with buckets as big as Olympic-sized swimming pools were easy to make out.

There was no shortage of port-a-potties in the construction

area. Danny loved their names. "Here's Johnny." "Willy Make It?" "Port-O-San, The Portable Can," and his own personal favorite, "Doodie Calls." He planned to make that his rallying cry to Emily when she had to change their son's diaper.

Their son. Or daughter.

Being with Emily was worth it, to raise their child together. He didn't know one person who was raised by a single parent who didn't have emotional issues later in life. No, his child would have them both around. Danny would be on the road a lot, yes, but when he was home, he'd be *home*, spending every moment being a father. That was the only thing he could imagine that was worth what he was about to lose.

After sliding in and out of divots and almost tripping over a raised curb that wasn't there the last time he made this trek, Danny finally cracked open the crash pad door.

The smell of mildew hit Danny like a slap. He'd hoped to be alone. Danny dropped his overnight bag with a thud.

"Sup," called one of his crash pad mates from the living room.

"SSDD, my man." Same shit, different day. "Another stint on reserve. Last time I sat here for five straight days." Danny surveyed the dirty apartment.

A very senior first officer, Jerry Joseph, nicknamed "Black," had his foot precariously balanced on the edge of the rickety thrift store card table in the living room. He'd gotten the nickname "Black Guy"—Black for short—in his new-hire class since, as usual, he was the only one. Now, he was sitting on the "good" chair—the one with the half-inch foam pad on it.

Danny pulled his phone out of his pocket, praying that maybe crew scheduling had called with a trip so he could get out of this hellhole and sleep in a nice clean hotel. No such luck.

"I'm hitting the head, then gonna get some sleep. You got a trip?"

"Yup. Tonight."

Black was a line-holder, so he only stayed at the crash pad if he had to commute in the night before a trip or couldn't get home after one ended.

"You know if anyone else is gonna be here over the next few days?" Danny figured it didn't hurt to ask.

Danny heard a grunt from Black. "Not me. Thank goodness."

Black was a decent guy. Respectful. Didn't say much but, really, what was there to talk about? After complaining about their respective commutes and schedules, the men who shared this temporary lodge had very little in common beyond their nasty surroundings.

A crash signaled the collapse of the card table. It was a recurring problem—the plastic tie holding one of the legs in place broke. Black didn't even react; CNN prattled on in the background.

"Very graceful," Danny chided Black. "Where the hell did Orange get these things from?" He joked, referring to another crash pad resident who everyone called Orange because, let's face it, that's what color his hair was.

"Goodwill? Or maybe the dumpster behind Goodwill, where they toss the stuff no human would want." Black fished a Leatherman tool out of his flight bag. The boxy black case was embossed with his full name "Jerome L. Joseph," and his Legacy Airlines employee number.

A quick look at the usual bedroom Danny slept in revealed that someone had already claimed the best mattress, and he'd have to blow up the camping bed. An exhausted sigh preceded his search for the plug-in pump he'd use to inflate it. It was an exercise in futility, since the mattress always deflated during the night, and he found himself on the cold linoleum floor in the morning. Hopefully, it would only be for one night.

"Tits, are you in there?" Black called, using his dreaded nickname.

"Yeah. I'm contemplating another comfortable night on the Coleman. Whaddaya need?"

"Wanted to tell ya the good bed's yours."

"You gonna pull your sheets or what?"

"Nah, you can do it. Toss them in a corner. I'll wash them," Black said.

Danny shrugged. At least he'd get to sleep on a decent bed tonight.

He pressed the number "1" on his phone's keypad. It used to be their number at home, but since Emily moved out, Danny had canceled the house phone. Now it was her mobile.

He expected voice mail but she answered. "Danny. I saw your number come up."

"Hey baby," he said, hopefully, as he always did, hoping she'd respond in kind.

A few seconds of dead air were followed by a quick "Hey, baby." Then Em's tone sharpened. "Have you told her? You said you were gonna tell her."

How could he tell his wife that he hadn't cut that piece of his heart loose, yet?

"I've called and called her. She's probably flying. Come on, Em, you don't want me to leave that kind of message on a voice mail, do you?"

A long pause preceded her next declaration. "I have a doctor's appointment tomorrow. Did I mention it?"

No, you did not. "My God, Em, are you sick?"

Her laugh sounded almost supernatural. "It's a little indigestion. Nothing to worry about."

"Are you going to Heather's doctor? The one she recommended?"

"Nope. I'm still seeing the one at Planned Parenthood."

"Why? Why do you still want to go there?"

She avoided the question. "When are you home?"

"The 12th. I traded some reserve days to get a full week off after that. I'll be home on Wednesday night."

Silence. "You promised you'd tell her. It's our future. Our baby's future. Leave her a message or something, Danny."

Easy. Easy. Don't scream.

"I said I'd do it, and I'll do it. I swear it, Em. Now call Heather's doctor. You don't want . . . those people delivering our child, do you?"

"Okay, baby," she said gaily, and hung up.

Danny's hands shook as he pressed down the #2 on his mobile, praying that Tris still wouldn't answer. After her outgoing message finished, he pressed End and called again. Listening to it brought him close to her, and each time the recording played, each time she failed to answer, meant at least a few more minutes, maybe even hours, that Tris would still be in his life.

Nine

INSIDE THE DOOR of her townhouse, Jannat hung her keys on the appropriate hook. Once she pulled the red poppy clip free, her dark shining mane streamed down the curve of her spine. So many were jealous of it, but unless her hair was wound into a tight bun and out of the way, it was mostly a bother. She stretched her neck and raised both arms to the sky to release stiffness in her back.

Today she'd earned some relaxation, having survived a two-leg trip with Sean, more wedding nonsense with Maman, and that tense meeting with Tris.

Tris's critique was not unexpected. Chuck's behavior reinforced his nickname—Cliché—after all, what was a cliché but a lazy trope someone used when they couldn't think of anything original? That described Chuck from tip to toe.

She'd worked with simpletons before. After intentionally pushing them as far as she felt reasonable, there was invariably some kind of chat with a supervisor. With a female Chief Pilot, she'd hoped that the rest of the team would be a bit more sophisticated. Chuck was the first indication that she'd be disappointed. At least he didn't leer at her. Male pilots frequently stared, and she'd have to flash her engagement ring to shut them down. Wedding bands didn't seem to have the same effect. They denoted settling. With an engagement ring, the union was all about possibility; something men respected more.

Her parents never pushed her to choose one man over another, although of course it would have been much easier on them if she'd picked a wealthy, well-educated son of one of the Muslim families they were close to, the boys she'd grown up with, celebrated *Nowruz* with, laughed with while they jumped over candles on *Chaharshanbe Suri.*

Randy's family was wealthier than her own. Their family furniture business started by his great-great-grandfather was phenomenally successful. Theirs was old money, and they lavished it on their only son and his bride-to-be. That's how the couple had been able to buy a townhouse in the trendy Lakeview section of Exeter.

Luckily, her fiancé's attitude toward material things was the same as her own. Despite his family's wealth, the only extravagance Randy craved was a new car every couple of years. He liked it easy, simple. Get take-out. Watch a movie. He enjoyed doing the little everyday things that Jannat hated. She'd grab clean clothes out of the dryer and ignore the crusty white toothpaste residue in the bathroom sink. He folded laundry and cleaned house with a smile.

Jannat picked up her mobile. The screen was empty, but her Blackberry buzzed. "?? r u," twice from Suzette. Suzette was a storm front moving in from the west, nothing like Randy—gentle waves lapping against the shore.

Jannat punched the number on her mobile that cued the waves.

"Mrs. Eller?" Randy answered the same way every time.

"Where are you?"

"Dry cleaner. Made it right before they closed. Good thing too—I need clean shirts. What's the latest?"

"Flowers with Maman."

A chuckle. "Wellll," he dragged out the word, "I think my daddy may have tried to teach me about the birds and bees the other day."

"Again?"

"Yeah. One track mind on that man. He'll write a check for whatever I ask—as a joke, I said you should arrive in a carriage drawn by Clydesdales—and he nodded and asked me if we were 'compatible' in bed. 'It's critical, son. Why look at me and your mother . . .'"

"Oh no."

"Oh yes!"

Randy's mother had prodded Jannat about the same thing once. To Maman's credit, she'd urged her only daughter not to consummate her relationship with Randy before marriage, but then left it alone. As close as they were, Jannat refused to discuss that part of her life with Maman. She and Randy had agreed to wait for the wedding night. If Maman knew, she'd be thrilled. If Mr. Eller knew, he'd panic.

"See you shortly. You're home for one night, right?"

"Yeah, baby."

Jannat snapped her phone shut and grabbed a bottle of water from the fridge. She looked up at the airspeed indicator clock on the wall. It was nine-thirty, early enough to call Maman. She wanted to apologize for being so distracted while they talked wedding planning. Baba was probably home, the two of them sitting in the kitchen, enjoying Maman's delicious stew.

Her parents adored Randy's Southern manners. His attentiveness to Jannat reminded them of how women were courted in Iran. Randy was the one who had suggested that he pick her up at her parents' house on their first date. To make that happen, he'd had to jump seat from Savannah, Georgia, change out of his uniform in the Legacy crew room at the airport, grab a rental car, and drive unfamiliar streets to the house in Avon, a suburb forty minutes away.

Their relationship grew in restaurants. They'd walk in, feeling the stares fix on the white guy whose hand rested on the shoulder of the not-so-white woman.

They'd talk for hours while their food got cold. Each felt the strength of their fit early on and the road to their engagement was short. Randy was her bridge, her path to a life she could manage.

Planning a wedding that meshed their two cultures was not the biggest challenge they'd face. "What are your plans for having a family?" Maman asked tentatively. Jannat swatted at the question as she might an errant fly that snuck in while the door was open.

Jannat drained the bottle of water and felt her stomach growl. She'd only had a small breakfast, and a taste of her mother's stew. Randy would be hungry, too. There was leftover Chinese food from the night before in the fridge, so she popped the containers in the microwave.

In the corner of the couch, wedged among glossy photographs of wedding flowers, Jannat assessed the benefits of promotion if the rumors that Tris was leaving were true. More money. More authority. More options to control her schedule and create the life she required.

Finally, she heard the front door open. "Hello, hello," Randy called, exactly as he always did.

"In here. I am buried in bouquets. Maman's last stand. I was firm about the catering, and the—my goodness I can barely say the word—*bunting* on the backs of the chairs. I would rather not carry a bouquet. But in this she is unyielding."

Randy passed behind her and squeezed her neck. She leaned back into his touch. He let his fingers play in the roots of her hair before he moved toward the kitchen.

The pop of a can was followed by Randy taking a long swig of something. "Why don't you have Suzette decide? Isn't that what a maid-of-honor is supposed to do? Take some of the stress off the bride?"

The sound of Suzette's name coming from Randy's mouth always caused a shiver. She got more and more used to it every day, but it would never sound completely natural. Randy and Suzette got along well, fortunately. Still.

"I suppose. You know Suzette. She is in and out of this process. I sometimes question her commitment." To the wedding process, for sure. To Jannat, never.

"Baby, I know you're trying to keep everything drama-free, but . . ." Randy sat down on the opposite end of the couch from his betrothed, separated by a sea of glossy roses, lilies and gerbera daisies. The scoop neck of the short-sleeved tees he wore to keep the armpits of his pilot shirts from yellowing peeked out below his already loosened collar. A can of Diet Pepsi rested on a coaster on the glass coffee table top.

"But it's not possible. Too many dramatic people involved." Jannat smiled. They shared a knowing look.

"Right. My mama." Both understood that Mrs. Eller's contribution to this union was to amp up the fuss with incessant nattering. "Yeah, she called me at least a dozen times while I was on reserve. I didn't get a trip, so I couldn't reasonably refuse to engage. That's exactly what I recommend you do, baby. 'Yes' is the word with my mama, whether you mean it or not. Then ignore her."

As if she could. Mrs. Eller. Maman. Too many mothers involved in this. Suzette pestered her, too. From Suzette, she could understand it. This wedding was more her idea than Jannat's—and a good one, on paper. The execution was another story.

"If it were only that easy. Come on, Randy. Weigh in on the flowers. Pick a photo that you like, and we'll be done with that part.

Then we can hang out, enjoy our night together."

Randy leaned over the photos, and, within seconds, picked a bouquet. Red and white roses, to go with his family's blue blood. "That's it. That's the one." He flipped the picture across the couch to his intended and reached for his soda. "So. Leftover Chinese, right?"

Despite being the daughter of a world-class Persian cook, Jannat was a disaster in the kitchen. When they'd shared an apartment after college, Suzette always cooked. She was a truly masterful chef.

"Already in the microwave. Grab it, will you?"

"Sure. You're kind of stuck there—I'll serve it up." His smile lit a warm path across the couch. He loved her, that was certain. He'd be good to her; of that she was also sure. Would she ever get used to the guilt, that horrible feeling of never being able to match Randy's devotion? It was obvious even now—Randy was the partner who loved more.

Part of her heart had been claimed years before, stamped and sealed with melted wax, hardened by resolve, and used to guard secret truths that could be devastating to her career.

The secrets had been useful. She'd raised them as a shield against the men who constantly vied for her attention. Then Randy got through, just a little, enough for her to think that the unthinkable was possible.

She would marry a man, have one kind of life with him, and another with Suzette.

She smiled as she pressed Suzette's speed dial.

"Suz. I'm buried in flower pictures. Randy chose the bouquet."

Loud laughter came from her best friend. "How handy that you have him around."

"So true. He's making dinner."

"Oh yeah? What's he warming up?"

"Chinese."

"Can't make *adas polo,* huh?" Suzette pivoted to the mention of Jannat's favorite Persian dish, which Suzette cooked to perfection.

"Stop that. Remember, you like Randy. *You* chose Randy, too. He's such a decent guy." Jannat picked at a loose thread on her sweatpants. "Sometimes I . . ."

"No, *you* stop it, Jannat joon. It will work."

"I know," she whispered. "But is it fair? Truly?"

Suzette replied wearily. "This again? He's getting what he wants."

"Baby, food's ready," Jannat's husband-to-be called from their eat-in kitchen.

Suzette sighed. "Sounds like chow time. When will I see you?"

Jannat looked around the townhouse like she was being spied on. "Randy's leaving for Boston again tomorrow night. Stop by sometime. For wedding planning and all."

"Got it."

Jannat hadn't noticed until that moment the rhythmic patter of rain on the roof. Fall weather had rolled in again.

Perhaps the skies would clear in time for Suzette's visit.

Ten

THE DEADBOLT on the front door clicked open at exactly 11:00 p.m. Then came the thump of something large hitting the ground—Suzette's enormous purse—and the clackety-clack of heels on the entryway tile. Jannat made no move to sit up in bed or turn on the lights.

Pilots were used to coming and going at odd hours. So little about their lives mirrored the world in which most people lived. Meals were eaten when they could be, and often Jannat found herself desperately trying to keep her eyes open during an oh-dark-thirty show time at the airport while eating a leftover turkey sandwich from a catering tray.

The lifestyle fit her. Nothing about it or her was predictable. She smiled and squeezed her eyelids together as footsteps traversed the kitchen, and the door to the refrigerator opened and closed, followed by the snap of a pop-top. A beer? Diet Pepsi? She'd soon find out.

Jannat had a guaranteed day off, a day where she could plan something or hang around the house without the threat of her pager beeping. It was one of the perks of working for a large charter operation run by a woman who understood the need for personal time. Jannat almost laughed out loud. Tris was at the airport every single day, whether she was flying or not.

No matter what time Jannat showed up for work, Tris was there. Her boss had a way of greeting her that made the junior captain feel special, valued. The pilots at Westin agreed on very little, but one thing they all believed was that Tris had their best career interests at heart.

Jannat was ready to move up, ready for more responsibility. The day-to-day requirements of being Chief, the paperwork, the scheduling, the training, she could handle that. While Randy was away on a five-day trip, she could easily work out her schedule to have time for Suzette. Woody wouldn't notice her coming and going unless there was a problem. He managed the bottom line and was mainly focused on bringing in business—doing charity events, going to Chamber of Commerce meetings, and getting photographed at community festivals with local influencers. If Woody didn't make money, his business partner Jimbo would have something to say about it. The last thing he had time for were the day-to-day details of the pilot group.

Jannat imagined herself in Tris' role. Could she mentor the rest of the pilot group the way Tris had? If Jannat questioned her own ability to be a role model, she knew Tris did, too.

First officers who assumed they knew more than the captain did and tried to run the trip from the right seat—like that know-it-all Sean—found that once they upgraded and had the ultimate authority for the safety of the flight, the world looked a lot different.

If Jannat didn't fully discharge her duties as captain she'd be called to task by Tris. Tris didn't let anyone get away with sloppy prep, bad execution or even an airplane that left the hangar in less than perfect condition.

I'll be an even better Chief. More diligent. Stricter. Even safer.

"What was that baby?" Jannat must have mumbled her thoughts aloud. "Care to repeat it?"

Jannat smiled in the dark. "Nope. But if you don't hurry up, I might not let you in bed."

"Fat chance of that."

Outside came the first clap of thunder from the approaching storm. With her clothes stripped off in what seemed like a millisecond, Suzette joined Jannat on the King-sized mattress that Randy's parents had sent as an early wedding present.

Eleven

AFTER A DEEP SLEEP, Rex had reached for Tris again early in the morning while they were only half-awake. A slow-moving encore capped off their acrobatics from the night before.

Tris rose reluctantly to grab a quick cup of coffee before heading home to shower and change for work. She missed her cats and liked to start the day in her own private space.

Rex got up and stood in front of the sink. His first action every morning, no matter what time, was to trim his already fussy beard. It was a thin strip of hair extending from his sideburn which took a 90 degree turn at his chin line, and finished its travels below his lip, where the tiny hairs met up with the carefully clipped mustache above them. Rex's daily facial hair coif routine to maintain the boxy L-shape on his face was the model of his personality. A little finicky, slightly over-tended, and very specific.

A cry from the bathroom meant some kind of nick. Rex never swore. Ever.

"What happened?"

"I'm a little distracted, I guess. Doggonit." He blotted the blood with a tissue. "So, when will I see you again?" He put his hand on her shoulder. Tris wriggled away as she put on her jacket. It was still raining.

"After Edinburgh. We launch on Sunday, back on Tuesday the 11th. Less than 48 hours on the deck." She took a final sip of coffee and placed her mug in the sink. Rex followed her toward his apartment's front door.

She could feel him behind her as she moved from closet, to purse, to exit. "Bye baby," he said, and leaned over to give her a kiss. This time, Tris moved too quickly, and his lips pecked the air as the door closed behind her.

A chill ran through Tris as she hurried out of her car in her condo's underground parking lot. It was going to be a soupy day yet the hair on her neck still stood up. She shook it off as being due to lack of sleep.

Deter showed up at the FAA, asking about her. It was too close, too connected. Rex ignored her anxiety, as he often did, dismissing it as a character flaw and assuming that it would pass faster unacknowledged than if he asked her what was wrong and listened to her tell him.

As she hurried to catch up with her routine, everything inside her apartment stirred into motion at a pace that matched her own internal churn. Both cats slid around her legs like a figure eight. Orion, the long-haired Tuxedo, complained the loudest. Falcon, a petite two-year-old black female, chirped like one of the sparrows that sung outside her bedroom window in the spring.

"Okay, guys, hold on a sec," Tris muttered. An attempt to hang her jacket in the hall closet failed, and it pooled on the floor over her work boots and an old umbrella. Mail was flung on a table in the entryway. Intentionally slowing herself down, she carefully placed her keys next to the answering machine and pressed the button to hear her messages while she checked their food and water bowls. All four were at least half full.

"Three. New. Messages," the synthesized voice announced. The mini cassette in the old machine sounded strained, almost out of breath during the rewind.

"Hey Flygirl, it's me." Danny. He'd once again resurrected the nickname Bron had given her. It belonged to another time, one that still evoked a persistent ache. It had taken years for the grief over Bron's death to fade and for the woman who had been *his* Flygirl to move on.

She should remind Danny again to stop using it. He'd been so stressed lately, maybe it was best to leave it alone.

"I've got some . . . uh . . . big news. Call me. No kidding. It's really important. So, as soon as you can. Okay. Peace out, Flygirl."

The tone of his voice, which was usually deadpan, rose and fell during the brief message. Lately, Danny talked non-stop about how he wanted to stay married. It made no sense. The divorce would rectify a bad decision. He and Emily had been miserable together, a bad match from the get-go. Danny was the most loyal person she'd ever known, and he'd want to keep the promise he made that day at the altar. Till death do us part, right? How many times had he repeated that hackneyed phrase? Instead of acknowledging that he was in a bad marriage, he was fighting to keep Emily.

How much more dear people seem when you're about to lose them.

Loss. Always hiding behind her eyes; she'd seen it looking back at her in the mirror so many times. On difficult days like Bron's birthday, or the anniversary of her first date with Mike, it was hard to resist remembering what had been good, why she'd loved them.

Sometimes she saw the same haunted look on Rex's face. His divorce had become final merely six months ago. She'd asked him about it, once. Rex shrugged. "Bad fit," was all he'd say. Like he was explaining a poor career choice at an interview.

Their relationship made some of her harder days a bit easier, and Tris hoped they did for Rex too. Sitting on her beat-up leather chair, fluffy Orion settled in between her thigh and the chair's arm, and Falcon's little frame curled in her lap, she saw the vision from her latest recurring dream: Bron, Mike and Rex in a circle, playing cards as a thunderstorm crashed down on them. There was a fourth person there, face obscured, wearing a pilot uniform.

The machine clicked, and two messages from Diana followed, each a quick, "Call me."

It had been a year since her friend and mentor, the woman who had taught Tris to fly all those years before, had moved back to Exeter in disgrace after getting fired from her job. Her flying career, one she'd more than earned after serving her country in the Air Force, hung by a thread. Diana had fought back. She'd challenged the neanderthal-like medical policies of the FAA that had forced her to make some bad choices. It took a year of battle until she regained her medical qualification. That, coupled with all her experience, helped her overcome the black marks on her record and find another pilot position.

The problem was where she found it. Diana flew for Tetrix, Inc., where Tris had spent the hardest year of her professional life.

Tris had implored her friend not to accept the job. Diana had heard all the wretched details of the horror show Tris had experienced. She'd spent so many hours listening as Tris detailed the bullying and abuse she'd taken during her year at Tetrix, how could she possibly accept a flying position there herself?

Diana responded with indifference. "It's not the same for me. Deter's the Chief Pilot now. He and I are both retired military. We have that in common. And, well . . ."

"What? What would make it easier for you, Di, knowing what you know? What could make you want to work for a man who blocked me at every turn, insulted me, bullied me. Because I was a woman—for no other reason." Tris still couldn't fathom how Ed Deter, who had never hidden his contempt for female pilots, could offer Diana a job. "What makes it different for you?"

"You were the first. I'm not," she'd said matter-of-factly.

They hadn't talked much since Diana joined Tetrix. Tris checked her watch and pressed her friend's number on her mobile phone keypad.

Diana answered on the first ring. "Tris? Hey, how's it going?" She was so excited she didn't even wait for an answer. "I got crewed on a trip to China. Flying the Gulfstream."

That was a trip Tris would have loved to make. Not for the first time, she fantasized about how wonderful the job at Tetrix could have been, should have been. If only.

No. She'd never want to fly anywhere with Diana's crew mates. She'd fly to China and places Tetrix planes would never go as a pilot for Legacy.

Keep your eyes on the prize. Now I sound like Cliché.

"Oh yeah. That's great. Who's doing it with you?" Tris asked, although she could guess.

"Deter. He wouldn't miss a trip like this. You know him. Now that he's Chief Pilot, he can fly any trip he wants."

"I'm sure I'll get to China with Legacy soon enough. And at least I won't have to spend all that time with Deter. That's a lot of dead hours crossing the Pacific Ocean with him sitting three feet away." Tris instantly regretted the words that brought her jealousy into the open.

Diana didn't hesitate. "It's China, Tris! Honestly, I never thought I would get there. He's not that bad. So, anyway, I've got more news. Deter sent your paperwork to Legacy."

Tris took a deep breath, unwilling at this point to share the news she had from Rex. "How do you know?"

"He knows we're friends. He told me. Tris, what's wrong? This is *good* news. Another box checked. He also asked me if you'd told Woody yet."

Her face flushed instantly. "That's none of his business. He didn't call Woody, did he?"

Diana tried to soothe her friend. "Tris, calm down. No, it wasn't like that. I think Deter was happy for you. I think he was making conversation. *Have* you told Woody?"

Tris concentrated on slowing her pulse. The memories of her working relationship with Deter still stung. She shook them off. Again.

"Not yet. I'm waiting for . . . I don't know what I'm waiting for. I want to tell him when I get back from Edinburgh next week. The class date will still be a month away. Yeah, when I get back, there's still plenty of time for them to get Woody's records, do all that paperwork."

Diana whistled. "You've gotta tell him Tris. You sure you want to wait?"

Her pulse again in a sprint, Tris walked in circles around her coffee table. "I want to wait. Until they get the Tetrix records."

"Why? You passed everything there, right? Deter said you did."

How could she explain it? It was done, but it would never be over. If Tetrix had any input in her career, no matter how small, the fear would live on.

"It's Tetrix. I don't trust them. Did Deter say anything else? Anything about the FAA?"

"FAA? No. Why? Why would they be involved?"

Why indeed. Tris couldn't shake the feeling that she'd never wear a Legacy Airlines uniform.

Orion bumped his nose against her hand as she sat on the edge of the bed. Thunder cracked outside a window Tris had forgotten to close before she left the house yesterday. She cursed the weather reports that forecast clear, sunny skies. The small stream of water running down the interior windowsill proved them wrong.

Diana was right. It was time to tell Woody about Legacy; tell him that she was leaving. Legacy human resources needed to contact Woody and were waiting for her to give her notice. They kept calling her; surely, they wanted to move forward with her background check. Unfortunately, Tris couldn't put it off until after Edinburgh. The time had come.

She and Woody had their weekly catch-up meeting this morning. She'd do it today. Once the initial shock passed, he'd be thrilled for her. Though he was gruff on the outside, the stretched-out pockets on Woody's Dockers were filled with compassion. His loyalty to Tris was unquestioned: he'd offered her the very first flight instructing job she'd ever had, and then took her back at the lowest point in her career, after she left Tetrix. Woody was the person who'd trusted her to fly his customers when he first started Westin Charter, and the one who made her Chief Pilot after the angel flight.

Today, she'd ask for his blessing. Sure, he'd be happy. Sad for himself. Happy for her.

Absolutely.

He couldn't have any reaction unless she got to the airport. The rain would double the length of her drive and complicate today's flight to Boston with Chuck. A quick shower, a few sips of coffee, and a brush through her hair were all she had time for before pointing her old Corolla toward the field that had been her home base for years.

By the time she pulled into the Chief Pilot's designated spot in the parking lot, her mobile phone had rung four times, and chimed three voice mail alerts. She listened as she gathered her things. Each one was from Danny.

Danny's messages were quick, each just a "call me," but in a voice that made it seem like he didn't really want her to. Tris would sort that out later.

Tris threw her phone in her bag, opened the car door, and put her foot directly into a puddle of standing water. Low, angry clouds swirled around her as she squished her way into the hangar, ignoring the pelting rain. Leaking water, she leaned against the metal door and peeled off her dripping sock. Limping on one wet bare foot, Tris practically ran into Woody, who barreled into the hangar searching for her.

"My office," he said when their eyes met.

Woody avoided looking at Tris as the two settled in their chairs. "Something you want to tell me?" he said, jaw set, eyes hard, tone caustic.

He was in a mood.

"Good morning, Woody. Sure, I have a few agenda items."

"Is this one of them?" He sputtered and threw a sheet of paper toward her. It landed at the edge of the desk and Tris caught it before it sailed onto the floor. "What am I supposed to do with all this, Tris?"

It was from the FAA. "PROOF COPY: Westin Charter Company: The Pride of Exeter," appeared in bold block letters. Pictures of Woody, Jimbo, and Tris sat below the by-line.

"What about it Woody? It's an FAA puff piece ahead of that *thing* they're doing next week. Didn't they quote you correctly? Why are you so upset?"

"Have you read it?"

"Not yet."

Woody sat back in his chair with such force, he almost toppled over. "I'll wait."

There it was. Paragraph four.

We caught up with one of Miles' previous employers, Tetrix Inc. "Yes, of course we were satisfied with Tris Miles. She'll be a great asset to Legacy Airlines," said Ed Deter, their Chief Pilot.

Leave it to Deter. Damn.

Woody's face was crimson. "You're leaving?"

Rex blindsided me. Again.

Heat filled her cheeks. Tris looked at her feet. "Woody, that's one of the things . . ."

"I built this company around you, Tris. I hired you as a no-time flight instructor, and then *again* after the beating you took from those Tetrix guys. I handed you the controls of my business. I stood by you through all the angel flight fallout, when they were investigating our operation like we were criminals. How could you do this to me? Crap on a cracker, Tris, you're my *Chief Pilot*." Woody's anger sizzled and popped in time with the thunderstorm booming outside.

Tris bent forward and released her hair from behind her ears to hide her face. Sitting there, in Woody's office, all power left her spine, and she feared that if she stood, her legs would not support her. She breathed heavily for a few seconds, hoping the storm that raged inside the room would pass.

"When's your class date? I assume you set one."

Tris couldn't look at him. "October 8th."

He jumped up out of his chair, poised to reach across the table. "A month. Only a month?"

As quickly as he'd sprung, he slumped back. Normal color returned to his cheeks, his eyelids drooped, and his lips extended in a pout. "What am I gonna do without you?"

Relieved and uncomfortable at the same time, Tris replied calmly. "Don't worry, Woody. We'll sort it out. I promise I'll have a plan in place when I get back from Edinburgh."

"When's that trip?"

"Out Sunday, back Tuesday. Woody, I wouldn't ever leave Westin, leave *you*, without . . ." Tris choked and couldn't go on.

Woody grasped the extra-large plastic container of Tums that was a fixture on his desk. He popped open the top and crunched two of the pastel discs. "Why Tris? What can they give you that I can't? Why would you betray me like this?"

"It's not like that, Woody. Not at all. Look, it's—"

A knock on Woody's office door interrupted her. Phyll stood there, holding her clipboard. "Tris, your passengers are set to arrive shortly. Time to get cracking, eh?"

"Woody, look. When I get back from Boston, let's pick this up."

Woody brushed her off with a hand wave and yanked his ringing cell phone from his pocket. "Yeah?" he bellowed into the phone.

Mortified, hurt, and royally pissed off, Tris left Woody's office. Outside, she turned her attention to the work she'd do in the cockpit, the one place where she could push everything else aside.

Her mobile phone buzzed again.

"Heading to greener pastures, eh?"

Chuck was at her side the second Tris entered the hangar, holding a fresh bucket of ice and his usual collection of snacks—one bag of M & M's, one can of Pringles, and a fresh bag of red licorice. He'd raided the storage closet for the first two and was never without the third.

The two were off to Boston shortly. It was not typical for the Chief and Assistant Chief to fly together, but they were the only pilots available to take this last-minute trip.

"Chuck, what are you talking about?" Tris kept her eyes on the flight plan in her hand.

"Wanna keep a secret? Don't tell anybody else. I could hear everything through Woody's office door from the stockroom. You're lucky that all our other planes are gone, so no one else is around."

"Ask me what you want to know, then."

"Are you leaving for Legacy Airlines?"

"Who else knows?"

Not one for subtlety, Chuck laughed out loud. "Everyone knows. We've all heard the rumor."

If one pilot repeated a piece of gossip, it suddenly carried the mark of truth.

"I had to tell Woody, but the rest of the staff . . . I'll call a meeting for when we get back tomorrow. Until then, Chuck, I need you to keep it to yourself. Yes, I accepted a class date."

Chuck's shoulders popped into the air in assent. "I know how you are about loyalty. Hey, I'm your Assistant Chief Pilot. I'm not gonna shit where I eat. I won't tell anyone, so your secret is safe with me. But it'll get out. You know this business."

Indeed she did.

"You leave, I'm up for promotion. Right?" Chuck often avoided looking her in the eye. This time, his gaze fixed on her like a laser.

"You'll be considered, Chuck."

"Considered?"

"Yes, you're a strong candidate. You're the Assistant Chief, and Woody . . ."

"Woody likes me."

Tris smiled. "He does, yes. I do too."

Try as she might to control her expression, Chuck gave her the side eye. If Chuck picked up on something, it must be glaring. "You're considering Madden. It's obvious how much you like her. Everyone sees it." It wasn't a question.

Tris flushed, embarrassed and more than a little annoyed that her favoritism showed.

"I've been here longer. I've been loyal."

Chuck and Woody were in the same bowling league. "Rivals under the same flag," Woody often said as he slapped Chuck on the back, referring to their two different teams. Tris would have to push Woody hard to promote Jannat, who he seemed to be a bit afraid of.

Tris handed Chuck the trip paperwork. "Put this in the cockpit, okay? I'm going to grab our passengers. Let's be ready to go." He sprang into action, directing the rampers to push the Falcon 50 out of the hangar.

Tris returned a few minutes later, chatting with three basketball players they were flying to a game in Boston. Each looked like they either hadn't slept the night before or dozed for only a few minutes after a night of partying.

"The early bird catches the worm, you know," Chuck said as they approached. Two of the three ignored him. The eye roll from a man in knee-length shorts and Air Jordans was obvious. "Make sure there's coffee," he growled as he bent over to enter the cabin that was way too low for him to stand in.

It might be fun to catch Chuck unaware for once. "So, what kind of bird are you, then?"

"Huh? What?"

Chuck never saw the humor. He believed the time-worn phrases he spoke had meaning. Studying for her masters in English Literature, Tris had learned the history of cliches. Turns out, they were an important part of the English language. How else would they become so entrenched in everyday conversation?

Tris slid into the left seat and briefed the trip. "Two legs today. One to Lafayette to pick up another player, hopefully more awake than our current passenger complement, then fly them out to Boston Logan. I've got the first leg; you've got the second. Any questions?"

"No questions," Chuck said crisply.

"Before Engine Start checklist, please."

They swiftly performed the well-trained activities designed to get them airborne. All cockpit conversation below 10,000 feet was limited to items essential to flight. The minute they broke through that barrier, with the autopilot engaged, and their passengers snoring, they could talk.

Chuck began with, "I've been working toward this for a while, Tris. You know that. I was Chief at a smaller operation when you hired me. I'm ready. Tris, I've stood behind you for a year. I had another Chief Pilot opportunity come up a few months ago and I turned it down."

Chuck hadn't mentioned it, but of course she'd heard. It was only a one-airplane shop and being Assistant Chief at Westin was a way better gig. Still, she always admired Chuck for not using the offer to try and leverage additional benefits at Westin.

"I waited. I figured you'd move on some day. Everyone does. And I'd be your successor."

Tris hadn't expected to have this conversation today and didn't have a demurrer prepared. "Chuck, you've done a great job. I support you for the position. But it's not guaranteed."

"Madden." He hissed.

Chuck gnawed at his already obliterated thumbnail. A habitual nail biter, it was the only one left that peeked past his cuticle. "Ma'am." Chuck drew the word into several syllables. "Are you really thinking of promoting someone who isn't the best candidate for the job?"

Tris ignored his question.

With that, she felt him pull away from her, already positioning his loyalty elsewhere. It wasn't uncommon in this career, where people moved around so often. Engage the person who could do you the most good. Local women's groups boosted Westin's profile, but the business Woody gleaned from that exposure would never compete with what came in through the old boy's network.

Luckily, Chuck recognized the need to change the subject. "So, Tris, since we're overnight, you gonna try and hook up with your friend? Am I having dinner alone?"

She still hadn't returned Danny's calls. His crash pad was walking distance from their hotel but with the Big Dig going on, too hazardous to navigate on foot. There was a restaurant in the Embassy Suites, where they were staying, and a bar close by.

"Not sure. Let's get busy with approach and landing items, shall we?" Luckily, checklists required the crew's immediate attention as they neared Lafayette. They went about the business of getting the aircraft safely on the ground, and everything else fell away.

Compartmentalization, the ability to cast aside unwanted emotions at will, was the best, and worst, characteristic of being a pilot. Today, she was grateful for it.

Once they landed, Tris switched her mobile back on. Her voice mail chirped. Danny had left two more messages. There was a third from a number with a Denver area code that she recognized. Legacy Airlines again.

Tris was about to call Legacy to tell them they were clear to call Woody, but the appearance of their new passenger propelled her into action. This freakishly tall gentleman looked like he was sleepwalking. He climbed into the cabin and, like his cohorts, promptly began snoring.

Chuck came up behind her. "I smell ribs. Do you?" he said, munching on a braided red rope. The air in Louisiana was thick and carried the aroma of thousands of barbecue grills.

"Brisket for lunch, I guess."

Chuck made a 360-degree turn on the ramp, sniffing the air. "Can't place it. Next time, I'm gonna track that scent down." He stepped up into the cabin to fill the ice compartment.

The fueler would be pumping for another minute. She scrolled to one of Danny's missed calls and pressed redial.

"What's up, Flygirl?" Danny yelled.

"In Louisiana. On my way to Boston. Where are you?"

"At the crash pad. Are you overnight? Can we hang? Can we? Please?" He sounded manic.

Her better judgment told her to say no. Tris wasn't sure she was up for another evening of weepy Danny, crying over the divorce. He was her best friend, but everyone had limits.

Then she recalled the hours and hours he'd spent with her as she cried over Bron, and then later when she agonized about Tetrix for weeks and months. Those were substantial deposits in the emotional joint bank account that friends like Danny and Tris had. Their history gave him a large positive balance she was more than grateful to honor.

"Sure. We'll be there in a few hours. I'll call you when we're on our way to the hotel. I'm going to need a nap, but if all goes according to schedule, meet me in the lobby of the Embassy Suites at six tonight? Okay?"

"That's perfect. See ya later, Flygirl." He abruptly hung up. Danny always said goodbye.

"Okay, let's get this show on the road!" Chuck popped his head out of the jet, beckoning Tris up the air stairs.

Her voice mail alert went off. Legacy again.

Twelve

JANNAT RUBBED HER EYES and turned toward the sleeping Suzette. Her maid of honor's thick eyeliner and mascara were mussed and streaked, making her look a bit like a round-faced Alice Cooper.

Jannat got out of bed and opened the curtains. The room came to life as dust swirled in the beams of sunlight. The smell of the morning's rain wafted in through the open window, along with typical weekday sounds: delivery vehicles and the occasional child playing. Both her neighbors worked regular nine-to-five schedules, so there was never any noise coming through their shared walls during the day.

Suzette lay snoring on top of the white comforter. She was tough to wake up when she was out like this, after a late night of intense lovemaking. Jannat decided not to try. Pulling her robe around her, she made her way to the kitchen to grab a cup of coffee from the carafe, brewed fresh a few minutes ago per the programming she'd set the night before. Jannat was thrilled to have a day where she could sleep in, and her body had let her.

Some nights she couldn't sleep at all, her duplicity churning in her body like a spin cycle. This morning, thankfully, there was no guilt, only complete satisfaction.

Jannat enjoyed the quiet for a few minutes before Suzette padded in, her flip flops slapping the tile floor. Her long black curls fell in front of her face. In the light, it was easy to see the few wiry grey hairs that had crept into her thick mane.

"Good morning, Soudeh," Jannat sang.

A sour look shot through the wall of hair.

Soudeh was Suzette's given name, but it never suited her. It meant 'touched' in Persian, and Jannat always joked that she was touched all right—in the head. Few knew her real name and no one questioned that she was, completely, Suzette.

"So kitsch it's almost cool again," Suzette muttered, a quote she'd read somewhere about her chosen name. "Remember that. I'm kitsch *and* cool!" She coughed, a remnant of her many years of smoking before Jannat threatened to end their relationship if she didn't quit. That was years ago, yet the hacking persisted. The only change was that Jannat didn't shame her for it.

Her throat finally cleared, Suzette sat on the barstool next to Jannat at the small kitchen island. "So. When's the boy coming home?"

"Not until Wednesday. The 12th, I think it is. His parents are coming to town for wedding planning this weekend and he won't even be here. Can you join Maman and me on 'Eller Duty?' I can count you in, right?"

Suzette laughed out loud, then succumbed to coughing. "You already know the answer to that. Your new in-laws are insufferable."

"Please? You'd keep his mom in check. I think she's a little afraid of you."

Suzette kissed the top of Jannat's head as she went to grab a coffee mug. "I'll think about it. They are quite annoying."

Jannat smiled. "True enough. But Randy comes with them."

Suzette poured coffee. "It's all going to work out, isn't it? You love him, right?"

Jannat nodded. "Very much. I can't imagine settling down with anyone else." When Suzette's brows cinched, she said, "No. Not even you." Jannat had always been up-front with her lover. She had no preference for men or women in her bed, but she wanted someone who offered a day-to-day commitment, which Suzette could never do.

Fake nails clicked on the counter. "Good. You know it's not what I want. I'm glad we found the right guy."

"Do you have to work today?"

Suzette was a nail technician at a local hair salon. "Later. The after five crowd." She yawned and rested her forehead on the marble countertop next to a small cup filled with chocolates. Without looking up, she felt around until her fingers found one. She finally sat up to pop a small piece of Dove dark chocolate into her mouth.

"Breakfast."

Jannat grabbed one herself. "Sounds great." The two women laughed as they chewed. Then Suzette took Jannat's hand, raised it to her lips, and kissed it. "You taste almost as good as this chocolate," she quipped.

"Almost?"

"Hah! I've missed you. Last night was special, Jan."

Jannat looked away, lips pressed together and curled down. Suzette had to know, after all this time, how sensitive Jannat was about their evenings together in Randy's own bed.

"Hey, I didn't mean to make you feel bad. I know we both have . . . other commitments."

Jannat's eyes opened wide as she turned back to her friend. "Really? Who are *you* committed to?" The two best friends grew up together in their tight-knit Persian community. Telling each other their secrets—and keeping them close. Their relationship had endured in shifting forms for over 30 years. It was one of the few things Jannat didn't question, probe or doubt. For someone who barely trusted anything she heard, and little of what she saw, that was saying something.

This was love, of course it was. Love not of greeting cards and staged photos, but the deep kind of knowing and being known that built over days, years, events, disappointments, successes. The two women could no more separate themselves from one another than they could voluntarily detach their own limbs. Suzette never strayed from her love of Jannat. She'd slept with many women but was beholden to only one.

Jannat worked in a world of men, homophobic men at that, so she'd learned to appreciate those few with finer qualities. Randy was raised around women, taught to fly by female flight instructors, and was perhaps the kindest, most gentle of the so-called stronger sex she'd ever known. He was a good *person*, which made him a good man.

Her home phone rang. She and Randy had turned up the sound on the answering machine so the two pilots could screen calls from their respective employers on off days. Jannat didn't want to miss a call from Tris if she was needed on short notice.

Finally, their recorded message finished, and the machine beeped for voice mail.

"Hi Jannat, it's Tris. We put you with Chuck and me on a trip to Europe this weekend. Ip will call you with the details, but I'd like you to come in tomorrow. I've scheduled an all-hands meeting for when we get back from Boston, and then I'll want to meet with you and Chuck privately. Enjoy the rest of your day. Bye."

There it was—a call to duty. Ip or Phyll could have made the request. For Tris to call herself, it had to be important.

The rumors must be true. Tris was leaving. The private meeting with Tris and Chuck could have only one meaning: Jannat was in the running for the Chief Pilot job.

Her relationship with Suzette would have to be more carefully guarded than ever. The more people who knew, the less likely she could keep her secret. She trusted Suzette. If word ever got out, it would not come from her. Suzette had watched her beloved fight to succeed as a pilot. No one knew her better than her very best friend, no one excited her more, no one fulfilled her physical needs better. Suzette would not risk losing that.

In the aviation world, being a diverse woman was already two strikes. Bi-sexual? That would be strike twelve. Marrying Randy was the smartest thing she could do for her career. And she truly loved him.

Jannat could have a successful marriage to Randy, keep Suzette close, and get ahead in aviation. She was about to become the next Chief Pilot of Westin Charter—she could feel it. If she could satisfy Randy and Suzette, she could do the new job, no problem. Effort always paid off.

Jannat moved closer to the dark-haired woman with the long ruby-red nails and smudged eye makeup. "Soudeh," she whispered, before planting a kiss fully on her lips. Suzette responded and Jannat let her tongue explore one of its favorite spots.

Thirteen

BY 8:00 P.M. in Boston, Tris was already yawning, and Danny had hit his stride.

"Bartender. Hey, Bartender!" he yelled over the din of revelers at the below-ground bar near the hotel. Danny said he wasn't hungry, just thirsty. She insisted on eating first, and he'd ordered a huge meal at the hotel restaurant. He'd wiped his plate clean of steak and French fries, then inhaled a large piece of chocolate cake before moving on to finish the mound of pasta Tris left on her plate.

His capacity to drink after that large meal amazed her. Danny consumed beer like water and was gulping number three.

"Another," he called when the bartender passed by. "And a menu."

After that dinner? She'd known Danny for years, traveled with him on trip after trip at Clear Sky, and had never seen him eat like this.

"What's going on Danny? Think Boston's gonna run out of food?"

"I'm hungry," he replied, and ordered a plate of loaded potato skins.

Sipping her beer, Tris looked around to see if there was anyone else in the bar she recognized, even so far from home. Best to be cautious. All the years of men approaching her in bars, asking what she did for a living. Tris sometimes said she was a forklift operator and sometimes an exotic dancer. Pilot was never the correct answer in a place where alcohol was served. People didn't understand FAA rules about drinking. Pilots could have a beer or glass of wine with dinner and still do their trips the next day as long as twelve hours had passed, and they didn't register illegal levels of alcohol in their system. Except the general public didn't make that fine distinction: all they understood was that someone who'd said they were a pilot sat in a bar with a drink in their hand.

Every bar she'd ever been to in Boston was laid out like "Cheers," horseshoe shape surrounded by tables, and this was no exception. "Cheers" never had more than a handful of regular customers at the bar. At this place the two old friends were lucky to find empty stools side-by-side, and people were three-deep behind them.

A trivia competition was heating up. Tris couldn't hear the questions, which made watching the participants that much more interesting. Some were a bit drink-palsied, leaning back or swaying in their seats. Others, clearly not drinking at all, tapped their fingers or popped their legs incessantly, hands perpetually raised, anxious to jump in and give their answer.

Danny loved participating in that kind of thing, although he never had the right answers. Tris hoped Danny would want to play some trivia tonight. At least that would mean no more talk about Emily.

No such luck. His conversation still played the divorce track.

"Emily's got me by the short and curlies," Danny said. The

bartender stuck what had to be a two-foot plate of steaming potato halves buried in cheese, sour cream, and bacon bits in front of him. Danny grabbed one with his thumb and forefinger, his other hand hovering below it to catch anything that might fall off.

"Seriously?" Tris said it loud enough for him to hear, yet he forged ahead by stuffing half of a potato skin in his mouth. Errant bacon bits and chopped scallion fell back on the plate and the bar. At least if he was eating, he wasn't complaining.

Tris had enough friends who'd divorced to know the legal dissolution of his marriage would be rough. Emily wouldn't make it any easier, either—she'd want to punish him for all his perceived failings, when in the end the only thing he'd done wrong was to be Tris's friend.

The buoyant sounds of a triumphant trivia team encouraged her to try and boost him with positivity. Perhaps explain how easy it would be for him to meet someone—after all, his airplane had four flight attendants on every trip.

"Big changes," Danny managed to say between bites. "So much happening." Danny snorted. "There's something I've gotta do. I've gotta do it. To keep it."

He wasn't making any sense. Tris stifled a yawn. "What?" she asked in the most disinterested tone she could muster.

"Hey, you want one before you're gone?" Danny motioned to the greasy plate.

"You mean before *they're* gone? Uh, no. Let's go, Danny. It's time." Her beer mug was no longer frosty, and she was tired. All she wanted to do was turn on some bad TV and relax. With so much going on—Legacy, Rex, Woody, Mike—she'd hoped flying this trip would give her a respite.

Danny sped through the last of the pile in front of him, wiped his mouth, and started talking again. "Randy, you know, that guy in my crash pad, the one who's getting married to your pilot. Sounds like he can't wait to get married. I hear him on the phone all the time with her, discussing the dress, the flowers, the hall."

"His fiancé? Jannat?"

"Yes. And his mother. His family is loaded. So's hers. They're both pilots. Randy says that pisses off both sets of parents. That's one thing they have in common, I guess. Seems like they can't agree on anything about this shindig. Or the parents can't agree. I told Em to do everything the way she wanted, and I'd show up." He rotated the now-empty stein in his hand. "Maybe I should have paid more attention."

Danny motioned to the bartender to fill his glass. Tris caught the woman's eye and shook her head. The check appeared instead.

"I'm cutting you off. Aren't you on reserve?"

Danny belched. "Not anymore. Home tomorrow for a night, then back to Boston. Schedule sucks."

Tris smiled. "Living the dream, eh?" She elbowed her best friend, who scowled.

"So. Emily. So." Danny stammered, running a finger over the empty plate to scrape off the crusty cheese and bacon bits. "Howsh that guy you're sleeping with?"

"Danny, my friend's name is Rex. Let's get out of here, okay?" She signed the credit card slip and put her card back in her purse.

Danny's head shook vehemently. Spittle flew from his lips. "Bad. He's a bad one. You need to get away from him." Danny met Rex years ago when he was a flight instructor and Rex was the FAA examiner giving check rides to his students. There was a rumor swirling around the airport back then that Rex was overly solicitous of the male pilot candidates while they were alone in the airplane during check rides. Of course, no details were ever provided, and Tris chalked it up to a disgruntled candidate who'd failed his ride making up rumors about the examiner who busted him. It wouldn't be the first time.

Rex had a naturally outgoing personality and was a habitual flirt. He'd pursued Tris insistently, and never failed to satisfy her in bed. The rumors were ridiculous.

"Oh, that's a lot of made-up crap from the past. If he were really interested in men, I'd know. Things with us are fine. He's a very decent guy. You don't have to worry about me."

Fine. Decent.

Acceptable?

She didn't dare tell Danny that she'd run into Mike. Mike's actions before and after the angel flight always wound Danny up. She hadn't read the letter, but she felt closer and closer to being ready. It was hard not to be touched that Mike still cared about her, which might lead to remembering the good parts of their relationship. Too much going on, with Legacy, choosing a new Chief Pilot, and the trip to Edinburgh. She couldn't focus on one more thing.

Danny barked a laugh, launching a cheddar cheese projectile from his lips. "Worry? I don't. I have to leave you. I have to go!"

"Yes, you do," she said. Danny's eyelids were half closed. "Let's walk to your pad."

"Pad? I guesh." Danny could barely stand, and after a couple of steps, Tris doubted that they could make the half-mile walk. Her hotel was a block away, and her room had a bedroom with a door that closed and a pull-out couch on the other side of it.

"Come on buddy."

"Back to Exeter. Home sweet home. Fuck scheduling. Fuck everything."

He was getting loud. She led Danny out the door and held his hand as the two of them started walking. No way he'd make it to the pad.

"Danny, I'm taking you to the Embassy. Sleep it off on the pull-out couch, and we'll talk later." She turned toward the hotel. He weaved and wobbled but moved forward. Then, half a block into their walk, he stopped. The cool evening air seemed to revive him. "You can't kill this! You can't take her!" he screamed at the sky, teeth clenched, pumping his fist.

"Danny, kill what? Take who? What are you talking about?"

"No no no no no," he repeated, pulling her by the arm toward the hotel.

All the way to her room, Danny alternated between crying and swearing, one moment angry, the next contrite. Tris sat him down on the couch while he muttered. She went over to the closet in the bedroom to grab an extra blanket and pillows, not knowing what else she could do for her distraught friend.

She was only gone a minute. When she returned, Danny was curled up, fast asleep.

Fourteen

"NO. I HAVE TO keep it. I have to. I need it so much!"

The digital alarm clock on the side of her bed read 2:26 a.m. At first, Tris thought she was shouting. It wouldn't be unusual for her to wake up, sweating and crying out. As her eyes adjusted and other senses followed, the sound seemed to come from the room next door. She'd bang on the wall and see if she could get her neighbors to shut up.

Then someone in the adjoining room beat her to it. "Hey. Knock it off in there. It's 2:30 in the morning!"

"It's done. It's done. She's gone. I swear it!"

This time, there was no mistaking Danny's voice, bellowing from beyond the door.

Tris didn't even try to find her slippers, breaking her own rule as her bare feet touched the hotel carpet that probably hadn't been cleaned since the property opened. She found Danny flopping back and forth on the sofa bed. When did he open the couch?

"Hey Danny. Wake up." Her hand pressed his chest, and his eyes opened.

"Whaaaaa?" Danny propped himself up on his elbow and looked around. The stale smell of beer wafted up as he yawned wide. There was a piece of scallion stuck in his teeth.

He looked into her eyes and began to sob.

"I'm sorry, Tris. I'm so sorry." He choked and coughed as tears fell in torrents. Stunned and confused, all Tris could do was sit next to him on the thin mattress, aware of the sharp metal frame below her thighs. *No wonder he's having nightmares. This is damn uncomfortable.*

Danny's forearm dragged a line of snot across his face. He lifted his t-shirt to wipe his nose. Then he buried his face in Tris's lap, moaning.

"It's okay, it's okay," she whispered. He'd had too much to drink; this was a bad drunk dream. He'd calm down soon, hopefully, since she had to be at the airport in a few hours for the trip back to Exeter.

She'd called Rex before she'd fallen asleep, to thank him once again for blindsiding her, this time with Woody. He sounded chagrined, pointing the finger at an over-zealous assistant, but she wondered. Rex had vehemently tried to persuade Tris not to go to Legacy. He wanted her at Westin, wanted her near him. Perhaps he was using a different tack.

They had a date for dinner and a movie last night, but Tris canceled when the trip to Boston came up. She was relieved to put distance between her and Rex. Despite all the therapy she'd had, when trouble brewed, Tris still retreated to the safe corner the cockpit provided.

With Danny bawling, his head in her lap, she wished she'd stayed home.

"I can't breathe." Danny hung his head over the side of the pull-out's metal frame and gasped for air, bringing Tris back to the present. She ran around the hotel room looking for a barf bag, but this wasn't her airplane where she could reach into a seat pocket and pull one out.

"Deep breaths Danny. Deep breaths. It's gonna be okay." Over and over, she crooned this mantra, hoping that she didn't have to call 9-1-1.

Danny bolted upright and raced to the bathroom. Gagging was followed by the sound of him vomiting multiple times. Finally, the toilet flushed, and Tris heard running water and then gargling.

Wiping his face and mouth dry with a thin, scratchy hand towel, Danny sat back down and buried his face in her lap. She rubbed his back while he sobbed. Raspy quick breaths slowed to a regular inhale and exhale. He lifted himself from his position draped over her thighs and looked at her. His eyes were wide open, full of longing.

Oh, that look. It was a look from their past, from before Rex. Before Mike. Before Emily. Every time that look met hers, her body told her no.

Up until this very second, Tris hadn't realized how much she'd missed that look, borne of the kind of connection that was built between friends, over good and bad times. A tight bond, the type she'd had from the start with the man beside her. With Danny.

Bron was dead. She didn't know if she could ever trust Mike again. Rex wasn't forever.

Tris was afraid, afraid of things she couldn't control, afraid of wanting love again in her life. That kind of love had been a visitor, a guest whose company she'd adored, but who she could never convince to stay.

Mostly, she needed a friend. They both did. Tonight, she would not back away.

Danny gently ran the back of his hand across her cheek. "I can't do it," he whispered.

Her eyes locked with his. "Can't do what?" His body was all too able and ready.

"Shh, no talking." Danny kissed her, his mouth tasting of her peppermint mouthwash.

He pulled back to look at her again, cocked his head slightly. A question or a request, she couldn't be sure. Regardless, her answer was yes.

His hand held her chin. How did it get there? It felt warm, like she'd thrown on a soft sweater over her t-shirt.

Tris lowered herself onto the mattress and laid down next to her best friend.

"Tris," he whispered, and sniffled. She was afraid he'd start to cry again. But that Danny had been replaced by a man she hadn't seen before, one who smiled with certainty, and let the hand that held her face migrate downward to a spot designed to bring her to the height of pleasure. Not once, not twice, but three times, working his magic again and again with such determination it seemed as if his very life were at stake.

Her eyes closed, and she saw Mike on the ramp. She nudged his face out of her mind, but the outline of the envelope remained, as if it had burned a rectangle in her brain. Yet as the two old friends felt their bodies click into place, the image faded away.

For years, Danny had needed her love, and she simply didn't have any to give him.

Tonight, for the first time, she did.

Their lovemaking left Tris breathless. As they lay in bed, both on their backs, spent and satisfied, Danny whispered to the ceiling, "I'm sorry, Emily. I can't."

Tris woke alone in her bed, where she'd returned after Danny fell asleep. For a second, she forgot he was on the other side of the door. After the first motions of morning, in the trickle of daylight streaming through a break in the blackout curtains, the memory stampeded back.

That was never supposed to happen.

Uncertainty overwhelmed her. What happens next? Could they ignore it? Not talk about it? Like Bron's death, would it hang there between them, an image projected from their minds and hearts, trotting along beside them forever?

For now, instead of the internal dread that so often accompanied her one-night stands, there was peace. The feeling of satisfaction she'd had after they made love was still with her. It was easy. Tris felt goosebumps raise on her arms. How many times had friends said of their relationships, "When it's easy, that's how you know it's right."

Danny was on the other side of that door. She'd sit by him on the sofa, and that's what she'd tell him. It was easy to be with him. Surely, he'd want to tell her how he felt—he'd never had trouble sharing his feelings for her in the past.

Maybe it was their time.

She was basically alone. He was getting divorced.

Slowly, quietly, Tris grasped the doorknob, ready to cross the threshold of her resolve to finally, after all the years of avoiding Danny's pursuit, take the next step.

Danny was gone. All that remained was a crumpled blanket and a single pillow. There was no note, no evidence at all that he'd been there.

He ran. It was a mistake.

Tris pounded her thighs with her fists, to knock some sense back into herself. How ridiculous, thinking that drunken Danny would sleep with her for any reason other than his libido on alcohol. He wanted Emily.

Here she was, wrong again.

The loud ring of the room phone cut through her escalating

panic, and she cried out sharply. It was probably housekeeping. They were always trying to get her out of the room early. She ignored it. Seconds later, her mobile phone rang.

"Tris." Phyll's unmistakable cockney accent. "Glad I caught you."

Tris hugged the receiver to her ear with her shoulder and checked the clock, quickly switching off the alarm before it rang. No, she wasn't late.

"Phyll. What's going on? Changes for today?"

Silence, a longer pause than was necessary to discuss flight details. "Not exactly, Tris. Look, I need you back here *quick as*," Phyll's accent amplified her concern.

"What happened? What's wrong?"

Phyll breathed hard on the other end of the line. "Woody. He's had a heart attack."

"Oh no. He's alive, right? Please tell me he's alive." The thought of Woody even slightly impaired was unthinkable Phyll swallowed and her crisp, business-like manner returned. "Yes. Yes. His family is with him. His wife says he'll be in the hospital overnight, a few days at most. Not too serious, she says, but you know Woody. He'll probably sneak out. Until he does, we need you here. You're all we have."

Indestructible, reliable Woody. He always said he'd never been sick a day in his life. Tris couldn't remember if he'd ever even had a cold in all the years she'd known him.

"Phyll, are you sure he's okay? You'd tell me, right?"

"He's already told the doctors to piss off. The company is what we need to concern ourselves with. Get back here."

"Right. On my way. If anyone needs anything, have them call my mobile."

"Quick as, Tris."

"Quick as."

The flight paperwork was stacked on an end table. Next to it was the half-empty glass of water Danny had sipped from. She touched it, as though it was a conduit, to tell him that whatever the reason he'd left without saying goodbye, she reveled in their lovemaking.

After all these years, he'd broken through. He'd reached her heart. Then he ran away.

The whirr of a vacuum cleaner right outside her room knocked her back into the moment.

Westin Charter was now her responsibility, and thoughts of Danny needed to be pushed aside. Tris showered, dressed, and collected the things she'd strewn about the room. Woody had a partner, Jimbo, a money man. In all these years, Tris had only met him twice.

Tris was Woody's *actual* partner, the second-in-command. Keeping Westin Charter going would be the thing that would make him better.

Housekeeping banged on her door.

It was go time.

Fifteen

FRUSTRATED PILOTS dotted the executive ramp at Logan, stalled by a combination of dense ground fog and zero wind. Aircraft sat with ground power running, in the hope that there would be a break in the near-zero visibility conditions. Each time one of their mobiles rang, all the stranded aviators in earshot checked their phones like Pavlov's dogs. Tris prayed that each call wasn't Phyll with more bad news about Woody, or Danny wanting to talk, or Rex, or . . .

Her angst had reached a crescendo when Chuck materialized in front of her. Tris cried out and stepped back.

"What are you so twitchy about?" he said.

"I've got to get back. With Woody gone . . ." she said, letting Chuck fill in the long list of responsibilities that had fallen on Tris, all of which were a thousand miles west.

"Oh. I talked to him. He's fine. Cool as a cucumber." Chuck said.

"You *called* him? In the hospital?"

"To wish him well. Let him know I was thinking of him."

She wanted to grab his shoulders and shake some sense into him. The owner of their company had a heart attack, and Chuck was campaigning for promotion.

Tris desperately needed to get out of Boston—and away from Chuck—yet time seemed to have stopped. Westin Charter operated under a very defined set of rules, one which held them prisoner to ground visibility. She couldn't see more than three feet in front of her, but still she raced through her pre-flight paces, reviewing the flight plan and making sure the catering was right.

Updated visibility reports were available every few minutes from pilots landing at the airport. They were not encouraging. She and Chuck weren't going anywhere.

In the light of day—the grey of fog—Tris still felt the warmth of last night's *mistake*.

Her phone rang. Danny. Damn.

What will I say? I had a great time? It felt right? I have feelings for you after all these years of pushing you away? You ran out before I could tell you . . . tell you . . .

Tris let the call go to voice mail. Danny's divorce was drowning him. He'd latched on to her as a lifejacket. Tris wasn't sure what she wanted but surely that wasn't it.

She'd put time and distance between them. *Then we'll talk.*

"Tris? What's going on?" Chuck's eyebrows were raised.

"What? Why?"

He pointed to her mobile, which she held out in front of her. "You've been talking to your phone. Were you on a call?"

She made a show of shoving the flip phone in the breast pocket of her uniform jacket, where it strained against the fabric. "No. Making sure that someone I don't want to speak to hasn't called." She realized how ridiculous and insincere the words sounded.

Chuck wasn't buying it at all. "So, you were saying *'Then we'll talk.'* Was that what you wanted to say to whoever you weren't speaking to?"

Challenging her—this was new for Chuck. His loyalty toward her continued to wane.

He pushed further. "Since our passengers aren't here yet, wanna get a head start on our meeting?"

Her brow furrowed. What was he talking about?

"You know," he continued, "switch mental gears? Talk about your successor."

Tris stared him down.

Didn't work. He shrugged. "You're gonna make the big announcement when we get back. You want to talk to Madden and me. It's about the Chief Pilot job. Well, let's get to it."

Changing mental lanes from a potential relationship with Danny to Chuck pushing the Chief Pilot conversation on her, Tris practically became airborne at the sound of a voice behind her.

"Excuse me? Captain?" A ramper had quietly positioned herself behind Tris.

"*What?*" Tris whirled around, the reaction sending the ramper stumbling backward. Tris tried again, calmer this time. "Sorry. What do you need?"

"Uh, ma'am, you have a phone call in the terminal. Can you come inside please?" She thumbed toward the building.

On the way toward the terminal her mobile phone buzzed again. She pulled it out of her pocket so quickly it fell, skidding across the damp asphalt. The little red light in the top corner of the flip phone blinked along with the silenced ring. She picked it up, heart pounding, praying it wasn't Danny, before it went to voice mail. That Denver number again.

She had to call Legacy. Between Woody's illness and Danny's— whatever this was—she'd forgotten.

The sliding glass doors that separated the ramp from the luxurious Signature Flight Support building had barely closed when both of her passengers approached. Tris donned the largest smile she could muster.

"Captain Miles?"

"Yes. Hi. I was coming in to update you on our departure time." No sooner had she finished her sentence than her mobile buzzed again. She peeked down at the screen. Chuck calling her from the cockpit.

No way Chuck would reach out this way unless there was something he didn't want the passengers to hear through the regular communication channels from the airplane, which broadcast audibly from a receiver behind the front desk.

"Chuck?"

Resignation dripped from Chuck's voice. "When you think it couldn't get any worse . . . I called for a clearance. Instead, I got an EDCT time. One hour." Chuck was right—their situation hadn't improved. Instead of receiving permission to leave for Exeter, the airport told them it would be at least an hour before they could even think of heading home.

With her passengers milling around her, Tris was limited in what she could reply. A string of expletives rolled by in her mind. "Thanks Chuck. Much appreciated," she said out loud.

During the few minutes it took to give her passengers the bad news, her mobile phone continued to buzz. Two more calls from Denver, two voice mails. No Danny.

"Captain Miles?" Another disembodied voice, female this time.

Tris couldn't help her terse response. "Yes. What?"

"Uh, your office on the phone? Remember? I can transfer it to a private booth if you'd like."

"Please."

The Signature employee was wearing a too-tight knee-length skirt in company colors. Tris followed the woman to a phone booth.

"Tris, Phyllida here."

"Phyll. How is he?" Tris couldn't keep the anxiety out of her voice.

"First things first, right? I've talked to the passengers' assistants about the delay. We've got them all sorted. Woody is out of the hospital, but on bedrest for a few days, quite against his will." They reviewed more scheduling issues created by the bad weather on the East Coast, which was affecting more than just Tris's flight. Phyll and Ip had gotten ahead of it all; Tris relaxed for a second.

"Phyll, I'm sorry, it's hard to focus. I can't help but think that maybe I . . . my news . . ."

Phyll picked up on Tris's concern right away. Her ability to read people was truly remarkable, and occasionally unsettling. "Tris, leave it will you? Please don't think you had anything to do with this. We do need you back here, though."

"As soon as I can." She ended the call.

Calm at last, Tris opted to remain in the booth for a bit.

Her phone buzzed again. She didn't recognize the number, but it was an Exeter exchange.

It could be Danny, calling from a different phone. I can't talk to him.

It could be about Woody.

Her finger trembled as she pressed the green talk button. "Hello? Tris Miles."

"Tris. Di." Thank goodness—a friendly voice.

"Hey. What's up? I'm socked in here in Boston and . . ."

"Tris, I'm calling you from the Tetrix maintenance hangar. The pilot area is full of people. Look, I heard Deter talking to someone on the phone about you."

Tris willed herself to sound calm, but her defenses were stretched thin. She couldn't pull it off. "What? What about me?"

Diana hesitated. "I'm not sure, but I think he was talking about you and Legacy Airlines."

"Deter?"

Tris started shivering, slightly at first. Soon, her entire body was trembling. Her grip on the mobile phone tightened.

"Tris, look, I could only get close enough to pick up a few words. I can't tell for sure, but he might have been talking to your old boss. That guy Zorn? Is it possible it could have something to do with the files? The ones he sent to Legacy?"

Tris couldn't hear her friend anymore. In her ear was Deter's voice, frustrated, angry, abusive, repeating over and over how she'd failed to measure up.

Sixteen

"YOU TALKED TO HER? You talked to Tris, right?"

Emily accosted Danny the second he walked through the door. Around the living room, boxes were still scattered, some with a few items in them, some full. The empty boxes Tris brought by seemed to have vanished.

Danny's head pounded, and so did his heart. He checked himself in the hall mirror. With bloodshot eyes and drooping lids, Emily would know for sure he'd been drinking. He searched his face for evidence of his other deeds. All he saw were pronounced lines looking back.

Is this what guilt looks like?

How could he have left the hotel without talking to her? Without telling her how much their evening meant to him—he'd been dreaming of it for years, and it finally happened. How often in life did an actual experience exceed his expectations?

This was one. There was no getting around it. His feelings for Tris were stronger than ever. None of that mattered, because here he was with pregnant Emily, trying desperately to be a good husband.

He sidled up behind Emily near the microwave, where she was warming some leftovers for lunch. "Hi, baby." He kissed the top of her head and patted her stomach. Some things were more important than happiness.

Hands on her hips, back stiff, Emily was waiting for an answer.

"Yes, Em. I talked to Tris. Let's move forward." He prayed that his wife didn't ask the wrong question, one that would require him to lie to her.

Who really knows everything about their partner?

Danny'd heard that somewhere before. Both of his arms slipped around his waist into a tight self-hug when he recalled who said it to him—Mike Marshall. The expert at keeping secrets from people he said he loved.

Emily moved to the kitchen island, and bit into leftover garlic bread while absent-mindedly turning the pages of the local *Pennysaver.* It was almost 11:00 a.m. in Exeter. Tris should be on her way home from Boston by now.

He'd been afraid to eat before his jump seat home, nauseated from last night's consumption. Now his stomach grumbled.

"Any of that left?"

"Nope," she mumbled, her mouth full.

He pulled a package of Hostess Ho Hos out of his flight bag. Emily's *Home is Where the Heart Is* cross stitch thingy was draped over the back of the recliner again. Their happy-faced couples' pictures had reappeared on the living room walls, walls that Danny now felt closing in on him, on his betrayal.

He crammed a chocolatey cylinder into his mouth. Then another.

"You wanna go out to lunch? See a movie?" Danny had a craving for burritos. There was a great Mexican place, where the portions were cheap and plentiful. People ate standing up at bar-height tables filled with bottles of habanero sauce named "One Alarm," "Two Alarm," and "Third Degree Burns." The stand was always packed since it was right across the street from the discount movie theater. First show of the evening—one dollar.

"Oh Danny. Don't be silly. I can't go to a *movie*." Em stood but didn't turn around and look at him. She opened the pantry door, her right hand rubbing a non-existent belly. "I'm exhausted. Being pregnant sucks all the energy out of me."

Emily was not showing, was never sick that he saw, but she'd turned into some kind of hermit. The only places she wanted to go were to her parents' house to talk endlessly with her sister about childbearing, or the doctor's office for tests. She *wanted* all the tests the doctors offered. Checking for birth defects, congenital defects, any kind of problem, like she was convinced that *his* child was in some way flawed.

It made a bizarre kind of sense. Emily wanted to have the perfect child. To somehow make up for her far-less-than-perfect marriage.

Danny cared too, but it was all *so much*. So many vitamins, so many magazines, so many *names*, and they didn't even know the sex of the baby. They'd find out as soon as possible. Danny didn't want to. Emily did. He pulled out a second package of Ho Hos and gobbled them down in a few quick bites.

All his airline buddies with kids told him the same thing—give Emily whatever she wants, let her do whatever she wants. "She'll be unreasonable. Like, friggin' out of her mind. Go with it." Danny was ready for midnight runs to the convenience store for pickles and ice cream. He hadn't anticipated her more onerous demands. Of all the unreasonable requests she could have made, her one and only ask was the most extreme.

Or so he thought at the time.

After finally making love to Tris, Danny realized that Emily was right. Tris had to be out of his life. He'd screwed his best friend, literally, and then he'd run out on her. He'd had the night of his dreams with the woman he adored and tossed her aside. He'd spend his whole life trying to shed the shame of dumping a woman who held one piece of his heart after cheating on the other, and his child.

"If you don't want to go out, should we order in? Or did you cook?"

Emily laughed so hard she felt the need to cup the bottom of her non-existent stomach once again. "My feet are really swollen. I can barely finish these dishes." At the sink, her back to him, she didn't see his look of despair.

The crash of a ceramic mug hitting the tile floor brought Danny to her side, eyes open wide.

Emily turned to him, her mouth open, eyes wide. "Oh, I'm so sorry, Danny. I know you loved that mug."

Danny bent over and tenderly picked up the largest pieces of the Clear Sky Airlines mug he'd bought back when he flew for the tiny commuter airline. When Bron was alive. When he fell in love with Tris.

Em watched as Danny tried to assemble the big pieces together on the countertop, prelude to an afternoon of glue and prayer.

His lips twisted from side to side, then he pursed them, concentrating on the ragged puzzle pieces in front of him. "We can try, right? Try to fix it?"

His voice rose at the end. After everything that had happened, he needed Emily to say something, do something, to make him believe it wasn't all for nothing. If Emily would only understand—the mug was his heart. She could put it back together, glue the broken pieces, make it whole. She'd done it before, after Tris had gently made it clear that he wasn't the one.

Care about the mug. Know how much it means to me. Say there's hope. Please.

"Throw it out. We have plenty of mugs," she said, stepping around the broken glass on her way to the bathroom.

Danny reached his arm out to her, an empty gesture that she never even saw.

"I'm going to get some takeout at the Mexican stand. What do you want?"

Emily responded as if by rote. "One Mexi-Max burrito, extra cheese. A side of guac and chips. And a side of refried beans."

"Uh, I might want something else this time."

"No, that's for me." He and Emily used to split that order.

Danny's fingers combed his pockets for the two Hershey's Kisses he'd lifted from the cupboard at the crash pad. He popped them both in his mouth at the same time and let the chocolate melt on his tongue as he left to run what he suspected was the first of thousands of errands like this.

"I may stop by the 7-Eleven to pick up a paper," he called to no response. On his way out the door, he tripped over the raised corner of the "This House is Not a Home until you Return," mat on the inside of their door and knocked his elbow against the wall.

Who in their right mind had a "goodbye" mat on the inside of their door?

As Danny was about to exit the car in the strip mall parking lot, he noticed his five o-clock shadow in the rearview mirror. Not shaving was the least of his worries. Hey, he was home. He could get as scruffy as he wanted.

He examined the menu at the Mexican place. Turned out there was nothing they could sell him that he wanted. He wanted more of what he'd had in Boston the night before. For so long, Tris had been remote—like a living, breathing sphinx—and then, suddenly, she was real. Eyes closed, he felt her again. Their lovemaking wasn't something out of a movie, her skin with a buttery glow, birds tweeting in the background. It was raw, honest. They were sweaty at the end. She had been satisfied. He could tell.

A fleeting thought that this might have been a mercy fuck changed the music in his head. No, it couldn't be. She couldn't have known it was goodbye, could she? They were so close, he barely had to speak, usually, before she started nodding that, yes, she understood.

That's the way it had been with them for almost seven years, since her first days at Clear Sky Airlines. A first officer who struggled in training; whose job Danny saved, not because he *wanted* her, but because he could tell she was the real thing.

Instinct. Her instincts were like none he'd ever seen before. On his lowest days, when his self-esteem was in the dumpster, recalling the moment that he begged the head of training at Clear Sky to give the struggling new hire another chance because this particular rookie pilot deserved a break, that kept his head up. He'd gotten her that final chance, the one that saved Tris's job, that enabled her to become one of the best first officers any of the captains at Clear Sky had ever flown with. He did *that*. As long as he lived, he'd know he had done at least one thing right. He'd helped someone who'd deserved it. He was proud of himself for that.

Look what she'd accomplished since: risen in the ranks at Westin Charter all the way to the top. Chief Pilot. Now she was about to summit her career peak at Legacy Airlines.

In his hands rested a rather impressive bag of chips from the 7-Eleven next door. He ripped open the bag of Sour Cream and Cheddar Ruffles and shoved the greasy chips into his mouth. He finished them while he waited for his food order. Crumbs bounced down the front of his shirt leaving tiny orange marks.

The Mexican food acquired, Danny started driving home. At the light, he decided to take the long way. His route curled around Exeter Airport past the Westin Charter hangar.

Was she back from Boston yet? He craned his neck to scan each car parked in the Westin lot, searching for the familiar Corolla.

Seventeen

FROM A METEOROLOGICAL perspective, fog was nothing more than a dense, watery cloud. That thick wet cloud that enclosed the flying Falcon in a soothing white noise, punctuated only by the clatter of instruments, brief exchanges between pilots and the rare instruction from ATC.

Climbing out of Boston, the cockpit was serene, almost cozy—Tris strapped into the pilot's seat, her flying partner silent, everything operational. Soon, the airplane's nose would peek above the clouds, and soar up into the sunshine.

At exactly 10,500 feet, after checklists were complete, Chuck resumed his crusade for promotion. The cherished moments of silent contemplation, of watching the airplane do what it was spectacularly designed to do, were over.

"We still having that all hands meeting?"

"Not possible. We're getting back too late. I couldn't ask the overnight crews to hang around and wait for us."

"Here's the thing, Tris. Straight up. Woody's gonna want me in the job. I can do it, you know that. I have been standing behind you, supporting you, for a year now. I'm ready."

Every word he said was true. It was what he didn't say, what he failed to acknowledge, that was more persuasive. For her, and for Woody.

"You're right Chuck. One hundred percent. But have you seen Jannat's resume? She has every bit of the experience you have."

"But not as your Assistant Chief Pilot." He looked squarely at his boss. "Not at Westin. Woody and I have known each other for years."

Whoever succeeded her as Chief Pilot had to prove they could get along with and lead people who were not like them. That kind of leadership was something the bosses at Tetrix never understood, and certainly didn't practice. Westin would never be a boy's club. She'd see to that.

Chuck had no idea how unpersuasive the old boy network was with Woody, since his primary confidante wasn't a member. As close as they were, Chuck wasn't privy to Woody's business strategy, the one that grew Westin Charter from one to four airplanes, including the high-end Falcon 50, in a mere year. Woody came off as a yokel at times, a practiced deception since he was no fool. He'd heavily leveraged the notoriety of his female Chief Pilot to mine charter contracts from women and minority-owned businesses.

Even companies outside Exeter loved the Westin "story," and hired them for charters. Tris crewed trips that launched from airports in Portland, Maine, to Portland, Oregon, and everywhere in between.

"Chuck, your support has meant a lot to both Woody and me. You're up for the job. So is Jannat. Please, I want you in the room when I tell her."

"Whatever you say, boss."

An hour later, the outline of the city of Exeter took shape below them.

"Descent and approach checklist please," Chuck declared, signaling the final stage of flight.

Tris complied, her head still firmly in the cockpit, but the back of her mind on the conversations to come with Phyll about Woody, with Chuck and Jannat about the future, and with Danny about last night.

Tris walked off the airplane and found everything at Westin Charter in a state of animation. Still reeling from Woody's health scare, Ip summed it up perfectly. "We're disoriented without Woody's disorganization," he'd announced, while shoving a pile of paperwork and phone messages into Tris's hands seconds after she'd walked the passengers to their cars.

From the moment she turned it back on, her mobile phone's voice mail buzzed consistently. She listened first to the one left by the Denver number:

"Uh, hello again, Miss Miles. We've been trying to reach you. I'm Regina Herbert from Legacy Airlines human resources. This is in regards to your application. We need to speak to you right away. Please call us."

Legacy had been calling for two days to talk about her *application*? Tris could claim a busy flight schedule for the delay, but she couldn't put them off any longer. Now that Woody knew she was leaving, there was no reason.

Chuck and Jannat were waiting for her outside her office door. "I *told* you there was time to get a cup of coffee. You did not believe me. If you do not believe me when I say *that*, what about—" Jannat said, pointing her finger at Chuck. She abruptly stopped when Tris approached.

"What's going on?" Tris asked.

"Nothing." Chuck shot a sharp look at Jannat, who forced a quick smile. Both pilots walked in and quietly sat in their boss's office. Tris closed the door.

"Let's talk about the future, the *near* future, and then the longer one. We have a trip to Edinburgh on Sunday. It returns on Tuesday. I want you both on the trip. I must assess your ability to work together. One of you is going to be the next Chief Pilot of Westin Charter. I am leaving for Legacy Airlines—yes, that rumor is true. On the Edinburgh trip, each of you will take turns handling pilot-in-command responsibilities, including managing the crew. *All* the crew. Including each other."

Jannat spoke first. "I am not sure what you mean. By *manage* the crew, you mean—"

"Whoever gets the job will have to work with the other, won't they?"

Chuck smiled. "Gotta work with her? Well, that takes the jelly right out of my donut!"

Tris laughed and Jannat smiled. Leave it to Cliché to diffuse a tense situation with one of his trite expressions.

"Then it's settled. Phyll will be the primary dispatcher on the Edinburgh trip, so see her for details. Chuck, I want you to order the international flight planning from Universal, and then I want you to review it with Jannat. When the NAT tracks are announced, I want to hear from *both* of you about which we should choose, and why. I'll make the final decision."

"Universal will recommend a track, won't they? Don't they generally suggest which preferred standard route across the Atlantic we should use? ATC wants all airplanes on the same route." Chuck spouted his knowledge of international procedures, trying to show up Jannat.

"That's correct Chuck. We *all* know that. Anything else?"

"Tris, when is your class date?" Jannat asked.

"October 8th. About a month." Chuck nodded to Jannat, a signal that she was asking questions they both wanted the answers to.

"Can we ask why? Why would you go?"

That was a question Tris expected to be asked over and over, and not only by the staff at Westin. The move fulfilled her dream of buoying the lives and careers of what she hoped would be thousands of pilots, so many of them women. How could she say that to two people who still needed her guidance to improve their own leadership abilities?

"It seems odd, I realize that. This place . . ." Her voice trailed off. If she didn't change the focus of her answer, she might choke up.

Maintain the majestic calm.

"Ultimately, I want to be in their training department, to improve it. To help innovate it—to focus more on confidence-building activities, learning how to achieve command presence. The things that are essential to being a captain, but that nobody teaches. The characteristics both of you have." She smiled at the two command pilots.

Jannat was about to speak, but Chuck beat her to it.

"Okay, Tris. We've got it. C'mon," he motioned to Jannat. "Time to make the donuts!" Jannat replied with a look like he had finally lost it. "We're having donuts?"

The junior captain with the ubiquitous clip with the red flower in her hair shook her head, then met her boss's eyes. Her lips parted to speak but she clearly thought better of it and followed Chuck out of the office.

Tris knew what Madden had wanted to say. *We need you to do that. We need you here.*

Tris rotated her wrist to check the time. Rex. She hadn't even thought about him, not once, after her night with Danny. Should she tell him?

Unsure what her obligation to Rex was, she rotated the watch around and around her wrist. She and Rex weren't committed. Danny was now taking up the emotional space where Rex had been.

Not now. Personal issues had to be pushed aside. Time to confirm with Legacy that they could contact Westin, and make sure they directed their inquiries to Phyll. No need upsetting Woody any further at this point. She'd tell Legacy about his health situation. Legacy wanted her. Surely, she could get this one small accommodation from them.

The Legacy HR representative answered on the first ring.

"Hi. This is Tris Miles. I'm so sorry about the delay getting back to you."

"Ahem. Yes. Well, we've been trying to reach you."

"The owner of my company was taken to the hospital unexpectedly while I was away on a trip, and—"

"Ma'am, actually, there's been a . . . something's come up. I've been asked to tell you that your class date is canceled."

Tris could barely hold the phone to her ear. "I . . . what? Are you sure you're calling the right person? That doesn't make any sense."

"Ma'am, I'm not at liberty to speak further about this. Legacy Airlines will not be proceeding with your class date."

"On October 8th? Or . . . when? When am I going to class then?"

"I don't have any information about that. It says here in the computer 'offer canceled.'"

"Can't you tell me any more? Am I no longer being considered? What's going on?"

"I'm sorry, but your offer of employment has been rescinded. Look, it might have to do with . . . something from a previous employer?

Goodbye and good luck, ma'am." She hung up.

The tips of her fingers went numb, and for the first time in her life Tris felt like she might faint.

She scrolled quickly through her phone contacts and found the number for Jennifer Prince. Prince had graciously offered her help with anything Tris needed during the hiring and training process. She could get to the bottom of this.

Tris got her assistant and gave her name.

"Who?"

"Tris—Patricia Miles. Captain Prince knows me."

"What is this about?"

"I . . . I'd prefer to tell her directly if I could. It's about my class date."

"Captain Prince is very busy. Would you like HR's number?"

"No, no. You don't understand. Captain Prince *knows me*. Please. Tell her it's Tris. Patricia Miles."

"Let me look up your record, and I'll let Captain Prince know. Please hold."

Legacy's advertising music touting its "industry leading safety record," filled the line. Finally, a click. "Ma'am, I'm sorry. Captain Prince directed me to tell you to call HR. Would you like their number?"

Tris couldn't feel the phone in her hand. Her jaw dropped, then she abruptly straightened up. Everyone walking by could see her— the sight of her sitting at her desk with her mouth agape would surely cause chatter.

Somehow, she found the will to whisper, "No." The line went dead.

It had to be Tetrix. Deter's visit to the FAA. The conversation Diana overheard. It all made sense now. He had his chance to bury her, and he took it.

The past always finds a way, doesn't it? Give the demons a little opening, let them squeeze in, then try and outrun them. You never can. They never die, they never leave, and they never stop trying to harm you.

Times change. Circumstances change. People don't.

After all this time, Deter couldn't help himself.

He'd finally destroyed her career.

Eighteen

RANDY AND MAMAN'S complaints about the Edinburgh trip reverberated around Jannat in surround sound. They had a point—the Ellers were getting to town on Sunday, the same day the trip departed, leaving Maman and Baba to host by themselves.

"It was not my choice." Jannat pleaded her case as Maman bustled in the kitchen, and Randy listened on speaker from the crash pad. "I did not ask for this trip. She put me on it. It is essential to my bid for the Chief Pilot job. Please understand."

Maman dropped a cast-iron pan on the stove a bit too loudly. "What are we to do, eh? Sit around, politely discussing the most intricate details of your wedding *without the bride in attendance*? Your wedding, Jannat joon. The rest of your life."

With little Randy could add to Maman's diatribe, he elected to remain silent. The Edinburgh trip was decidedly inconvenient, that was true. Maman and Baba had offered to let the Ellers stay at their home, fully expecting the Ellers to decline in favor of a luxury hotel.

"Oh, Lolly," Mrs. Eller replied, mispronouncing Maman's name. "We'd be honored."

That threw Maman into a bit of a snit but knowing that her daughter would be there to cushion her against Mrs. Eller's peculiarities comforted her. Now this.

"Randy, say something," Jannat begged her fiancé. "Can't you drop reserve days? They're *your* parents." She regretted the words the moment she said them. How dare she guilt Randy. This mess was her fault.

As usual, Randy started off with, "wellll . . ."

Jannat grappled for any solution. "Can't we put them off? Can't they come another weekend? This trip is critical to my career."

Maman practically shrieked. "Your *career?* Jannat Madini, your wedding is in six weeks! Hundreds of people will be there, your Baba and I are working day in and day out, spending hours on a labor of love *for you.* This does not make sense, no sense at all."

Jannat leaned on the kitchen island, head in hands, hoping for inspiration. Maman was right. Randy, in his silent agreement, was right. Jannat was decidedly putting her career ahead of her wedding. Aviation had a way of queering the most important of plans.

Jannat's frustration boiled. On the verge of being put in charge of a growing, complex pilot group, her career advancement could be put in jeopardy not due to inability or injury—but all for some big party that everyone else seemed to want more than her.

Even Randy had fallen into step with Maman.

It's like he's marrying Maman. Or like he's becoming Maman.

Maman continued to crash around the kitchen, expressing her displeasure without words. Everything happened around food in their culture. Anger and disappointment were no exception.

"I think, baby, that your mother has a point here," Randy started softly. "We've had this scheduled for some time."

Jannat straightened up. "What was I to do, Randy? Tell Tris no? It's only three days. It is a shame that the trip leaves the morning your parents arrive, but I'll be back on Tuesday. We can make all the decisions then. Maman, I'll persuade Suzette to join you if you think you can't handle the Ellers on your own. Which I fully believe you can."

"Mrs. Madini, could you help us make this work? I know we're asking a lot, ma'am." Something about Randy's formal southern manner always seemed to smooth over the rough moments between this mother and daughter that loved each other fiercely but were way too alike to always do so peacefully.

"Of course, that will be fine," Maman said, and turned her back, returning to her dinner preparations. She was making Kabob Joojeh, Baba's favorite. The only thing he loved as much as Maman herself was her superb Persian cooking.

This latest wedding crisis was averted for now, yet more would surely follow. If Jannat became Chief Pilot, it would happen right before the wedding. She'd have to juggle both events, cope with both sets of parents, satisfy both lovers. Suzette would only be minimally helpful in this; she wanted Jannat's attention and would demand it if she wasn't getting enough. She had not changed a bit since they were children. Whatever her needs were, they had to be satisfied immediately. She needed Jannat.

Jannat began mentally parsing the words to explain this latest turn of events to her best friend. Suzette was almost as zealous about Jannat's career as Jannat. With the trip put to her as an opportunity for promotion, she prayed Suzette would agree to help with the Ellers.

Instead of getting a cooperative maid-of-honor on the other end of the phone, she met with a Suzette that had decided Jannat should come clean about their relationship to Randy now, instead of after the wedding.

Suzette had done some research. "Polyamorous. That's the word. What we would be. You and me. You and Randy."

"Suz, that sounds great, but I think we need to wait before we spring it on Randy. Right now, you and I are a bit ahead of him on this."

"Randy loves you."

"I love him. What's your point?"

"Jannat, I am not entirely comfortable with this. Not as the wedding comes closer."

Neither woman was. It tugged at Jannat's conscience too. She had no second thoughts—she wanted Randy, and she would never lose Suzette. In her current frame of mind, what Suzette might say, the reveal that the Ellers might provoke in Jannat's absence nagged at her.

She'd made a promise to Maman that she'd ask Suzette to step in while she was in Edinburgh, but she wouldn't keep it.

It wasn't the first time she'd dodged the truth.

Nineteen

"I CAN'T BELIEVE what you're telling me. Why didn't you tell me sooner? Why did you wait to call them back?" Rex's voice rose an octave as he spoke, hurt betraying his attempt to sound measured.

Tris bristled. How had this become about Rex? "I thought they just wanted permission to call Woody. I was in Boston on a trip. I didn't have time to return their calls right away. I only just found out myself."

They were standing in the local Starbucks. It was almost 4:00 p.m., but the late afternoon coffee crowd still formed a line that snaked around the store. Tris was tired and distracted from the trip home from Boston, the meeting, the Legacy disaster. Last night.

"You got, what, *how many* messages from them? You didn't think anything was *wrong?*"

Calm down. He's not blaming you. He's upset for you.

"I was late out of Boston, Woody's in the hospital, and . . ." And Danny. No way she could tell him that.

Rex abandoned any attempt to stay calm. "You had a *class date.*

You went through the entire interview process, were offered a job, *accepted it*. Now it's gone?"

She hissed her answer. "This is happening to me, not you. I need your help, not your hysteria."

Rex coughed into his hand. Another affectation, something he did when faced with an important work decision.

"Okay. There's nothing I can do, officially. This law, this Pilot Records Improvement Act, is so new, no one is expert in it yet. I believe there's a provision about 'fair and timely treatment' by an employer. You think this was Tetrix?"

"I'm convinced of it. I have my Clear Sky records—they sent me a copy. Whatever Tetrix sent to Legacy, I haven't seen."

"You asked for a copy?"

"Of course. I haven't received it yet. No wonder." She didn't want to see the documents. How could she bear to read their lies, the things they made up that would cause a major airline to blackball a qualified applicant who was personally invited to join the company by their top pilot?

"There has to be something I can do. I don't know what."

Danny. Danny had warned her this might happen. While she was still at Tetrix, he'd discouraged her from challenging their harassment. "It'll come back to haunt you," he'd pleaded. It was inconceivable. It was true.

Nothing in aviation was ever behind you, ever finished.

"Call him. Ask him for help."

"Who?"

"Ed Deter."

"Are you out of your mind? He's the one who screwed me." She shuddered.

Rex paced back and forth in front of the baked goods display. Paranoia was setting in. Did Rex know more than he was saying?

"Rex, when he came to the office and talked to you, what *exactly* did he say?"

Rex looked to the sky. "I don't remember. Something about you belonging there, at Legacy. Made me think he was happy for you."

Deter hated airlines and airline pilots almost as much as he did female pilots. Her heart sank.

Rex picked up on it. "Look, so what? Stay at Westin. Woody doesn't want you to go. Don't go." He paused. "I don't want you to go."

Tris let herself smile, seeing how much it meant to Rex for her to stay where she could spend more time with him.

Then it hit her.

"It's more than Legacy. Don't you see? This will destroy any opportunity I choose to pursue. Those records will follow me *everywhere*. I must fix this. But I don't know how."

"Call your friend over at Tetrix. She can help you, right? Come up with a plan to talk to him, see if he can straighten it out." Rex twisted his lips.

He had no idea. Tris would use her contacts, her intelligence, and whatever influence she could muster to save her career. She'd do *almost* anything.

She would not beg Deter.

Twenty

WALKING INTO O'SLATTERY'S Irish pub was the last place Tris wanted to be. She was about to leave the country on a trip. There was simply too much on her mind—serious things, life-changing things—and too many joyous revelers around. Usually, the live Irish music cheered her, but tonight it sounded like a bunch of crashing pots and pans.

Diana insisted that they meet after Tris gave her a snapshot of what had happened. Tris agreed: she needed to look someone in the eye and speak honestly about what frightened her.

Woody was slated to return to the office on Monday. He'd likely be there to meet the aircraft when she landed in Exeter late on Tuesday night after the quick Edinburgh trip. He balked against spending even one day away from the office.

"I have no idea why they're keeping me here. This is ridiculous," he'd told her from his hospital bed. His wife Giselle was in the background talking over him, "You fell down. You couldn't breathe. What's so ridiculous?" Giselle was from New Jersey, and despite twenty years in Exeter, nineteen of those married to Woody, her edgy accent was strong as ever. "You have got to be kidding me," Woody yelled back at his wife, but right into the phone. "It was nothing. A little indigestion."

Woody might be able to help her, give her advice about what to do next. More likely, he'd be so happy that Legacy pulled her class date he'd jump around like a kid with a new bike.

Tris followed Diana, single file, though the weekend throng. O'Slattery's never used to be this crowded. Diana stopped to talk to someone she recognized. "Tris, can you get us a pitcher and find us a table?" Diana turned to finish her conversation.

Tris had a plan. First, they'd come up with a strategy to reverse the Legacy decision. Then she'd tell her friend about Danny.

People crowded the bar. Tris worked her way to the edge, and there was not an empty stool to be found. Tris didn't recognize either of the bartenders. Probably some new "young lads" the owner brought over from Ireland to work for a few months, get some experience, and head back to literally greener pastures. She caught the eye of a skinny young man with fair, almost white skin, wearing all black except for the bar rag he held in his hand. She gestured to him for a pitcher of Guinness. He nodded and put a frosty jug under the tap.

"Di, there's a table outside," she called to her friend over the din.

The live Irish band was in full throat, the lilting, heavily accented voice of the lead singer swirling the crowd into a hand waving, foot-stomping frenzy. She hefted the pitcher in one hand, and two chilled glasses in the other. Snaking through the crowd, it took some time for Tris to finally get close to the narrow ramp that would take her out to the pub's patio.

"You're here." The soft voice snuck itself in between loud yelps coming from the stage. Tris couldn't see the speaker. The voice was unmistakable.

"What are you doing here, Mike?"

"Waiting for you."

Tris took a step back, hands full.

"Let me help you with that." Mike reached for the two frosted mugs that looked about to slip from her hands. She jerked them away and one crashed on the floor.

"Damn it. Mike, please. Go away." Tris looked left and right, trying to figure out what to do first—drop the beer off at a table, or tell someone about the broken glass.

"I've got it Tris. Relax." Mike gestured for her to wait and grabbed a passing busboy. Once the busboy had cleared the path to the patio, Tris headed out to an empty table. Mike watched her go.

Diana joined her, poured a Guinness and chugged half of it. She gestured toward Mike.

"What happened? Why's he here? Were you two planning to meet?"

"Di, no. No."

The pub had a small utility bar set up outside. Mike leaned against it, drink in hand, eyes on the two female pilots engaged in deep conversation. Tris couldn't do anything about his presence, which made what she had to tell Diana even more nerve-wracking.

Diana started right in. "What was in the documents? Doesn't Deter have to give them to you if you ask? What could be in there that would cost you a job?" After a second of thought, Diana's eyes widened. Her face twisted.

"Oh man. A lit file?"

"Huh?"

Diana shook her head. "The guy that preceded Deter. As Chief Pilot. Brian?"

"Zorn. Right." Tris nodded, anxious for her friend to continue.

"Shit. That trip—Luxembourg. You also said something about

a weird event in the simulator? During your captain upgrade check at Tetrix? Damn."

"Diana, what are you trying to tell me?"

Her friend placed her mug carefully on the small round table and leaned toward Tris, her eyes fixed on Mike. "Can he hear us, you think?"

"With this music? No. But keep your voice down. So many pilots drink here. You never know who's listening."

Diana's eyes closed tightly for a moment before she spoke. "There was something they used to do at my former company, probably still do. When they have someone who's a 'problem,' but there's no good reason to let them go. Not like me. I made it easy." Diana shook her head ruefully. "They start writing things up that are, well, not exactly true. Small things, little mistakes, that they make look big. Something that happened on the ground, you know, where no one can get hurt. They report that it happened in the air, threatens safety. They make it official, using memos and such. Company letterhead. I've seen them do it."

Danny warned me.

"But I . . ." Tris stopped abruptly. That flight to Luxembourg, when Deter screamed at her in the cockpit, calling her those ugly, insulting, abusive names. She'd considered her options to fight back, but Danny talked her out of them all—to save her career.

Companies lie to protect themselves against people, he'd said, against pilots who would never be part of the group. Outsiders, like Tris. "It's what they do," he'd said matter-of-factly. Exactly like Diana had.

Tris silently picked at the edge of the plastic tablecloth. Her face reddened as she realized what had been done to her.

"I don't even . . . how do you . . . how *could* you?" Her anger at Diana rose as she fumbled to find words. "How could you work with him? How can you even look at him after this?"

Diana shrugged. Always someone who took meticulous care of herself, she looked way older than her fifty-one years. In all the time she'd known Diana, Tris had seen her angry, self-assured, embarrassed. Until today, never weary. How often had she heard the kind of story Tris was telling her from other women? Even Diana hadn't totally escaped the wrath of an industry that flat out favored men.

Tris put herself in the place of her Legacy interviewers. They'd asked her why she left Tetrix. She'd told them it was a bad fit, which was true. These ginned-up records must have told a very different story. One that made her look like a liar. No wonder Jennifer Prince cast her aside.

The sheer devastation left Tris with tingling fingertips and a body that felt rooted to its chair. She couldn't imagine where she'd find the strength to stand.

"What can I do?"

"Ask Danny for help. He's still at Legacy, right?" Diana poured herself more beer.

"Danny's not . . . available right now."

"Anyone else?"

The sound of shuffling and stomping feet on a hard surface floor wafted out from the stage. It was late, right around the time that the group of partiers started mimicking Riverdance.

"Can you help?" Tris whispered. "Di, talk to Deter. He'll listen to you. You can . . ."

Diana looked away. "I can't. You know I can't."

"Because?"

"Because? Things are good for me. I can't jeopardize the goodwill I've built with him."

Tris huffed. "With Deter. You realize, Diana, that he could turn around and do the same thing to you someday."

"Never happen."

"You don't think so?"

"We're ex-military. He and I. We're comrades."

Tris swallowed. "Di, please. Talk to Deter."

Diana traced a jagged line in the condensation on her beer glass. "I can't take the chance. I need this job."

"You know this is wrong."

All the years they'd been there for one another. Nothing each wouldn't do for the other, blah blah blah. Those promises, that connection, turned out to be strong only if no risky action was called for. Wasn't friendship all about the willingness to take a risk for someone else?

"I can't, Tris. I'm sorry. I can't. I'll lose my job."

Diana was betting on the wrong horse. If she didn't realize that to Deter, she belonged in a kitchen, she'd be blindsided when he finally took aim at her.

Tris dug her fingernails into her palms, an old habit she thought she'd broken for good. Desperately, she looked around for a cigarette. Something to dull the feelings of helplessness, anger and sorrow.

Tris asked Diana first—she'd been up to a pack a day when she first moved back to Exeter. "You got a smoke?"

"Sorry. Quit. Deter convinced me. You know, he said something that finally hit home with me about smoking."

Tris banged her hand on the table so hard that Diana pushed her chair away.

"Tris, calm the fuck down. Look, call Danny. He's got to have an idea. He flies there. Maybe he knows someone in HR."

Danny. What choice did she have? This was too important. She fished her phone from her purse, shot Diana a hard look, and pressed his speed dial number.

Voice mail. Tris didn't leave a message. She set down her phone.

Grasping the end of the table, Tris leaned toward her former mentor. "I don't know who else can help."

Diana's eyes moved toward where Mike was still drinking at the bar. Her lip curled.

"What about *him*? He used to work there. Think he can help?"

Twenty-One

STANDING AS FAR AWAY from him as she could and still be heard over the music, Tris considered the man in front of her, looking for traces of the one who'd loved her. Surely some part of that Mike remained, was real. Maybe the parts *she'd* loved as well.

"I can see you're still clenching your fists. Careful, you'll bleed." He'd seen it so many times before when she'd been rigid with tension, talking about Tetrix. Or holding back tears, talking about Bron. He sipped his beer. She hated how well she'd let him know her.

"Did you read it?"

His letter. In the wake of the emotional earthquake of the last few days, she'd completely forgotten about it.

The slight shake of her head caused a flash of pain to cross his face. It vanished as quickly as it appeared.

Tris pulled at the neck of her black mock turtleneck; it felt like it was choking her.

"If you haven't read my letter, why are you standing here? Want to know how to prepare for your class date? What to expect? Tips?"

Someone pushed her and she grabbed onto a barstool to steady herself. She apologized to the woman sitting on it, who shot Tris a dirty look and returned to her highball. Tris glanced helplessly over at Diana, who nodded and urged her forward.

"Why are you looking at her? Look at *me.*"

"She's my . . . friend." Did that word still apply?

Mike smiled. "Anyway, it's your class date, right? Want to know what to wear? What it's like up there at the world's largest carrier? What is it, exactly, I can do for you, Patricia?" He chuckled. "Patricia. None of the newscasters ever called you that. They all called you Tris, like they'd been friends with you forever. They didn't really know you, did they?"

"Diana suggested I come over. She thought you might be able to help me solve a problem. About my class date. How did you even know about it?"

"Come on, it's aviation. Tell one person, everyone knows. I try to keep up with your news. You're not in the paper or on TV anymore, but I still have sources. Tris, I still care about you."

Tris backed up a step, to gain physical distance from the source of the emotional onslaught. Pain hovered beneath the surface of his words. Was he hurt or did he want to hurt her?

"It is about Legacy, Mike. Do you know anyone in their HR anymore?"

"Possibly. Why?"

"I—I need some help."

He bent over and rubbed the calf of the leg he limped on then straightened up.

"Help *you.* I was *shot.* While I was recovering, you took my job."

Those words exploded like they blasted out of a cannon, throwing her back directly into someone dancing to the music.

"Hey lady. Time to stop drinking," the dancer drawled.

"Sorry. Sorry." Tris righted herself and turned back to Mike. "*Your* job? You lied to Woody about your past to get that job. Then you lied to me. Again and again." She put both hands up, palms out. "Forget it. This was a mistake."

Tris turned to rejoin Diana at the table.

"Tris. Don't. I'm sorry. Let me try to help you. I want to. Talk to me. Please."

She'd started this, and she'd finish it. Tris cleared her throat and told Mike what had happened.

He listened thoughtfully, his thumb and forefinger curled under his chin. "Something in those records spooked them. They've black-balled you. Is it possible that you missed something? Didn't remember some critique or a bad flight?"

Her heart beat like a snare drum. "Nothing. I told Legacy everything I thought could hurt me. Full disclosure. Diana thinks Tetrix had a lit file."

Mike's expression softened. He moved toward her. "A lit file? Stuff the employer makes up? Yeah, I've heard of that. It starts with a shred of truth. Maybe you had a bad landing—and who hasn't—and it turns into a memo about your inability to fly. Some question you ask, or some idea you share, instead of being valued input makes you look like a . . ."

"A what? What, Mike?"

"A bitch. It's twisted, turned around. To hurt you." He took a few deep breaths. Any rancor his eyes had held earlier fell away, replaced by genuine concern. "You're in a no-win situation. On the face of it, it looks like you lied to cover bad job performance. Arguing that you were set up—well, you know what message *that* sends from a female pilot."

"At the interview, I couldn't say I was harassed and bullied at Tetrix. I'd sound like a victim. So, I said I quit because it was a bad fit. It *was*."

Mike reached out to touch her shoulder. She let him.

"I can help you. Read my letter. Then we'll talk."

Mike drained his beer, placed the empty stein on the bar, limped off, and was swallowed by the crowd.

Twenty-Two

EMILY FLED THE living room in tears. The bedroom door slammed hard. Photos haphazardly replaced on the wall swung back and forth on hastily placed nails. They were still in boxes when Danny left for Boston. Had Emily tried to re-create a quick feeling of family?

"You didn't tell her. You said you did but you didn't!" Emily shrieked more than yelled from the other side of the door. It was usually Emily who stayed the course; Emily who showed no emotion. Except about Tris. Always Tris.

She had a real reason to be upset, but not the one she thought.

"Emily, I did talk to her. I didn't get a chance to . . ."

"To *what*? She's *calling you*. I saw the missed calls. Answer the phone and tell her. Or leave a voice mail. You promised me, Danny. For our family."

Danny looked to the floor. He didn't lie, exactly.

Yes, he did.

How could he have left his mobile out in the open? He always had it on him. Why was Emily checking it? Thankfully, Tris didn't leave a message or Emily might have heard something to send her running straight to an abortion clinic.

This reaction was bad enough.

Danny's mind raced. He had to consider his options, but there was too much noise in his head. Surely there was something he could say to calm Emily down. A partial truth might be better than a half-lie. It couldn't get any worse.

First, he had to coax his wife to unlock the bedroom door. He gently turned the knob, expecting the door not to move. It easily swung on its hinges. Emily sat in the corner rocking chair, staring at him wide-eyed. He imagined their child in her arms. He had to fix this.

"Em, I saw her in Boston. We had dinner." Emily's eyes widened even more. "I know what you're thinking," he started. Whatever it was could not possibly be as bad as the reality. "I tried to tell her. I got drunk instead."

If there was anything Emily hated more than Tris, it was when Danny got drunk.

"I knew it. I knew you'd never tell her. Why did I even think you would? I have no idea. Stupid stupid stupid." Emily's quiet rambling continued unabated while Danny waited it out. The less he said, the less chance he had of telling her the whole truth, which he could never, ever do.

Emily stopped mumbling and beckoned to him to sit down next to her on the bed. When he did, she took his hand. Surprised, he moved away slightly.

He regretted the visceral reaction and shifted closer. Emily wanted peace. She absent-mindedly ran her hand up and down his arm and moved into his side when he put his arm around her. Her touch calmed him, giving him hope they could get past this, that she might forget, or soften her harsh demands.

The couple squirmed to find a comfortable position, and finally lay down next to each other. Danny adjusted so that his wife's shoulder would fit into its familiar slot under his arm. Yet it felt as though he were forcing a puzzle piece into the wrong place.

Nothing was the way it used to be.

Twenty-Three

OVERNIGHT STARS were obscured by cumulus clouds that dropped a misty rain as Tris pulled into her garage. There wasn't a sound around her until the elevator dinged.

The cats were sleeping so soundly when she opened the apartment door that neither stirred to greet her. The numbers on the living room wall clock announced how late it was.

What a night. Legacy. Diana and Mike at O'Slattery's. Exhausted by the emotional slalom she'd just run, she dragged herself to the bedroom.

Tonight, she'd invited Mike back into her world. She opened a crack, and he slid right through it. He wasn't all the way in. Not yet.

As she pulled off her clothes and draped them on the bedroom chair, Tris caught a glimpse of herself in a mirror lit by the moon. What she saw was a woman much older than her own thirty-nine years. Tris couldn't blame the pressurized environment of the airplane for the deepening lines framing her face; not this time. No, the grooves she noticed were borne of choices, responsibilities, and the bubbling anxiety of love.

She pulled on her favorite big t-shirt. In the dark, Tris could still make out the boxy shape of her flight bag, stashed next to her bookcase. Mike's letter was in it. She turned away and padded into the kitchen.

Without turning on a light, Tris placed a glass under the water dispenser in the door of her refrigerator. She'd finally gotten used to the more luxurious accoutrements in her new apartment. The new sofas and bookcases were Rex's idea, and a good one. When she moved in, she'd hoped to leave behind the detritus of old relationships that had leached the hope from her heart.

Surely the old haunts and hurts would remain with the used furniture she'd donated. Mike was part of the memories she'd erased. So she'd thought.

The answering machine light blinked twice. Tris was sure one of the messages was from Rex. He'd paged her while she was at the bar, had been trying to reach her all night. She couldn't concentrate on anything but Legacy. And Danny.

Falcon and Orion finally rose from their slumber, stretched out and stood on alert, tails raised and fur erect. Tris moved to the entranceway to see if she could hear what their sensitive ears picked up. The cats ran to the door. Orion pawed at it. A light knock caused both felines to meow.

"Yes?"

"Tris?"

Mike.

"What do you want? How did you know where I live?" He must have followed her. Hadn't he left before she did? Had he waited in his car? Watched her as she exited?

He stalked his ex-wife. She got a restraining order. Should I?

She blinked furiously, a new habit she'd picked up when she felt anxious, to try and dampen the unease.

"I only want to talk. I checked my contacts. I know someone at Legacy."

Tris quickly pressed the button on the side of her watch and lit up its face. "Showing up at my house at 2:30 a.m. to talk about it? You've got to go, Mike. Please. Don't make me . . ."

"Call the police? Yeah, I get that. Look. Tris. If you won't read my letter, then at least let me help you. I owe you a lot."

A long pause. Both stayed on either side of the door, separated by mere inches, yet emotionally continents apart.

It was a bad idea. First Tris turned the deadbolt, and then the door handle. She stepped to the side as Mike walked in.

He stood on the tile entryway. "I know how this looks. I know what you're thinking. I'm not that guy anymore. Look, let me tell you. Please." He did not move to touch her. Orion wove through his legs, meowing.

"I'm . . . you need some water?" Tris moved toward the fridge, which had a phone right next to it. Her eyes were on Mike. He shook his head.

Mike sat down on the couch and Orion jumped up beside him. Tris took her flip phone from the counter and sat on the edge of her leather chair, the furthest seat from him.

He looked toward the phone in her hand and nodded slowly. "I don't blame you."

The former lovers considered each other silently. Mike looked anything but threatening. He was not drunk, even though he'd been at O'Slattery's before she'd arrived.

"How do you know where I live? Did you stalk me?" She rose abruptly. "Look, I'm tired. You need to go."

"I'm going to earn you back, Tris. I'm going to do it by finding out why Legacy rescinded your offer—what it is they thought they learned from Tetrix's records. I'm going to ask them to give you another chance, a chance to set the record straight."

Tris laughed. "Yeah right. You can do that."

"I think I can. I think I know the right person to ask."

Tris sat back down. Engaging with Mike could be dangerous. Or get her back in class at Legacy. She was so tired she couldn't think. A yawn escaped, and her head fell into the back of the deep leather chair.

"I almost didn't make it back, Tris. I'd lost so much. I'd lost you," he began. As he spoke, her eyelids drooped. She would rest her eyes while she let him talk for a minute. Then she'd ask him to leave.

Tris woke with a start, unsure how long she'd slept. Falcon was curled in her lap. On the other side of the living room, bent over on the couch where he'd fallen asleep, was Mike, Orion sleeping by his head.

She shivered, grabbed a throw and twisted it around her body. It was always cold in the living room. She got up and looked out the window. The sky was lighter, the drizzle had stopped but it was not yet morning.

Mike snored. The familiar sound brought back memories of so many warm, comfortable nights. She'd been convinced that she'd be listening to it for the rest of her life. It was as close as she'd come to forever.

"Hey. Get up." Gently nudging his shoulder, the words were like an alarm clock. He startled, sat up, and rubbed his beard.

"No one wants me to give you a chance, Mike," she whispered, more to herself than to him, as he twisted off the couch and stood.

"What?"

"Nothing."

"You sure?"

Am I?

Her arms tingled and her breath quickened. There was no getting around it. She was still attracted to Mike. It wasn't the deep connection she had with Danny, or the playful sexiness she shared with Rex. It was lust mixed with the remnants of something precious. Something forgotten.

He rose, stretching in ways she wasn't familiar with. When he stood up, she could see that one side of his body was noticeably shorter than the other.

"Yeah, this is left over from the . . . you know. I'm always stiff after I sleep, no matter what, uh, surface, I've slept on. Gotta stretch a bit before I can move around."

"Is that it? The only permanent . . ."

"Damage?" He finished her sentence. "Physical, yes. The psychological impact is permanent, I think. Anyway, I don't want to talk about that now. I want to help you with Legacy. That's why I came. It's what you want, right?"

Tris looked at her watch, still fastened on her wrist, "It's five a.m. I need to get some rest. I'm leaving for Europe tomorrow. This, you . . . this is not something I can do right now." She turned to walk him to the door.

Mike picked up the signal, sighed, zipped up his jacket. "You need my help?"

Tris rubbed her eyes. "I need someone's help."

He nodded and followed her to the door.

As he walked out, the tips of his fingers brushed the tips of hers.

"To be continued."

Twenty-Four

JANNAT PUTTERED around the townhouse, packing for the trip to Edinburgh. It wasn't a complex trip but given the length of the flight and the number of time zones traversed, the crew had to be on the ground for at least twenty-four hours per company rules before flying home. They'd leave Europe on September 11th, the day *after* the Ellers left Exeter.

She'd miss their whole visit. And Suzette refused to stand in for her. Poor Maman.

She could plead her case to Tris, but the timing of this trip made it too important. The last thing she wanted to do was ask for personal time when career advancement was at stake. The news that Tris was leaving, that either she or Chuck would be the new Chief Pilot was all over Westin. Most of the buzz was about how loyal Chuck had been, and how Jannat was trying to jump the line. Chuck and Woody were tight. She wished she'd made more of an effort to get to know Woody.

Asking off the Edinburgh trip was the right thing to do for her family, her marriage, and the absolute worst thing she could do for her career. She'd suck it up and go, and she'd deal with the personal fallout later. Maman. Randy. Suzette. They'd still love her.

Jannat looked around. The place she and Randy bought with the down payment money they grudgingly accepted from their parents was nothing fancy. They didn't want to start off by buying too much house, scrimping and saving for the barest necessities. Neither would permit their parents to support them. No need. The money would be there if they wanted it—plenty of it. If Jannat became Chief Pilot, she'd be the primary breadwinner. At least until Randy got the captain's seat at Legacy. After that, her earnings would never catch up.

It was unusual to be a pilot and not have to worry about money. Financial security, so rare in aviation, brought choices—financial insecurity brought panic. So many pilots she'd known were thrown into making bad career decisions because of money. Leaving jobs that were good for them, chasing the dollar. The bigger the airplane you flew, the more money you made.

There was also the prestige factor. How she'd love to be Captain on a 777, like Tris would be someday. To walk up to an international gate with hundreds of passengers gawking at her petite, brown-skinned self, and her more-than-likely-white male co-captain and first officer calling her "ma'am" and "Cap."

Jannat loved being called "Cap." Suzette always called her Cap in bed.

She looked around, double checking to make sure she was alone even though no one else was in the house.

"Hey, Cap," she whispered to herself in front of the full-length antique mirror her parents bought her as a housewarming gift. It symbolized the beginning of the life she was building.

She hadn't heard her mobile ring at first and answered seconds before the call went to voice mail.

"Hey, Chief," Suzette said, trying out the title. "Where ya been?"

"Ha ha. Not yet. Working, Suz. You know. Wedding stuff. Getting ready for the big show."

"Still going through with it, eh?"

Both women laughed at their private joke. "Of course. Exactly as we planned it. But there's a wrinkle."

Suzette laughed. "You mean besides me?"

"I haven't been able to persuade anyone to stand in for me with the Ellers. Like my maid-of-honor."

Expecting a laugh or caustic remark, Jannat was shocked when Suzette said, "Call off the wedding."

This again. "Suz, please."

Jannat could almost hear Suzette's frustration crackle over the mobile phone line. "If you won't tell Randy before the wedding, at least tell your parents the truth. This is ridiculous. How can you live like this?"

How indeed. All her parents ever wanted for her was to settle down, the way they had, with someone she liked, could talk to, lusted for. That was exactly what she was doing.

Jannat wanted both people she loved, and she would have them.

Her eyes closed, and she took her time before opening them, regulating her breathing, fingering the clip in her hair. She and Suzette had been like conjoined twins since they could crawl. More than close, they were committed. Suzette would never leave her.

She was also prone to impatience, and it wore on Jannat.

"What can I do to make it easier on you, Suz? The wedding's moving forward, like we planned, and we're still together. You've gotta back off a bit."

Finally, her life-long friend laughed. "Well, okay, as long as you don't make me wear that dress." Jannat had to agree on that point.

Suzette's maid-of-honor dress was awful.

"You let Maman pick it. You know if it had been your mother, she'd have picked one with more chenille."

"I can't believe I agreed to wear it. I must have been temporarily insane. Like I am when I'm with you." She purred into the phone.

Oh, that voice, the incandescent hum behind it. Weakness overcame her again. "Can you come over? We can talk about it."

It took a long time for Suzette to answer. "I can come by. What's my excuse this time?"

"Don't need one. Randy's back in Boston. Bring Chinese. And grab some extra chopsticks."

"I think we can make good use of those wooden sticks. Don't you?"

Now it was Jannat's turn to soften. "Mmm-hmm. For more than the dumplings."

"Now that's what I'm talking about. See you soon."

"Soon," Jannat said as she pressed the END button on her phone. She pictured Suzette, with her full sleeve tattoos on both arms, Goth-black hair, and large hoop earrings that she never removed—not even to shower.

Suzette wasn't of Jannat's world. She *was* her world.

Jannat removed the red poppy clip, fluffed her hair, and spread some gloss across her lips; the time-honored process she'd developed to prepare for the furious turbulence to come.

"I'm tired of this discussion." Jannat stood her chopsticks in a container of pork fried rice and plunked it on the nightstand. "I'm not telling them. Especially Baba. He'd lose his mind."

"They'll find out eventually." Suzette said off-handedly as she cracked open a fortune cookie. "Look to the sun to see the future," she read aloud. "Who writes this crap? Anyway, maybe *I'll* tell them. Yeah. Your father loves me. He'll accept anything coming from me."

It was true. Baba had always adored Suzette.

"I don't think the news that I'm bi-sexual would be acceptable, even engraved on a solid-gold plaque handed to him by Nobel laureates."

"Live your life, Jan. Your real life. Be who you are, out in the open."

Jannat fingered her engagement ring and caught a glimpse of her wedding dress hiding in a bag in her closet. She pointed to it.

"That's who I am too," she said.

Suzette smacked her shoulder, and the two women began to fake-fight on the bed, Jannat playfully pushing Suzette down and straddling her. Suzette tried to sit up, and Jannat was about to shove her down again, when she noticed the look of horror on her friend's face. She spun around and froze.

"You have forgotten the white rice again, Jannat joon." Her mother stood at the bedroom door, holding a Chinese food carton and a spoon. "Hello, Sudeh joon."

As Suzette yanked the comforter to cover her bare breasts, Maman gestured to her to relax. "Always good to see you." She smiled and stepped to the bed, where she handed the carton to the frozen Jannat.

"I'll wait for you both in the kitchen," Maman said, turned, and walked away, heels clicking on the wood floor.

PART II:
THE END

September 9-12, 2001

Twenty-Five

SUZETTE HID under the covers. Jannat bumped her lightly with her fist. She spoke softly, so that Maman, just a few feet away in the kitchen, couldn't hear.

"Did you know about this? That Maman knew?"

"Are you friggin' kidding me?" Suzette hissed from underneath the sheets.

Jannat pulled Suzette's cover off. "I don't know what to do."

"You've gotta talk to her."

"Come with me? Please Suz."

Suzette considered it. "I think the two of you need a minute alone."

Jannat nodded. That made sense. She slid on her robe and slippers.

Maman was standing by the sink rinsing some coffee cups.

"I took these out of the dishwasher. They are still dirty. Have you cleaned the dishwasher, Jannat? You know it requires regular maintenance, like all your other appliances." Maman spoke without a hint of rancor or, frankly, any other emotion. As though she were picking up on an inane conversation about housekeeping that they'd been having all morning, instead of surprising her engaged-to-be-married-to-a-man-daughter in bed with her lesbian lover.

"How did you guess?" Jannat croaked.

Maman picked up a dishtowel and dried the cups.

"A mother knows, Jannat joon. A mother always knows."

All the worry, the guilt over keeping a secret from her parents.

"Does Baba know?" Jannat held her breath.

Maman inhaled deeply. "He has not spoken of it to me, nor have I to him."

"Randy." Jannat whispered, her expression twisted with concern.

Her mother sat at the island in Jannat's kitchen, considering her offspring with nothing but love in her eyes.

"Ah yes. Randy. *Azizam*, you must decide what you will do. He accepts this?"

"No Maman." Jannat's cheeks reddened.

"He does not accept it? Then how are you marrying?" Maman glanced toward Suzette, who now leaned in the doorway, eyes trained on the floor.

"Maman, he doesn't know."

"You must *tell* him."

"I can't. Not yet."

The older woman pushed. "When then?"

Suzette and Jannat exchanged guilty looks. "The plan was . . . well, is . . . we thought . . . I'm going to tell him after the wedding."

Her mother gasped. "Jannat, *no*. You cannot do that. He is to be your life partner. How can you keep this from him? How can you let him marry you without knowing?"

There was no easy way to explain it. It somehow sounded so commonplace, so easy to accept, when she discussed it with Suzette. Maman's reaction was a muted one compared to what Mrs. Eller might say. Or do.

"Maman, please. Please let me do this my own way. I love Randy. I *want* to marry him."

Maman's gaze softened. "Of course you do, *Azizam*. I understand this." She gestured toward Suzette. "The two of you are the closest of friends. Your love for each other is of such long standing. Soudeh, dear, of course we know your preference. You must be true to it. You, Jannat, you are experimenting."

Suzette looked toward Jannat, her eyes silently imploring her friend to tell the truth.

"Maman. It is more than friendship. Suzette and I love each other in many ways. Emotional and physical."

"Yes, yes, I understand. Now that you have chosen to make your life with Randy, you must say goodbye to this . . . activity."

Jannat stepped up to her mother and took her hand. "You don't understand, Maman. Suzette and I will always be lovers. As we've been." She threaded the older woman's fingers through her own.

Maman jerked her hand away. "You still plan to do . . . *this? After you are married?*" She flung her arm toward Suzette. "No. I raised my daughter to be faithful. My daughter would not do this."

"Laleh," Suzette began, but Maman cut her off.

"No! This is not a negotiable issue, not an intellectual exercise where ethical judgment is malleable. This is right and wrong in its purest form. Jannat, you must tell Randy, and then you must choose. My daughter would not be duplicitous. My daughter would *not* keep such a secret." Maman had tears in her eyes.

Jannat's nostrils flared. "Then I am not your daughter."

Her mother recoiled, slapped both palms on the kitchen island, and turned her back on her only child.

As quickly and efficiently as she'd entered the bedroom, Maman was gone.

Twenty-Six

"DANNY?" Tris whispered sleepily. Sweating, she flung her Wedgewood-blue-and-cream comforter to the side. Both cats were curled up on the pillow next to her.

It was midnight and she'd only had two hours sleep. Fully awake now, Tris was afraid to close her eyes and miss her alarm. She couldn't be late for the 2:30 a.m. show at the airport. Years into her career, with fourteen Atlantic crossings in her quiver, Tris still didn't know whether it was better to sleep a little or stay up all night. She'd be exhausted either way.

She snatched her mobile from the nightstand. No messages. No missed calls. Danny hadn't called her back. In all the years she'd known him, even after he got married, when she'd needed him, he'd been there.

Something felt different. She looked around her dark bedroom for a new addition, sniffed the air for an unfamiliar smell.

Mike in her apartment had jolted her. Staring death in the face changed people—it was one of the only things that truly did. As he poured out his vulnerability in awkward words, as he'd begun to reveal the price he'd paid for the things she'd held against him, the lies he'd told, the people he'd terrified and hurt, the anger she held onto started to drip away.

His words had cleared a pathway.

When Danny held her, it was like soaking in warm honey, a sweetness that stuck. She'd felt something real then, too. She shook it off. Their timing had never been right. Danny was consumed with his divorce. Their night together meant nothing.

Still, they'd had sex. Sex changed the strongest of friendships.

Parked in the Chief Pilot Only spot in the Westin parking lot, Tris sat in her car with the motor running, collecting herself. Her focus had to be on the trip, observing the two pilots who would doubtless be overstimulated by their competition for a job that might not even be available.

So much stress could be avoided if she said, "It's off. I'm staying."

Then Deter would win.

Two years ago, she let him off the hook. Not this time.

It took a few moments before Tris turned the Corolla's key, and the old engine clunked, sputtered, coughed, and finally shut down.

Chuck's Chevy was already in the lot, as was Jannat's Infiniti. It was still twenty minutes before show time.

Phyll called her yesterday to alert her that the Legacy news was flying around the office; all the pilots were talking about it. If it were that easy for them to hear that she was going to Legacy, how long would it be before it leaked that her class date was canceled, and why?

The whispers, the stories people who had no idea what happened would tell—she lied at an interview. They pulled her class date.

Tris would be a cautionary tale.

Jannat cracked open the door to the crew entrance and waved.

"Hey," Tris replied, as she swung her expertly assembled overnight bag from the trunk. Years of carrying way too much stuff on the road had cured her of the tendency to overpack. She'd purchased a second set of items that lived in her bag—seemingly insignificant things, like slippers and a thin robe, that made being away from home a little easier to bear.

"Tris, I have some questions for you," Jannat said in the lilting, impatient voice that always made Tris smile. At times Jannat's tetchiness annoyed her, but how could she argue with someone who was wearing themselves—and sometimes Tris—out trying to be her best? She'd need to temper that quality if she were the Chief.

She could do it. Tris would teach her how.

"We'll talk inside." Tris waved her off.

The younger woman nodded and let the door close without holding it for her boss. No, it wouldn't occur to Jannat to wait. Her quick mind was already focused on the next task.

In the crew area, Chuck dove into his brief without saying hello or making any time-worn remark. "Here's the detail," he said, handing Tris a thick computer printout. "It includes the tracks. Our service suggested one, but we can use whichever we want."

No smile, none of the usual banter from him before this early departure. No talk of how boring it was to cross the Atlantic, what they'd eat, where they'd stay.

The stakes were high. Both candidates were feeling them.

Tris grabbed the track information. The NAT tracks were suggested routes for U.S. departures over the North Atlantic to maximize fuel burn to Europe. Each of the four tracks was assigned a letter, depending on the direction of flight. Eastbound, toward Europe, they were W, X, Y & Z.

Four separate paths, each with their own characteristics, weather, winds. These unique routes took airplanes step by step across the vast expanse of the Atlantic Ocean, where they floated past the point of no return, into spots that no radar could see them. "Trust us," they whispered. "Follow us. We'll get you safely to your destination."

There were always four: Bron, Mike, Rex—no, not Rex. Danny? Who else? Like four arteries pumping blood, who occupied that last direct route to her heart?

"I can handle the charts. I don't need any assistance." Jannat's sharp tone distracted her.

"Divide and conquer," Chuck said, but without the sly smile that usually accompanied a cliché. He reached over Jannat's head to pull a book of charts off the shelf.

"Excuse me!" Jannat.

"Give me that." Chuck.

They were so much alike.

"Okay. You two. This ends now," Tris said. "I'm not kidding. Don't you realize that I'm assessing how well you'll both work together? Make it a team effort, or I'll tell Woody to hire from outside." Chuck smirked. Tris turned an icy gaze on him.

"If *I* tell him to do it, he will. Count on it."

It was excruciating to keep up the façade that she was leaving, which was no longer assured. She had to. She'd find a way to get to Legacy—the successful completion of that maneuver could not be in doubt.

"Jannat, *please* let me handle the charts. Labor of love. You know how much I love charts," Chuck cajoled.

Jannat did indeed and nodded her assent. When Chuck first joined the company, if he got nervous, he would regale Tris on the intricacies of aeronautical charts; what each discrete symbol meant, the tricks and little-known idiosyncrasies. She had to be careful here, though. These two wouldn't have her to diffuse conflicts in the future.

"Like I said, you two work it out. I'm watching. Now, is the airplane ready to go?"

Both Chief Pilot wannabes shook their heads.

"Let me know when it is." Tris moved toward her office where she had put together her own trip information package. She'd been to Edinburgh before, but it had been years.

Theirs was a rare flight leaving the U.S. for Europe early in the morning. Their passengers had to make a brief stop in Newark, then they'd all cross the Atlantic.

Jannat came back a few minutes later and Tris steeled herself to be barraged with questions. If only she'd had more sleep.

"Can I grab your bag, Tris, and put it in the plane?" Jannat asked.

"Nope. I got it. What's left?"

"Catering and coffee. I'll handle it." Jannat had a way with Westin's antiquated Bunn-O-Matic coffee maker. None of its bizarre meltdowns—spitting water out the side, a burner failing to warm— seemed to occur when she operated it.

Tris's mobile rang and she checked the screen.

Danny. At last!

It was 3:00 a.m. Tris pressed the Talk button on her phone with relief. "Danny. I'm so glad you called."

There was no one on the other end.

He'd hung up before she could answer.

Twenty-Seven

THERE WAS A LULL, a time between preparation and execution of every flight, when the workflow slowed. It came between weather reporting periods, that golden hour before launch when the forecast remained unchanged, and there was simply nothing left to plan.

Tris considered her two exceptional captains, who stood bent over the company's operations manual. The team at Westin would follow Chuck because they were used to him. They expected him to be promoted. The same team didn't quite understand Jannat, but, in time, they would follow her too. She'd garner a high level of respect, and it would be borne less of expectation than their own experience with her. That was the better way.

Her phone buzzed again. Danny. She'd been aching for this call. Would he speak to her this time? What would she say to this man she'd been friends with for so long?

"Tris? Are you there?"

"Where are you?" Pilot speak, location first.

"The crash pad."

"It's what, 7:00 a.m. there? Look, I want you to know—" she began, but he cut her off.

"I'm so sorry. It was all my fault. Tris, it—"

Was Danny going to tell her it was wonderful? That he'd never felt so good before? That he'd felt wanted and needed in a way that he couldn't explain, in a way no one had ever made him feel?

"It was no one's fault. I mean, it wasn't something anyone would find fault in. I think it was something that had to happen, right? Danny, listen. I want to talk about this with you. That night. It was . . . amazing. But I'm leaving for Edinburgh shortly, and there's a problem. It's Legacy. It's my class—" She stopped abruptly when she heard Danny crying.

"Danny? Are you okay?"

A cough, followed by aggressive throat clearing. "No. Tris. It *was* a mistake. Don't you realize? Oh, God, this is all my fault. I screwed up."

The smile that curled the corners of her lips, her relief at being able to talk to her best friend, to ask for the help he'd do anything to give her, vanished. "You're right. I don't understand." Tris fell back against the wall, grasping it for support.

"Okay. I'm gonna spit it out, before I go back to Em."

"Back? To Em?" Tris repeated slowly.

"We're back together. Em and me. She's pregnant. Tris, I'm going to be a father. Em's agreed to reconcile. There was a condition; well, more of a demand. I agreed to it. I didn't want to. It's my child, don't you see? My child. Em said she'd get a . . . get rid of it." With that, he cried harder.

"You can't be my friend anymore? Because you're having a baby?" Her voice rose, and the murmuring of crew members around her in the hangar stopped. After all, their Chief Pilot was standing in the middle of the hangar.

Be careful. The majestic calm.

He spoke haltingly between sobs.

"Tris, that night was the best night of my life. I lo—my feelings for you will never change. But I can't see you anymore. Can't talk to you. It's my *child*. I have no choice."

Emily always seemed severely lacking in the intellect department. Turned out, she was brilliant. She'd figured out the perfect way to get what she wanted.

"Danny, please. Wait. I'm getting ready to cross the Atlantic. I have a long overnight in Edinburgh, I'll be back on Tuesday. Let's talk more, okay? I need your help."

Danny acted like he hadn't heard. "Let's face it. I tried. People move on. Maybe that one night is all we get."

Her head shook furiously. It moved her entire torso and attracted the attention of a couple of Westin mechanics. Her entire body was saying "No" in the sharpest, most emphatic terms.

Neither pilot spoke, nor did they hang up. Tris held the phone so tightly she thought she might crush it, her mind racing through its internal catalogue of words and phrases, desperate to conjure the one to turn this moment around. She always grabbed the right one in the airplane.

Why couldn't she do it now, for Danny? Why?

"That night … something changed. I have to tell you something, something important. I need you. Danny, I know how you feel, how you've always felt and I …"

"No you don't. I don't love you." The line went dead.

The concrete beneath her vibrated like rolling surf. Her legs wobbly, Tris clawed at the wall with her free hand, fighting to stay upright, and grabbed hold of the mounted first aid kit. It came loose, spilling its bandages, pills and salves all over the hangar floor.

"Damn it. *Damn it.*"

The two mechanics pulling the Falcon out on the ramp stopped and ran to her. Her tongue ran across her dry lips. Despite the chill in the hangar, the armpits of her shirt were soaked.

The two men each grabbed an arm to keep her from falling.

"Thank you. Thank you. I'm okay," she muttered. She straightened up. "I'm okay." The mechanics exchanged a look, released her, and walked away.

What was it about her? She stared at her hand. It looked normal. Her arms, legs, fingers and toes—the correct amount, all attached. What was it about her that caused every man who meant something to her to vanish?

Her father. Her grandfather. Bron. They'd all died. Mike was shot. Now Danny. Loyal, logical, long-term Danny. Gone.

Could everyone see the blood spurting from her heart as it shredded itself into pieces?

"Tris?"

"Chuck! What?"

"Uh, excuse me, but you asked me to come get you when it was time to go over the final weather report?"

Who was this stranger? What did he want of her?

"You okay, Tris? Something grab you by the balls, or what?"

Her laugh was shrill. "Got some stuff going on. What do you need?"

"Ip needs you. When you're done with him, please come inside and review the latest weather." Chuck turned away. Ip stood behind him, holding the clipboard.

She shouted. "You're here early!"

Ip involuntarily leaned back.

"You know I like to make sure my crews are taken care of. No one but me is gonna come in for a 4:30 a.m. departure, are they?"

Tris placed a hand on his shoulder. "Thanks, Ip. Did you finally get hotel information for us? Where are we staying?"

Ip thumbed through a thick stack of papers. She was amazed how he could rifle through so many sheets and find exactly what he was looking for in a snap.

"The Caledonian. Wow." He whistled at the name of the famous Edinburgh hotel.

He scurried away to consult with another captain who was headed to Teterboro. Tris faced the wall. One of the papers Ip had handed her was a phone message from Woody. He'd asked Ip to write, "We need to talk. Call before you leave."

Tris crumpled the pink message slip in her hand.

"Tris?" Jannat poked her head through the door that led to the office. "Do you have the final crew assignments for today?"

"One second." She collected herself, plastered a neutral expression on her face, and put her hand to her chest.

Calm. Calm. Calm.

Her crew waited, arms folded across their chests.

"Chuck, put the trip book together, and let me see it. Have Jannat watch you so she can see how to do it correctly." A quick wink and slight gesture toward the ramp where three other Westin crews were going about the steps to launch were meant to remind him that people were watching. If he was going to be Chief Pilot—here or anywhere—his example would be emulated by others. "They're always watching. Remember that," Tris whispered.

"Yes ma'am," both captains said in unison.

Tris quickly reviewed the latest forecast. No changes. "Chuck will fly us to Newark. Jannat, you'll be in the right seat, and I'll take the jump seat. Then Jannat and I will fly us across the Atlantic to Edinburgh."

"Excellent," Jannat said. The younger woman squared her shoulders.

"I'm ready," Chuck said.

Chuck and Jannat disappeared to make their own final preparations.

Tris was left alone—confused, heartbroken, and in command.

Twenty-Eight

DANNY PULLED OFF his T-shirt and used it to wipe the tears from his face. After years of trying—of hoping, of dreaming—it had finally happened. He'd been intimate with the love of his life, and it was everything he'd hoped it would be, everything he wanted.

Except his child.

This is nuts. This is soap opera shit.

The crash pad smelled of sour milk and body odor. His sheets were dirty, meaning someone had slept on them without permission, and Danny didn't have any quarters for the washing machine. Which didn't matter, since someone had also emptied his Extra-Strength Tide, despite the "DON'T TOUCH—DANNY'S," written on it with a thick black marker.

He had to get out. Unfortunately, his only assignment was a deadhead on Tuesday to LAX, then fly one leg to SEATAC, and another deadhead back to Boston. His bag was ready, his socks were laid out on top of each shoe. All he had to do was wait until Tuesday.

The only bright spot was that Legacy didn't have a departure that got him to LAX on time, so they were flying him out and back on American. He liked that far better than flying on-line on Legacy. Other airlines' flight attendants treated him better than they did on company. He detected a barely disguised dislike of pilots from the cabin crews at Legacy.

Danny flopped back onto the mattress and rolled over, trying desperately to find a spot to bury his face that didn't stink. Nausea rose again, and the only thing close by were his shoes. If he had to, he'd puke in them. He deserved it for what he'd done.

He'd connected with Tris. It wasn't just sex. Then he'd left. For his child.

I'm gonna be a father. Big fucking congratulations to me.

Someone flushed the toilet. Hopefully, they'd only peed, but the chances were slim. None of those guys flushed when they peed. Sure enough, a pungent smell wafted into his room.

His mobile buzzed. Emily. His chest was heavy, his breath labored. Was this what a breaking heart felt like? Could he get enough air into his lungs to talk to his wife?

"Hey," was all he could say.

"Danny, baby, please. Tell me it's done."

It. She wouldn't say Tris's name. *It.*

"It's done. Let's move on." He didn't want to start crying again.

The line was silent for several seconds.

"Danny?"

He discerned notes of relief mixed with distrust. And why not? He'd disappointed his wife so many times.

"Danny? Are you okay?"

He lied. "Sure. Fine. Anything new?"

Emily brightened considerably and detailed her plans for the day. Crib shopping. Pedicure.

"Which one do *you* like better?" she said sharply.

He hadn't been listening and couldn't be sure what "one" she meant. "Whichever you like, baby. Listen, scheduling is ringing. I've gotta go. Later." He lied again and ended the call.

Tris was coming to Legacy. Surely there'd be a way for them to see each other, maybe even fly together some day. He was due for recurrent training. He'd call his friend in the training department and find out her new-hire simulator schedule. Maybe he could bid a training sequence for the same time. They could partner together, like when they met so many years ago at Clear Sky.

There'd be a way to see her again. He'd find one. He stood up and walked out of the room. Exhaustion kept him in his dirty sweatpants. Right now, he didn't have the will to do anything but think about breakfast.

On his way into the kitchen, Danny tripped over one of the fully packed overnight bags his crash pad mates always kept by the door before they went to bed.

Randy Eller sat at the card table in full uniform, despite the early hour. He'd probably slept with one eye on his mobile phone. When reserve pilots weren't staring at their phones, willing scheduling to call with a trip, they sat around watching TV, ready to run out the door.

"When did you get in?" he asked the other pilot, who held his flip phone in one hand.

Danny didn't listen to the answer. His first goal was to make it to the kitchen sink to splash some water on his face. The bathroom was still polluted.

Breath came hard. Head in hands, he stood at the sink letting water drip through his fingers onto the countertop. He didn't hear Eller come up behind him.

"Tits, you okay?" How he hated that nickname.

Danny muttered a reply and grabbed a dish towel. Held up

against his face, it smelled like a combination of grease and mildew. It probably hadn't ever been washed. It was dry, however, and that was what Danny settled for.

The air around Danny shifted. Eller touched his shoulder, and Danny recoiled.

"What?" He said, louder than he intended.

"Nothing. Checking to see if you're all right. I mean, look, it's none of my business, but it sounded like you were crying."

Damn. Damn. Get it together, man.

He tossed the reeking towel to the side and rubbed his nose with the back of his hand. "Nah. It's my allergies. The dust in this place is insane."

Eller shrugged as he walked away. "You can dust any time you want."

Both men laughed. As if. This wasn't the kind of living situation anyone took seriously.

Danny opened the fridge. He thought he'd seen a package of hot dogs in there. If they didn't smell too bad, maybe he could boil some up.

The sound of air being released from the tightly sealed door caused Eller to call out, "Hey? You looking for something to eat? Wanna go to the Dump?" That's what they called the local 7-Eleven, which smelled as bad and was as dirty as their pad. It was the only place within walking distance to purchase food. Danny could usually stomach their pizza, which frequently looked like it had congealed in a pan for days. He didn't mind.

"Ok. Yeah. Give me a minute to get my shoes on."

It was already a gorgeous day in Beantown. The two pilots looked bizarre walking together, one in worn-out sweats and a pilot shirt, the other in full uniform, both wearing their lace-up work shoes. No one they passed gave them a second look, a testament to how many flight crew crash pads were in the neighborhood. The whine of jet engines taking off and landing provided a non-stop soundtrack.

Danny's eyes never left the ground.

"I'm sorry about your divorce," Eller said.

"Divorce is off," Danny said, as he stepped over a low metal fence. "We're pregnant." His tone sounded like he'd been taken prisoner. "Yup. Havin' a baby. We'll be a family."

Something in Danny's voice must have alerted Eller that sadness lurked behind this usually buoyant news.

"Good for you," he said carefully. "Jannat and I aren't interested in kids, but I suspect our families will put pressure on us. So that was it? The baby got you two back together?"

Danny couldn't bear to let his crew mate see the tears in his eyes. If he began to speak, he'd lose it. Luckily, his mobile rang. Scheduling, for real this time.

"Danny Terry." He answered on the first ring. *No one at Legacy would believe that I was begging to hear from the enemy.*

"We've got flight details for you for Tuesday."

"Go ahead." Danny grabbed a pen from his shirt pocket.

The scheduler's voice was almost drowned out by the sound of aircraft passing overhead.

"You're deadheading to LAX Tuesday, on American Airlines Flight 11, AA 11, scheduled to leave Logan at 7:45. Your confirmation code is Papa X-ray Romeo, the number six, Whiskey Victor. Read it back, please."

Danny scribbled the code on his hand. "Got it. PXR6WV. What am I flying out of LAX?"

"You've got one leg to SEATAC and we'll work on your deadhead back to Boston from there. That pairing is in your schedule."

"Hey, any chance you can deadhead me back to Exeter at the end of the trip?"

"You know the rules. Back to base. Thanks." The scheduler hung up.

At least it was positive space on American. No begging for the jump seat. No worrying that some American pilot would kick him off the plane if it were full. He'd be on duty in uniform. Hopefully, the gate agent would upgrade him to First Class. They had the last time.

Danny blinked back the tears that kept wanting to come. How could he live like this? The corners of Eller's gleaming smile fell as he saw the despair on Danny's face.

"Holy shit. What were your wife's terms?"

Danny's throat constricted around the words as his mind whirled.

I sacrificed my dream. I abandoned Tris.

It took a few seconds before he could answer.

"Unconditional surrender."

Twenty-Nine

THE HUM OF PRE-LAUNCH departure amped up, and Jannat threw herself into it, grateful to have something to do to distract her from Maman's surprise appearance in her bedroom.

The Exeter ramp was dark, lit only by taxiway and runway lights, and the flash of moving aircraft. What would happen if an aircraft suddenly went out of control, careening across the grassy areas, cutting through taxiways, ending up T-boning her Falcon on the takeoff roll?

Disasters and worst-case-scenarios had spun out in Jannat's head ever since she was small. It was one of the many ways she realized that she was not like other kids, and not like her parents. Nothing could befall, threaten, trick, deceive or delude her that was worse than what she created in her own imagination. As an only child, she'd been the heroine of all these potential tragedies. She could hold back an airplane speeding down the runway and keep the Ayatollah from killing her grandparents.

Baba. If he found out . . . Best to put off thinking about it. She'd have plenty of time to herself to come up with a strategy in Edinburgh. Trip preparedness. Life preparedness.

Randy answered her call on the first ring.

"Hey. It's me."

He cleared his throat, and she heard the scrape of chair legs against an uncarpeted floor. "Getting ready to go, right?"

"Passengers arriving any minute. We're ready."

"Home on the 11th?"

"Yes, Tuesday. I'll have at least two days off after the trip. But, Randy," her tone tightened, "You need a heads up on this. Tris will probably make the Chief Pilot decision as soon as we get back—once she can clear it with Woody."

"What about our wedding, Jannat? It's only a few weeks away. How can you manage all that and the wedding?" Pouty Randy was not her favorite version.

"I'll make it work. We'll make it work. This is so big, Randy. I have to focus on my job. You understand, I know you do."

Randy had been bested. Her career would always come first. "While you're in Europe, I'm getting together *over the phone* with the brain trust to review the menu. You know how my mother is obsessed with the couple's first dance, so I'll deal with that *from the crash pad.* Then there's the throwing of the bouquet and garter. She has some relatives she wants you to target with all that. Since you won't have the time to work that out, *I'll* do it." Randy prattled on, tossing in constant reminders that he'd be the one managing things from afar.

How had Maman known? Why had she never spoken of it? Maman was vocal over Jannat's choice of career, so pointed in her efforts to push her daughter toward science, "the family business," she'd said. She'd been thrilled when Jannat had gotten engaged to Randy.

How long had Maman kept her own counsel about Suzette?

How long had she known about her daughter?

When Jannat was in college, one day her roommate, a boisterous woman from New York who she studiously avoided, came walking out of her bedroom half naked, and grabbed a snack from their tiny fridge. Jannat could not take her eyes off the bare-chested woman—and not because she was shocked.

Jannat placed her hand on the woman's bare shoulder. Instead of shrugging her off, her roommate turned and kissed Jannat deeply, putting one hand on her breast, the other between Jannat's legs.

From that day forward, Jannat sought her satisfaction from women and men, and got pleasure from both.

She and Suzette had grown up together, so Suzette's sexual preference was well known at an early age. Her parents embraced it, but Suzette feared she'd be bullied if she were out in the open. They joked about the choice she made to keep her homosexuality private while they were in high school. "Must be musty and dark in that closet," Jannat always said.

The first night Jannat and Suzette made love ended with the two women spent yet still grasping for one another. Jannat felt, for the first time, exactly herself, not a reflection of someone else's vision, some avatar or cartoon image of reality. Jannat and Suzette would live other, different lives. They'd never sacrifice the one they shared together.

All these years, and no inkling whatsoever that Maman suspected. To never say a word about it? How well did Jannat know Maman?

"Baby? You still there?"

"I've gotta go. Tris is walking out with the passengers. I'll call you from the road. Be safe," she said, and clicked off.

The wedding couldn't come soon enough. She'd walk down the aisle, say "I do" and mean it. She loved him, they were good together in ways she and Suzette never could be.

She'd marry Randy.

Then she'd tell him the truth.

Thirty

HALFWAY ACROSS the Atlantic, at 30° West longitude, the ocean's white-capped waves appeared more like ripples from thirty-seven thousand feet. In the calm of the cockpit, Tris could almost hear the sound they made lapping against the shores of two continents.

Stacked one on top of the other at different altitudes, airplanes flew east in a sort of formation. They couldn't see one another, but their reported positions dotted the radio frequency, a line of explorers sailing toward land. Errant sounds of scratchy feedback from their HF radio, the hum of the engines, and the occasional rustling of their passengers provided the only background noise.

Chuck and Jannat had indulged in the verbal equivalent of chest-thumping from Exeter to Newark, each trying to show Tris how much more knowledgeable they were. Tris shut them down before they left for Edinburgh with a line about leadership being more by example than exclamation. It was an expression Bron had used over and over. It stopped their bickering.

Chuck snoozed in the jump seat, and Jannat monitored the

instruments as the flying pilot in the left. Stable and aloft, the airplane working perfectly, Tris couldn't keep the outside world out of her mind.

Solve the Legacy problem. Find Danny. Tell him how you feel.

Getting her class date back didn't guarantee that Danny would come with it.

Legacy Airlines had 10,000 pilots, and seventeen crew bases. What were the odds she'd get based in Boston? If she did, would Danny still be there? When she finally, inevitably, ran into him, what would she do? What if Emily and their child were with him? Could she stand in front of his wife and baby, profess her love, and beg Danny to leave them?

She'd promised Chuck and Jannat that one of them would be the next Chief Pilot at Westin. She wished she hadn't let Woody's call go to voice mail. So preoccupied, she'd forgotten to call him back before they launched. They'd talk in Edinburgh. She'd have plenty of time on the ground. She could explain it all to him.

Would he let her stay?

She could still leave Westin, apply for other jobs, go somewhere else... but the records. They were out there. Every potential employer would see them. She'd be combating this enemy for the rest of her career.

When did being a female pilot get easy? When did the battles stop?

Moments like this brought back her father's story of how she got her name. Not a well-educated man, he loved Latin and taught himself the ancient language. He'd convinced her mother to name their only child from Latin roots.

"Patricia is Latin for 'noble.' And Miles is Latin for 'soldier.' A warrior. Noble Warrior. That's what we named you. And that's what you are." He'd said and stroked her hair.

"I don't want to fight."

"No, no honey. A warrior is someone who sacrifices themselves for the good of others. Someone strong and big-hearted—who fights for right, who helps people."

"I'm tired of fighting, Papa." Tris must have mumbled aloud because both Chuck and Jannat stared at her.

"Uh, everything all right, Tris?" Chuck asked, yawning.

"Sure. I have a lot to think about."

Jannat hesitated for a second. "About your successor? Of course. It's a big decision."

Other people always assumed you were thinking about them. How amusing.

Chuck, his eyes closed again, chimed in. "Yes. A sticky wicket for sure, boss."

"Only because you and I are in contention. May the best person win." Jannat shot back.

Chuck laughed. "Yeah. Clash of the titans. Butter sure wouldn't melt in *your* mouth."

"Stop. Right now." Tris had heard enough. "Honestly, Jannat, how you managed to know what I'm thinking without special powers is a mystery to me. And *Cliché*," she carefully enunciated her Assistant Chief Pilot's nickname, "maybe you should go back to sleep."

"Nothing ventured, nothing gained," Chuck replied, propping the pillow up against the metal bulkhead and closing his eyes.

Jannat looked straight ahead, cheeks slightly flushed. Still so much for her to learn. Who would teach her?

Tris let her thoughts churn like the big water below her until the shores of Europe began to take shape. As objects on the surface of the earth became larger, more defined, so did her resolve.

To choose between Jannat and Chuck and promote one to Chief Pilot.

To fight for her career, for the job at Legacy.

To fight for love.

To be the person her father saw in her.

With no more than a nod, she and Jannat began the procedures designed to bring them safely to the ground. Checklists were requested and run, clearances received, systems reviewed, and approach procedures briefed. Tris focused her mind on their special language, a favorite symphony whose notes guaranteed a safe approach and landing. The two pilots worked in perfect harmony.

As the Westin Falcon touched down in Edinburgh, and taxied to the ramp, Tris looked around to see if there were any other aircraft she recognized. There was only one.

The Tetrix Gulfstream.

Thirty-One

FOUR GRUESOME *thunderstorm cells loomed above her, blackening the morning sky. Hail fractured the airplane's fiberglass wings. Tris held the yoke in a death grip like a beginning flight student. The force of the storm ripped open the cockpit. All protection from the elements was gone. Exposed and alone, Tris had only one chance, but she had to choose which of the four sunlit paths that loomed ahead would take her to safety.*

Two of the routes were already closing.

Another sported the fingers of building cumulonimbus clouds, poking out accusingly on all sides. It was unreliable, she couldn't trust it.

The fourth was straight, open—the likely choice. She steered toward it, but the closer she got, the smaller the entrance became. If she tried to force her way through the ever-shrinking opening, the storms on all sides would rip her wings off. She'd die for sure.

She was cold and wet. She'd never fly alone in weather like this. Where was her partner?

Tris pounded her pillow and heavy rain doused her. Except she was in a dry t-shirt, and the only thing wrong with her pillow was that it was now compressed like a pancake.

Another nightmare.

The numbers on the digital clock glowed in the dusky room. It was 6:00 a.m. in Edinburgh, which meant it was . . . what back home? She started a quick mental calculation, then stopped.

Today was a ground day. She'd promised to tour some of the highlights of Edinburgh with Jannat and Chuck. The room's drawn curtains were backlit by a rising sun. She opened them and was treated to a rare view of Edinburgh Castle from the historic Caledonian Hotel.

The Caledonian was fascinating; its structure a throwback to another era. Its two wings spread out in a V shape, a testimonial to the days when it was a hotel on one side, and the entrance to the Edinburgh train station on the other, connected so visitors could easily traverse the two.

European trips were high workload and exhausting. The benefits were being able to visit cities like Edinburgh, stay in places like the Caledonian, and learn their histories.

As a treat, she'd stuck the hangtag outside on the door handle to order room service breakfast. It wasn't going to be delivered for another forty-five minutes, give or take, so she checked her BlackBerry for any issues that may have come up while she was out of touch.

There was a short message from Leo, one of Westin's other captains, letting her know his trip had returned on schedule. He was heading home to get some sleep before returning to the airport to fly a top executive of Sacker, Inc., one of Exeter's largest corporations, to their annual Executive Retreat in Aspen, Colorado. It was a trip Tris would ordinarily do herself. She'd chosen Leo, who she trusted, to make sure that Westin Charter made a good impression, and hopefully get more business from the company. Leo's silver hair and practiced manner, like those of the executives he flew, had a way of putting them at ease.

Eyes closed, arms extended above her head, Tris automatically ticked off the names of Westin Charter's crews, where they were, and whether she needed to check in with them, a habit honed by repetition. This mental taking stock was part of being in charge. She'd hungered for a career with even more responsibility.

She'd had it. She'd lost it. She'd get it back.

No messages on her mobile. Nothing from Westin. No updates from Mike.

Tris pulled herself out of the featherbed-topped mattress and headed toward the water closet. When she was halfway done brushing her teeth, the message alert on her mobile phone chimed. There it was, Mike's new number. It was the middle of the night in Exeter, if that's where he was. He could be in London, or in the next room. The life of a charter pilot.

He said he'd help her, and maybe he had.

She knew one thing for sure: it was time to read his letter.

She knew precisely what pages it lay between in her work folder and could visualize its corner sticking out of the pile.

Open it. Read it. How much can it hurt?

Her fingers tingled as they touched the plain white envelope with "Chief Pilot Tris Miles" written on it.

"Room Service." A lilting brogue sang from outside her door, accompanied by a series of knocks.

Moments later, the white gloved attendant uncovered a sumptuous breakfast of scrambled eggs, cooked well-done, blueberry scones and clotted cream, along with an elegant silver carafe filled with coffee. Nothing on the tray took her mind off the letter.

Of all things, in addition to the usual business-sized manila envelope that her daily flight service messages always arrived with, the hotel's office team sent a white letter-sized piece of paper, with a note that read, "Thank you for staying with us, Captain Miles."

No sense putting it off. She stopped again, gripped by the chilling thought that the letter might contain some diatribe. Perhaps his advances were a smokescreen, persuading her that it was safe to read his missive, which was really a blow-off, like the one Danny had given her.

Danny. Her eyes moistened as she recalled the slight scratch of his fingernails on her back, his hot breath in her ear. She was determined to hold that memory tight. It would live among the many memories of him that she would carry.

She lifted the envelope. Was Mike still unstable? There was no way of knowing.

Could she risk more loss?

She grasped the silver letter opener on the desk in her room, which had ornate scrollwork fit for royal communication. Tris tucked the sharp tip of the shiny tool into an unsealed crack in the corner of the envelope. It slid through the folded flap like a hot knife through clotted cream. Inside were three folded pages, written in Mike's clear, bold hand.

To the Love of my Life:

How did we get here? How did you end up leading Westin's pilot group while I got two bullets in my body and lived in hospitals and rehab facilities for a year?

It was all my fault: my action, my inaction, my behavior. You don't care about my past, I told myself. So what if I'd said Christine was dead? Far away in the frozen wilds of Canada, she might just as well have been. You deserved all my heart, and telling you that Christine was still alive, you'd have thought a piece of it still belonged to her.

Yes, I lied about my ex-wife being dead. You'd never find out, right?

Then I betrayed you again. I told Woody about you seeing a shrink. I knew what the consequences could be, but I wanted the Chief Pilot job. Woody favored you. So, yes, I played golf with him, went to lunch, shared a few at O'Slattery's.

I needed Woody to trust me *like he trusted you. I couldn't tell him about my past, the police, the restraining order that Christine got, how I left Legacy Airlines.*

I wanted to be someone that you looked up to, not just a peer. I swear the only reason I went behind your back to get the job was so that you would admire me. I was so focused on getting the Chief Pilot position, I was blind to what I might lose if I did.

That's how I betrayed you. Every day we were together, I kept that secret, another betrayal. Every time you asked about my life before, my ex-wife, my time at Legacy Airlines, and I lied to you—yes, that was another betrayal.

I'd say that I've kicked myself over and over for not letting you know before Christine appeared, in the flesh, as our angel flight passenger—because what were the odds?—but I couldn't kick anything with either leg, not for a very long time.

Recovery from the gunshots was long, painful, and demanding. The hardest part was therapy, not the physical therapy but learning why I did the things I did. I didn't realize that I'd been addicted—addicted to Christine, what she'd meant to me. I hung on to her too long, tried desperately to stay in her life. I thought she was all I'd ever have.

Until I met you.

Look, I can't say that I'm "cured." I guess you know from therapy that there is never that moment. But I know myself better now. I own my mistakes.

You were not one of them. In talking with this great therapist I was seeing, I learned that you were probably the sanest, realest (is that a word?) person I'd ever met. If I wanted any chance at a happy life from here on out, I'd have to make it work with you.

I was really screwed up, Tris.

Maybe being shot was the best thing that could have happened to me. It shook me up. Made me get better, get my medical back, go back to flying. I'm here, back in Exeter. I did it for me, I did it for us. I can work anywhere, but wherever I flew, every place I went, I'd look for you. I dream every night of you walking up to me, of the two of us on the wraparound porch in our house, the one in that painting—remember?—where we'd sit in the winter, warmed by the wood burning stove as snow fell around us. We can still find that house, Tris. We can have that dream.

We'll live happily ever after in that house. If you give me another chance.

Let me show you how much you mean to me. I'll go at your pace, as slow as you want.

So now you know—all the dark corners, the secrets, the miserable, embarrassing truths. You know the good stuff, too. The things that we had before I ripped us apart. You can't tell me they didn't mean something.

I don't want to start again. That's not what I'm asking, since that would assume we are the same people we were.

The angel flight changed us all.

We can begin from where we are now. Make the past our friend, make it part of the fabric of our future.

Can we try that?

Let me back in, Tris.

I know you.

Mike

The sun was up. Outside the window lay a carpet of grass so green it seemed unreal. Open fields were dotted with trees, rocks, and rounded corners. They blurred in the distance, connecting earth and sky to make one continuous, undulating living thing.

Life was like the rippling scene outside. Her past with Mike was part of her—the way she'd loved him; the ways he'd failed her.

Tris thumbed the pages of the letter again. They jabbed at her fingers like shards. She ripped them into the smallest pieces she could and tossed them in the trash bin.

Her scones still looked appealing, even though they were ice cold. She took a bite from a corner of one and found that while it wasn't the perfect warm treat it had been when first delivered, it was quite delicious. She wiped her lips after enjoying every bite.

Thirty-Two

"HEY, YOU READY?" Chuck called from outside her hotel room door.

"Yep. Stand by," Tris said.

Tris, Chuck, and Jannat piled into a hired car bound for St. Andrews, the legendary golf course. The grass sported colors of deep green, yellow-green, and wheat. The roughs were easily distinguishable—Tris had picked up a lot of golf lingo flying with obsessed pilots over the years—as were the bunkers. Lining the perimeter of the course were hotels, inns, and what looked like pubs.

Jannat wandered around the clubhouse, in that way she always did, not simply taking in the sights, but assessing them, grading them somehow. Something about her was forever putting the world in order.

"What's this?" Jannat stood in front of a display that featured an oversized golf club.

Chuck raised his eyebrows slightly in wonder, as he did every time Jannat asked about something that, in his opinion, was a scion of popular culture.

"Uh, that's a Big Bertha."

Jannat took in the wood paneled clubhouse around her. "You two go walk around the grounds. I'll sit in this very masculine room and wait for you to finish playing with balls." A rare double entendre, executed with a smile. Chuck ate it up.

"Well at least I've got the balls to play . . . golf!"

The sound of the two competitors joking was heartening. Men who weren't afraid to make mild, slightly sexist jokes generally had the most respect for women; the women who could laugh at them had the strongest potential to be successful in their industry.

The others, the men who blushed every time they swore, who constantly apologized, who called her "ma'am," or the women who pounced on every one of those small indiscretions, were destined to be unhappy as pilots. Play fighting, humorous jabs, and a thick skin were the keys to survival—and even joy—in this decidedly upside-down career.

Later, with her crew in a limo that was taking them to Edinburgh Castle, Tris's blackberry buzzed with a message from Diana.

"Call me."

She keyed Diana's mobile number into the Sat phone and heard the two quick rings that usually meant the number she was calling was located outside the United States.

"Diana Estes." Of course, she wouldn't recognize the number.

"It's Tris. You're here in Edinburgh. I saw the Gulfstream parked on the ramp."

Diana hesitated. "Yes."

"Where are you staying?"

A scratchy sound came over the line. "The Balmoral. Iconic. Old. I would have preferred the Marriott, but that's where the passengers are staying. You know the rules."

Indeed she did. Tetrix crew and passengers never stayed in the same hotel. Crews didn't want the passengers to see them enjoying themselves on the road.

"Do you want to come have a drink with us later? We're at the Caledonian."

"I'm a bit jealous." She paused. "Sure, why not. I'll come over for a drink. And, Tris," she hesitated, which was not like her. "Look, I'm here with Deter."

"So?"

"You know I can't leave a crew member behind in the hotel without at least asking. May I invite him to join us? All the way across the pond, Deter could not stop talking about you, about Legacy Airlines. I told him what happened. He kept asking if I was sure, what they'd do, whether they'd give you another class date."

"Bullshit."

Did Diana seriously think that Tris would have a drink with Deter?

"Tris, he didn't *add* any negative comments. He said his trip reports were sent exactly as he'd written them after your flights. It was the previous guy, Zorn. He said, 'Tris needs to know how this happened.' He wants to *explain* it to you."

"Nobody is that cavalier about sending records required by the government. Deter was an officer in the Navy. Sorry. He made no mistakes."

"He's not who you think he is, Tris. He's changed, really. Have you thought about that?"

Her body stiffened. People didn't change. Circumstances changed. Environments changed. Rules changed. Absent shattered earth, a brush with death like Mike experienced, or unimaginable tragedy, people, at their core, did not change.

Deter might be sorry for what he'd done. He was still Deter.

Diana sounded desperate. "Tris, please. Look. You and I, we have so much history. Deter . . . he's my boss. We get along, I like him. I can't be in between the two of you. This is friendship, but it's also business."

"Then take yourself out of the middle. I don't want to have a drink with him, Diana. If that means you can't meet up with me, I can live with that."

In all the years she'd known and revered Diana, she couldn't imagine ever speaking those words to her. The filters of friendship faded against the weight of what Deter had done.

If she didn't take back what she'd said, she might lose Diana.

"Di, wait. I don't—"

"Nope. I got it. Have a great time in Scotland."

The line went dead.

September 11, 2001
Boston

DANNY WOKE to the sound of an emergency vehicle shrieking by outside the crash pad. In a flash of thought, a tiny scrap of optimism, he expected rescuers to bang down the door and let him out of this cage he'd built for himself, where he had to shed one dream of happiness for the promise of another. Where he'd told unimaginable lies to both women he loved.

In the cockpit, whenever the airplane jerked from side to side, up and down, slammed by turbulence, rising and falling a thousand feet at a time, he'd push aside his own terror in the moment and ride it out. It always ended. Always.

This would, too. Somehow it would end.

Make up your mind. Decide to be happy. This is what you wanted.

His mobile buzzed. Company. "Danny Terry."

"Hey, it's Destiny from Legacy training in Exeter. You left me a message?"

Danny fumbled the phone and almost dropped it. He wedged it against the pillow he leaned on and yelled, "Hey. Sorry. Hold on," before he finally stabilized himself enough to talk. He had to get this right. Destiny was his road to Tris.

"Des, a friend of mine has got an upcoming class date with us, sometime next month, I think. I wanna see if I can schedule my recurrent around that time, you know, surprise her at the training center when she starts." He thought of Emily and closed his eyes tight to force her out of his mind.

"Sure. What's the name?" Typewriter keys clicked in the background.

"Miles. Patricia F. Miles." He looked around the room, expecting to see Emily's eyes widen, the look she got right before she got angry. Guilt, his new constant companion, surged as he again broke his word to Emily. He was in it now, though. No movement but forward.

"Miles. Huh."

"What?"

"She was scheduled for October 8th, but she's not on the list anymore. Let me check something." More clicking. "I'm sorry, Danny. I can't say any more. She's not scheduled for class. Is that all? Anything else I can help you with?"

"I don't understand."

"Sorry. I'm so sorry. Her class date got pulled. It's confidential."

Confused, Danny muttered, "Okay, thanks."

It was early morning in Denver. He quickly ran through his list of phone contacts. Surely there was someone he could call, someone in training who could tell him what was going on.

If Tris wasn't going to fly for Legacy, he'd never see her again.

He scrolled through the names of people he'd met in training at the airline and found Britt Rosen's number. Britt was a captain in the training department. Somewhere, he'd heard that Britt was involved in pilot hiring.

Hopefully the number he had was still good. Pilots changed cell phone numbers more often than girlfriends, which, he'd learned, was the reason they got new numbers.

The phone rang several times. Danny was composing a voice mail in his head when he heard the rushed voice on the other end.

"This Britt."

"Hey, Britt. Danny Terry. Remember me? From that training sequence a while back?"

Silence. Then an explosion of laughter. "Tits! Hey. Sure, I do. What's going on?"

"Yeah, man, I've got a favor to ask." Danny quickly explained what he'd learned from HR.

"Hmmm. Yeah. That's odd. Hold on a minute. Let me see if I can find her name on the computer." More typing. Then Britt whistled into the phone. "Danny, how well do you know this girl?"

"Very. We flew together at Clear Sky, back in the day. One of the best pilots I've ever flown with. Why?"

"Look man. I'm not sure what happened between then and now. There's a note here that's kind of an internal code. Not a good note, if you know what I mean. You sleeping with her?"

Danny chuckled. "It's not like that. She's important to me. She deserves this. She's faced some shit, you know?"

Britt hesitated. "Tits, you didn't hear this from me, okay? Apparently, this girl lied at her interview. Maybe she's not who you think she is."

Danny almost dropped his cell phone. "That's not possible. Not possible," he repeated more softly, almost to himself.

"Hold on. Okay, here it is . . ." Britt recited the story of a former employer, who had included a statement in Tris's training records that she was a poor crew member, divisive, didn't play well with others, didn't take criticism, and that those negative qualities affected her ability to fly the aircraft safely.

What did those fuckers do to her?

That's what Tris tried to tell him, why she needed his help. He didn't listen. Why didn't he listen?

Appalled that any aviation employer would go to such lengths to keep a fellow pilot from getting a job, Danny pressed his plea. "Britt, I know how it sounds, how it must look, whatever they said. But it's wrong. I'm telling you it's wrong. There's backstory there. If anything they wrote was true, she'd never lie about it. I *know* her. There must be something . . . someone . . ."

"Dude, I'm not sure—"

"*No.* This isn't right. Look, hire her, or don't. But this isn't right. Listen, okay?"

The sound of typing in the background drove Danny crazy but he kept talking. Whatever amount of goodwill Danny had with Britt, he was determined to use it all. This wasn't fair. Tris already paid for what happened at Tetrix, time and time again. He couldn't let her dream die like this. Danny told him what Tris had endured, how she'd come out the other side, how she'd kept her counsel no matter how bad things got. He told Britt the whole story, including what had happened on the way to Luxembourg. What Deter had done; what he'd said.

A long silence followed. Danny heard a brief side conversation. "Yeah, gimme a minute," Britt said, followed by the sound of a door closing.

"Are you sure about her, Tits?"

"I'm sure."

"You're off probation, right?" Danny shuddered. Could asking for Britt's help harm *him*?

"Yeah. Why?"

"Dude, you know how this works. If I make her case *for you*, your name and hers are gonna be tied together at this company forever. Everything she does, any misstep or bad training report, well, that'll come back on you. If what was in those records, if *any* of it is real, it sticks to *you*. Then things will get difficult, and I won't be able to help. No one will. You *sure*, Tits?"

Danny didn't hesitate. "I'm sure."

"Okay. Let me see what I can do." Britt hung up.

Every bit of energy he possessed disappeared. His arms, all the way from his shoulders to his fingertips fell to his sides as he flopped back down on the soiled sheets. There was no strength for anything but his devotion to Tris.

The crash pad door slammed, startling Danny. He'd dozed off. His flight didn't leave until 7:45 a.m., and he had no preflight responsibilities on a deadhead—all he had to do was be at the gate on time.

He lay back down and closed his eyes. Another bang caused the thin wall separating his bedroom from the apartment next door to vibrate. It was also a crash pad, this one for flight attendants, and there was one guy who stayed there who always dropped his overnight bag on the ground like he was trying to send it through the floor. If Danny hadn't seen it with his own eyes one day when he was hanging out over there, he wouldn't believe it. Day or night, regardless of the time, that guy slammed his bag down.

Sleep was over. Danny stumbled to the kitchen to make coffee and passed Eller, who stood at the sink. The two grunted at each other, and Eller headed to the other bedroom.

After two cups of coffee, a beef jerky stick, and a shower, Danny made his way to the terminal. He was early, so he walked. The sun was out, and he easily navigated the land mines created by the Big Dig before Boston's rush hour traffic made it a death-defying act.

Logan Airport's curbsides were already two deep with cars, limos, vans. Airline terminals and their passengers fascinated him. Who were these people? Where were they going, and why? Some wore their very best clothes, like they were headed to a wedding, or church on Sunday. Others appeared with sweatpants, bed head, and morning beards. How many of them who peered at him through sleep-crusted eyes were going to end up on his airplane? Would he recognize the people who'd be sitting next to him?

Danny sipped from an almost empty water bottle and made his way to the gate area for American Airlines flight 11. He checked in, got a boarding pass, and pulled the latest copy of *Aviation Week* out of his bag. The gate agent glanced quickly at his uniform and upgraded him to First Class, so no need to buy breakfast in the terminal. This morning, he'd be served.

In line to board, he rolled his head side to side, but couldn't relax. His plea to Britt was passionate. Danny felt his voice crack several times. Was Britt convinced?

Did it even matter? Tris would never forgive him for the horrible things he'd said.

If he could do this for her, if she got her class date back because of him, then she'd listen. He'd tell her the truth—how that night meant everything to him. She'd understand that he had to say something, anything, to save his child. He wouldn't have to convince her that he really loved her—his voice, his touch, his eyes would prove it.

Buoyed by his newfound optimism and a first-class boarding pass, Danny didn't notice his mobile buzzing. It buzzed again a few seconds later. Maybe it was Britt calling with more information. He stepped off to the side in the jetway next to the gate-checked luggage.

"Danny Terry," he answered hopefully, as two men clutching their carry-ons tightly to their bodies, boarding passes in hand, entered the cabin.

September 11, 2001
Edinburgh

TRIS WOKE, eye level with the soft white sheets that covered her bed. She hugged herself, expecting to be soaked. She was completely dry and safe. She'd had the thunderstorm dream again, but this time the four paths, tracks—whatever they were—were all blocked.

She padded over to the desk where she'd read Mike's letter. Only the envelope remained.

Relationships were about trust.

There'd been no further contact with Diana. She and Deter had probably already left for wherever their next destination was. Tris wondered if Tetrix still did an annual ten city European tour they called "The Ball Buster." She'd flown it once—the crucible in a series of unpleasant experiences during her time there.

Her mobile chirped. Probably company, more than likely with some last-minute changes, even though she'd confirmed the trip details with Ip yesterday.

Rex.

"Tris Miles," she answered, as if she didn't know who was calling.

"Tris. You haven't called." Hovering under the surface of his sleepiness was hurt. "Are we still on for tonight?"

She'd promised to have dinner with him when they returned.

"Uh. I guess so. Can we see how I feel when we land? I might be beat."

"I was going to cook something special and be waiting for you at your apartment. I need to go to feed the cats anyway, so . . ." His voice trailed off.

As much as she lacked the emotional capacity to deal with Rex right now, she couldn't end their relationship, such as it was, on the phone from thousands of miles away.

"Rex, please . . ."

He cut her off. "I've been thinking about you so much since our last night together."

Tris had to smile. She'd enjoyed it, too. "Let's see how I feel tonight. I'll call you."

A deep sigh made its way over the trans-Atlantic phone line. "Love you. Bye." Click.

She held the receiver as far away from her as she could without dropping it and stared it down. He *what*?

She'd guessed how he'd felt, and now he'd said it. His courage inspired her. She checked her watch; the gift Rex had given her.

It was early out east. Slowly, she punched in all the numbers that would connect her Sat phone to his mobile.

Please please please let him still be at the crash pad. Please.

"Hi. You've reached Danny Terry. Leave a message." What if Danny was home and Emily was checking his call log or voice mail? That was something Emily would do. Her finger hovered over the red "End" button. Tris cradled the phone in her hand so long, the recording ended without her ever saying a word. She hung up.

It didn't matter if they had no future. It didn't matter if he wasn't there to hear her.

She had to say the words.

"Danny." His name came out involuntarily, like an epiphany. "Danny. You're more than my best friend. It wasn't a mistake. I'll hold our night together in my heart forever. I understand what you have to do. I love you."

The bedspread heard her. The curtains heard her. Her dirty underwear, toiletries, shoes—all heard her. Maybe, somehow, Bron heard her.

Danny did not.

Tris was thirty-nine and alone. She'd almost settled down with Mike. He'd overcome so much. Could she find a way to understand the things he'd done, the things he regretted?

Mike would help her get back to Legacy. Maybe he already had. He still wanted her. Their relationship ended with gunshots, not by agreement, or design.

Mike said they weren't finished.

He was right. Half-right.

Tris and Danny weren't finished.

Desperate for distraction, Tris looked around her hotel room. A habitual flinger who'd toss clothing around within minutes after arriving, this time she'd outdone herself. Tris enjoyed the ritual of walking back and forth, back and forth, picking up like items to place them together in her bag when it was time to go.

A t-shirt here, a t-shirt there. Shorts hanging on a doorknob, a night shirt. Check. Toiletries, first hair products, then skin, then makeup. The makeup part was always the quickest. Mascara and lip gloss. Check. Any more put her look too much at the whim of the weather. Too hot, foundation ran. Too cold, her eyes watered, washing concealer into them.

The distinctive ring of the Sat phone interrupted her packing.

"Tris, it's Mike. Hey."

She looked at her watch. "Early where you are? Which is where?"

He paused. "On a charter in Bangor."

Tris took a deep breath. "First time back?"

"Yup." The angel flight ended with an emergency landing in Bangor, Maine. Mike rolled out of her airplane on a gurney; Christine was in a body bag.

"You okay?"

"Yeah. Hey, I'm sorry, Tris. I couldn't get past the gatekeepers at Legacy. All they said was that they couldn't tell me anything."

Tris took a deep breath and let it out slowly. It was becoming more and more clear that she might have to approach Deter directly. Instead, she threw a Hail Mary. "Mike, do you know anyone in Legacy scheduling that can tell you if Danny Terry is flying?"

"Danny? You think *he* can help you?" Mike's jealousy thrummed on the other end of the line. "Aren't you still friends with Danny? Don't you have his cell?"

"It's complicated. Check if you can. If you can't, then—"

"I can. I will. Tris, did you read—"

"Yes. I read your letter. I . . . I don't . . . Thank you, Mike, for saying those things. For apologizing. It meant a lot to me. I'm getting ready to fly home right now. We'll talk when I'm back in Exeter."

"You promise?"

"I said we'll talk." An easy promise to keep.

"I'll call you back when I find out Danny's schedule."

None of the Westin pilots spoke on the way to the airport, lest any sound detract from their ability to take in the beauty of the countryside that slid past. There was something about this place, something about Edinburgh, how easily such an old, traditional city accommodated the new, that both stunned and relaxed them. Each wore a look that said they wished they could stay longer. Pilots never got to stay anywhere very long; their world was motion.

Their Town Car pulled up at the Signature Executive Terminal, beside another hired car sporting the same livery as theirs. Its rear doors swung open, and out stepped Diana and Deter. Tris let Jannat and Chuck exit the car first, pretending that she'd received a message on her BlackBerry. Which, while she was pretending, she did.

D on his way to LAX on AA11. Launch 7:39 EDT. M

Mike was trying. He really was. Another sign of change.

Danny was working today, so he'd have his phone on him. There'd be no danger in leaving a message. It was 1:30 p.m. in Scotland. Tris did the mental math—it was 7:30 a.m. in Boston. He might not have boarded yet.

"Chuck, you and Jannat get started. I need to make a call," she said to her number two. Chuck nodded and grabbed Tris's bag without another word.

Their passengers were due in an hour, and they'd be ready to go as soon as they arrived. Both Chuck and Jannat had been studying the documents for the two legs home. They'd stop in Reykjavik for fuel, and then head non-stop to Exeter. Easy.

She'd have dinner with Rex. It was time to be straight with him. Mike was back in her life, and Danny still knocked at her heart. There was no emotional space for him. He'd said he loved her, and she simply couldn't let it continue. Rex wasn't the one.

She pressed #3 on her speed dial.

Voice mail.

"Danny. I know I'm not supposed to call. I know you're deadheading to LAX today, so that means you're working, and hopefully this message won't cause you any trouble with Em. I need you."

She stopped. She'd planned to say she needed his help. This felt more real. "I know you're back with Em, but I really, truly need you. That night. In Boston. It wasn't a mistake. It was right. Finally, completely right. Call me. Talk to me. I'm crossing the Atlantic today, on my way to Exeter. Use a go-between, do something. I must speak to you. I can't shrug my shoulders and let you go out of my life."

She caught her breath. Made a decision.

"After we—after that night, things felt different. I realized that I—"

The automated voice mail attendant cut in. "If you are satisfied with your message, press 1, or just hang up. To mark your message as urgent, press 2. To delete your message, press 3."

No, this wasn't the way. She pressed "3" and turned off her phone. She'd wait until he answered.

Above her, the sky darkened. They needed to get out of there before weather rolled in. Get home.

She'd talk to Rex. She'd deal with Mike. She'd find Danny.

Tris stepped out and walked toward the ramp. The majestic tail of the Westin Falcon 50 rose above the security gate.

Get me home.

"They're what?"

Chuck shrugged. "They're already here. Early. Our passengers finished their business early."

"Then why didn't someone call us?"

Chuck tilted a thumb over to the three men glued to the big screen TV in the terminal. "They like soccer. They came here to watch. This place is pretty nice. Catering's here. Jannat is on the phone with Universal changing our departure time. We can go early."

Tris lightly touched his shoulder in thanks and exited the sliding glass doors to the ramp. Jannat had the Falcon ready to go any time. All she had to do was get their clearance.

Tris gritted her teeth in frustration. Both pilots deserved to be Chief. They had earned their shot at the top spot, and, at this point, it was possible neither would get the nod.

A familiar sound stopped her cold. That step, that shuffle, the motion of shifting weight from side to side of someone who was severely bowlegged.

"Hello Captain Miles." Deter.

Tris continued her climb into the cabin.

"Tris."

She took another step up and steadied herself by grabbing one of the cables that supported the door. Anger swelled, and she breathed deeply to keep it at bay. What could this man possibly want?

She turned, high above Deter, gazing down at him. "Yes? I'm busy, and our passengers are here early."

"Let me talk to you while you get ready."

A shrill laugh escaped, and Tris shook her head violently. "You are not invited on my airplane. Say what you have to say, say it quickly, and let's move on."

He bristled. This wasn't the Tris he was used to, the one who took the verbal blows, the insults, the ignorant remarks, and let them bounce off. His words had scarred and strengthened her.

Deter stood his ground. "It was Zorn, Tris. He wrote some things in your file. He was afraid of you. We all were. What you'd do. What you'd say. Would you sue us? This was never about anything else but him. Even hiring you, that was—"

"You think I don't know? It was to make him look good— hiring a female. It was never about me."

Deter's piercing blue eyes bored into her. "Okay. Gotta get *my* airplane ready to go." He gestured toward the Gulfstream, the sheer size of which made her Falcon look like a plastic toy, and he wobbled away.

Tris decided to fly the leg home from the right seat, to see how Jannat handled non-flying pilot duties on the captain's side. And because Tris felt an overwhelming need to handle the controls. The encounter with Deter made her want to prove it again, prove it once more, even if only to herself. She wasn't who Tetrix said she was. Even if only she knew it.

Jannat expertly rolled the Falcon slowly onto the taxiway in the direction of Runway Three-Zero. Tris called out items on the taxi checklist. Short of the runway, she notified ATC.

"Edinburgh Tower, Falcon November Four Whiskey Charlie, short of Runway Three-Zero, ready to go."

"Falcon November Four Whiskey Charlie, Edinburgh Tower. Climb runway heading to 3,000. Wind Two-Nine-Zero at one-five knots. Runway Three-Zero, Cleared for Takeoff."

The power levers full forward, Tris lifted the graceful jet into the sky. Things happened fast after that, as gear and flaps were stored, and the swiftly climbing jet had to be leveled and slowed.

"Falcon November Four Whisky Charlie… standby." Tris expected a handoff to departure. The radio was silent for way too long.

"Jannat, give them a call please."

The younger woman clicked the mike. "Edinburgh Tower, Four WC. You want us over to Departure?" Surely a frequency change was required.

"Uh, no. Falcon November Four Whiskey Charlie, you are cleared to the Edinburgh Airport via direct. Turn left to a heading of Zero-Four-Zero, vectors for a visual approach to Runway Three-Zero."

Tris didn't hesitate and turned the aircraft while Jannat queried the bizarre clearance.

"Tower, Four Whiskey Charlie did not request a clearance back to Edinburgh."

More silence.

"November Four Whiskey Charlie, call us on the ground. If you still need to. You are prevented from entering U.S. airspace at this time. You are re-routed to Edinburgh per your company's request. Say intentions."

"What the fuck?" Chuck blurted from the edge of the jump seat. He practically thrust himself into the instrument panel.

One thing they all realized—they couldn't solve this riddle in the air.

Tris keyed the mike in lieu of a frowning Jannat. "Falcon November Four Whiskey Charlie cleared to Edinburgh via direct. Let us know when we can turn toward the field."

As pilot-in-command of this trip, Tris was irked that no one at Westin had alerted her. She'd power up the satellite phone as soon as it was safe and call Phyll.

This better be good.

On the ground, as soon as they taxied off the runway, a ramper in a Follow Me vehicle blocked the Falcon. Jannat abruptly pressed the brakes. The ramper began waving his arms and then crossing them above his head. The ramper held his hand to his ear, which wasn't a standard signal.

"Edinburgh ground," Tris said, "we've got a ramper in front of us signaling for an emergency stop. Are we in distress?" Could something be on fire? Tris checked the warning lights. There was no indication in the cockpit of anything amiss.

The controller spoke sharply. "Falcon November Four Whiskey Charlie, Follow-Me will escort you back to Signature along with the airport police. This is for your own safety. Call your company. Or turn on the TV."

"Edinburgh Ground, we don't understand. Are we in distress?" she asked again.

"Everyone is," was all the controller said.

Jannat didn't flinch. She guided the Falcon behind the golf cart back to the ramp. The ramper that they almost ran into on the taxiway led them to a parking spot.

"Chuck, get inside and find out what's going on. Jannat, shut her down and I'll talk to the passengers." What would she tell them?

Their lead passenger was out of his seat. "Why are we back here? What's going on?"

Tris summoned all her strength to remain calm. What words for "I have no earthly idea," would ease his anxiety?

"Relax. There is nothing wrong with the airplane. Something else has happened. I'll find out." She grabbed the satellite phone and walked toward the ramp for privacy.

Before she could key in the international operator code, Chuck dashed up the stairs and practically ran into her.

"Tris. Tris. You won't believe it. Attack. We're being attacked." Chuck could barely speak, he was panting so hard. Commotion picked up among other crews on the ramp. Some ran to the terminal. Chuck spoke so quickly nothing he said made sense. It sounded like, "plane hit the tower." Had he lost his mind? He had no color in any part of his face. Chuck began hyperventilating, doubled over, and gasped for air.

"Jannat, hand me a barf bag." Tris grabbed it and made Chuck breathe into it. She turned to the passengers. "Folks let's head inside. On the double."

Still gasping for breath, Chuck shouted, "Airplane crash. Building," over and over.

The crew and passenger complement of Falcon Four Whiskey Charlie rushed into the terminal they had exited less than thirty minutes before. A crowd stood in front of the TV. There was no sound, other than a television reporter's voice.

"Here is a scene from the New York financial district. Debris is falling like heavy snow from the fire in the North Tower of the World Trade Center, due to an American Airlines jet flying directly into it. People are fleeing the area to escape any further explosions. Police and firefighters, however, are trying to access the area around the buildings, desperate to help anyone trapped inside, and searching for survivors of this deadly crash."

A phone in the terminal rang and rang, but no one at the desk made any effort to answer it.

Again and again, the video showed an airliner flying into the North Tower of the World Trade Center.

"I don't understand. Is this a computer simulation?" Tris muttered.

"It's real," someone said.

Chuck was by her side. Their passengers stood together behind them.

Where was Jannat?

"American Airlines Flight 11, Departed Boston's Logan International Airport at 7:59 a.m. bound for LAX with a full load of fuel. The information is coming quickly now. It is being reported that crew members in the rear cabin of the flight—flight attendants and possibly someone who was jump seating from another airline— attempted to report the incident to American Airlines flight operations. But it was too late. The cockpit was overcome by hijackers who—heaven help us—flew the airplane into the North Tower."

Boston to LAX.

Danny.

Where was her phone? Desperate to find it, Tris jumped up and started digging through her purse.

Chuck shuffled behind her, eyes wide in horror. "What are you doing? Tris?"

"I've gotta call a friend. My friend. He was deadheading to LAX this morning. Out of Boston. Oh no. Oh no."

Sat phone in hand, she tried to still her trembling fingers to dial and realized that she'd only ever pressed a memory button on her cell phone. She didn't know his number by heart.

"My mobile, my mobile," she mumbled, and tore through her purse until she located the flip phone. It slid around in her palm as she struggled to hold onto it.

She almost had it open when a horrified voice reached out from the TV.

"And now . . . oh my . . . this is . . . another airplane has flown into the World Trade Center, the South Tower. The South Tower has been hit. It's been hit. Parts of the plane have fallen off. Have hit the ground. The South Tower of the World Trade Center in New York City has been hit by an airplane. We're hearing that . . . the airplane was hijacked. The South Tower is now burning. Thousands of terrified people are literally running away from it, trying to escape the falling debris. Yet police and firefighters continue to run toward the calamity, to find survivors, people who might be hurt, who need medical attention."

Tris and Chuck stared at the television. The newscaster pressed in his earpiece, then spoke into the camera.

"We have just received word that an airplane has crashed into the Pentagon. The Pentagon is on fire. It's on fire."

The reporter lowered his glasses for a moment, eyes pinched closed. It took a few seconds before he recovered. He finally spoke.

"How did this happen? And when will it end?"

Danny's mobile beeped a continuous busy signal each time she called. Tris hadn't taken her eye off the Sat phone's keypad for what seemed like hours. Yet only minutes had passed since her plane was forced out of the sky, and the world changed.

She twirled the wheel of her BlackBerry around and around, keying in on Mike's message. "BOS TO LAX. AA11." It wasn't possible. He had to be wrong.

Nobody could turn off the television. Four airplanes had been hijacked. Who were the people that did this? Was it a horrific coincidence, or part of a ghastly plan?

Who could hurt so many people?

Airplanes were crashing all over America, her country, and all Tris could do was grasp a Sat phone, sick to her stomach. There was no way to fathom the damage, all those planes and passengers, and the many hundreds of people in the towers. People who got on the elevator on a sunny Tuesday morning with their brown bags filled with buttered rolls and regular coffees. All those crews. Every one of those four airplanes had pilots, flight attendants. Jump seaters. Non-revs.

Her people.

The news reported that a flight attendant on AA 11 called company dispatch during the hijacking. Had others?

How terrified they all must have been. Not only for their lives, but for their impotence. To watch helplessly as airplanes, *their* airplanes were turned into flying bombs, and be powerless to stop it.

Pilots went to work every day knowing their lives were at stake, yet not one ever thought they could die. Quite the contrary—Tris and every pilot she'd ever known believed that they and they alone had the power, the skill, the guile, the *training*, to *save* their airplane in an emergency.

You're a coward. You couldn't say I love you.

Danny died not knowing she loved him. Exactly like Bron.

No calls were getting through clogged U.S. phone lines. Acting quickly, Phyll had notified their international handler, and that led to the Falcon's dramatic landing back at Edinburgh. American aircraft outside of the U.S. were diverted to places they'd never imagined, nor intended, to be. Everything in the air was allowed to land anywhere but home. U.S. airspace was dark. It was incomprehensible. The New York air corridor, the busiest in the world, shut down. Exeter airspace, shut down. Chicago to Denver to California. Shut down.

They were stuck in Edinburgh.

Stymied crews and delayed passengers flooded the Executive Terminal. "Why not crash an airplane in Edinburgh," an edgy Citation captain with a Midwest accent said. "It's in the UK. Everyone's still flying here. It could happen. Why not?"

"Shut the fuck up, Dave," his co-pilot said. "Aren't we all freaked out enough?"

Incredibly, Chuck was able to get the crew the same three rooms they'd vacated hours before at the Caledonian. A car was on its way to pick them up. Their passengers had already departed by limousine, back to their hotel.

Jannat sat alone, far from the television, where the hub of activity was, everyone talking at once, propounding their theories on how and why, and when the next attack would come. Or simply stood, mouths agape, watching the news, the tapes of airplanes hitting buildings, hitting the Pentagon, hitting the ground.

Tris sat down beside her crew mate. The younger pilot's eyes were red. She whispered to her boss, "What will be next? Who will be next?"

What was she talking about?

The petite daughter of Iranian immigrants continued. "My father goes to the mosque every day. My mother volunteers at the community center for senior citizens of my culture."

"I don't understand. You're Americans. You did nothing. No one knows who did this. No one will blame you."

"You *don't* understand. How could you? I must speak to my parents."

A bank of pay phones across the room had all been occupied. As soon as one came open, Jannat rushed to grab it before someone else snuck in ahead of her. There, she began the desperate task of dialing the U.S., with a fingers-crossed prayer that she'd be the one to slip into an opening in the choked phone lines.

It was almost midnight in Edinburgh. The continuous loop of airplanes hitting the towers, the Pentagon burning, a smoldering hole in Pennsylvania, the crumbling World Trade Center played in the dark hotel room. Every replay hit like clubs, beating her again and again and again.

Emotionally exhausted when they arrived back at the hotel, Tris had implored her crew to try and get some sleep, knowing none of them could.

There was no way to plan. Tris had no idea when the U.S. would let them come home.

She'd accounted for all the Westin Charter airplanes with help from Ip and Phyll. Only one besides the Falcon was stuck in a place that it had not intended to be. The Royal 350 was grounded in Detroit. If necessary, the crew could drive back to Exeter. For right now, they were staying put.

Everyone else was home, safe.

The death toll mounted. The last Tris heard, it was over 2,000 people.

Plus one. Plus Danny.

She'd reached Mike at WhisperJet. He'd gone there to get out of the house and found most of the company's other pilots in their hangar, watching TV, talking. Looking for comfort from their own.

"American Airlines 11. Are you sure?"

He sighed. "I checked and rechecked. Remember, he's married to my cousin Emily. His schedule said AA11." Mike's voice caught. "I'm so sorry."

Not possible. It was a mistake.

Whenever Tris forced her eyes closed, she saw flames, and the ash that dropped like confetti on New York's financial district. People running for their lives. Airplanes flying into buildings. She'd push her eyes closed even tighter, but the sight of the towers falling was burned into her eyelids.

Those august structures, the ones she'd relied on so, so many times to guide her approach into LaGuardia. Gone.

Out in the hallway, overnight guests, involuntary and otherwise, mingled for hours, their room doors ajar. United in tragedy, it was a way of coming together, to buffer their pain. Tris had met a couple from Germany on the elevator up to their rooms. They barely spoke English, but the three of them clearly communicated through universal expressions of sadness, loss . . . and fear.

With the TV off and the hallway finally quiet, the hours ticked by. Tris heard what sounded like a vacuum cleaner. Its motor waxed and waned as it conquered the hallway carpet. Someone with a strong accent asked about bed sheets, and said, "have a soap."

A siren sounded outside, loud enough to deafen any living thing in its range. It blared and blared, well beyond any normal length of time. Tris curled up on the bed, cell phone gripped in one hand, and pressed a pillow to her head.

Her television off, she could still hear the words of the stricken reporter.

Here's American Airlines Flight 11, a Boeing 767 jet, which departed Boston's Logan Airport at 7:59 a.m., hitting the North Tower of the World Trade Center. First responders estimate that it hit somewhere between floors 93 and 99. It is uncertain how many people were able to exit the tower before it collapsed at 10:28 a.m. eastern time. No one on the aircraft survived this brutal attack on U.S. soil, the worst ever reported.

She felt Danny's hand, warm on her shoulder, the way he'd touched her that night, as he pulled her into his body so closely their hearts collided.

Thirty-Three

MAMAN. BABA. Jannat couldn't think of anything else.

Sleep was out of the question.

Who was Al-Qaeda, the group suspected of launching the attacks? Their leader, Osama Bin Laden, was the son of a wealthy construction magnate. What was a privileged kid like that doing out in the desert, plotting to kill people?

She was embarrassed that she hadn't heard of him, or Al-Qaeda, but it had been so long since she'd picked up a newspaper. The wedding. Chief Pilot. Her career. Her future.

What did any of it matter now?

Try as she might, she still couldn't get an outside line from her room. Maybe the lobby. Maybe there was a pay phone. Maybe the desk could help her get through. She could explain about her parents. Her Muslim parents. How she feared for their lives.

As long as she carried her pager, Tris could reach her. Jannat slid on some sweatpants and a Westin Charter t-shirt.

On the way to the elevator, she stuck her head in Tris's room, making eye contact with her boss who sat cross-legged on the bed, papers spread around her, talking on the hotel room phone, with the Sat phone and pager at the ready, buried in the details of Westin Charter airplanes that had been flying all over the U.S. at the time of the terrorist attacks.

Jannat grabbed a piece of note paper with the hotel's emblem on it from next to the phone and scribbled a note, "Can I help?" and placed it in front of Tris. The Chief Pilot smiled briefly and shook her head, while scribbling furiously on a pad in front of her, which bobbed up and down under the weight of her pen on the bouncy mattress.

Down in the lobby, people moved quickly, but looked like they were going in circles. There wasn't a sense of urgency, not like the one she felt, to do something, anything, to be of assistance. That's the thing about terrorism. There's nothing you can do.

Randy. Suzette. The wedding confab. Everything facing her at home. U.S. airspace was closed. She was stuck in Edinburgh. Here, she could avoid it all. The dread that had blanketed her for hours about her relationship with Suzette, her upcoming marriage—gone. Replaced by a far more sinister panic.

Would they be safe to fly home?

As soon as she exited the main part of the lobby, she heard someone say, "There's one of them!" Her head swung around, but no one was there. Wait, someone was pointing toward her. Jannat turned around to look behind her. No one.

One of who? What's happening?

In a thick southern accent that could have originated nowhere but the United States, she heard it again. "She's one of them. Terrorist!"

A woman wearing leggings and a tunic over her apple-shaped body sat in a divan crying. Her husband kneeled on the carpet next to her.

"She killed him! She killed Tom!"

The woman pointed in Jannat's direction. Jannat again searched for the person this distraught woman was referring to, but no one else was there.

"Beverly, stop, will you? This girl had nothing to do with it."

"But look at her. She's one of them." Then the woman, this Beverly, started to cry louder.

"How could you have killed all those people? How could you kill my brother?" Beverly let out a scream that stopped all movement around her.

Jannat clasped her ice-cold hands together and raised them to her heart. "I . . . I . . . I . . . I'm so sorry for your loss."

The man led his wife away and called to Jannat, "She doesn't know what she's saying. Her brother was in the South Tower when it collapsed. He's a banker. He *was* a banker.

All the way into the elevator Beverly kept muttering, "These people. Why? Who are these people? Why did we ever let them in?"

Jannat heard the echo of the grieving woman's words bouncing off the walls of the hotel lobby.

She saw Jannat—a dark skinned woman—and put her in a box with Al-Qaeda.

If this could happen to her thousands of miles from home, Maman and Baba weren't safe.

Thirty-Four

TRIS SPENT THE MORNING trying incessantly to reach Rex. He'd know how to check the passenger manifest for AA 11. It must be crazy at the FAA today, with the airspace closed. For Tris, he'd find a way.

She tried his office, and his mobile. The lines were still clogged. A day ago, she'd avoided him. Now, his absence felt like another loss, lumped in with the thousands in the towers when they fell, with the unsuspecting pilots and cabin crews whose duty turned to death. The crashes were jumbled together. She couldn't parse any of it.

Fueled by grief and tempered by lack of sleep, Tris worked to carry on the business of getting home. Westin had faxed some hypothetical routings to her, but she tossed them aside. It was impossible to plan a flight when you were a prisoner on the ground.

In the background, the TV screen locked on images of New York City burning.

Tris wished she were there, in New York, to help. She could support an injured person fleeing the scene, give a bottle of water to a firefighter or police officer. Put her arms around a devastated pilot at the airport. They could hug her back. How nice that would feel.

This was an injury that cut deep. While no one was looking, a team of terrorists learned the basics of piloting an airplane so they could attack Americans on U.S. soil. What would this do to flying? Would passengers ever want to get on a commercial airplane again?

She hadn't moved, at all, in several minutes, yet her heart raced. She needed to get up and do something. Enough ruminating. Work. Work would make it better.

Sat phone in hand, she called the home store. "Westin Charter, Phyllida speaking. Can you hold please?" Phyll didn't wait for her to answer, so Tris had to listen to the wonders of Westin Charter being extolled on their recorded hold message. Was there some company that specialized in making these ridiculous tapes, with corny parade music in the background and the voices of actors pretending to be satisfied customers?

"Westin Charter, Phyllida speaking." The unusually cool voice carried only a hint of stress.

"It's me. Any word on when we can get out of here?"

"Not yet, but we're hoping Thursday, uh, tomorrow. We put in an order for a flight plan with Universal's service, but who knows . . ."

Who indeed? "Phyll, what are you hearing? It's hard being so far away."

"There's nothing you could do here. Everyone is fine. All the planes are down. No one is hurt. Woody, Ip, and I have things well in hand."

"There are people I need to account for. So many people I know." Tris knew that Phyll could hear and feel her sadness.

"Quite. I'm sure. You concentrate on that, Tris. We'll mind things here until you get home. And you *will* get home."

Tris choked up. "Thank you Phyll," she said, softly, and pressed the End button.

Tris scrolled into the Sat phone's call history and found Danny's number. She selected it, pressed redial, and waited.

Beep. Beep. Beep. Frustrated again, she ended the call.

The Sat phone immediately buzzed. She didn't recognize the number. "Tris Miles."

"Tris, it's Diana." The background noise sounded like a busy bus or train terminal.

"Di. Where are you? My god, the attacks . . ."

"I know. I know. I'm at the airport."

"Why? Where are you going? We can't get home and—"

"It's not me, Tris. I need your help. Can you come? Can you meet me? I need your help. Look, I know you don't care—"

"Don't care? About you? C'mon Di—"

"No. Him. About him. I'm at the airport. It's Deter. He's losing it, Tris. He's getting the airplane ready to fly. Or trying to. The rampers don't know what to do. He's yelling at the people at the Executive Terminal. Screaming for the fueler. I can't talk him down."

"What do you want *me* to do?"

"He says he needs to talk to you, to explain what happened. With the records."

"That's crazy. He's running around the airport like a lunatic to make me talk to him? Come on, Di. You can't possibly believe that."

Diana's tone became more urgent. "He wants to move the airplane. He wants to *fly*. We can't leave our passengers here. He's asking for fuel and calling for flight plans. Our handler called *me*, the first officer, asking what the hell was going on. I don't know what to do."

"Di, this doesn't make sense."

"What makes sense right now, Tris?"

In a time where people ran screaming from smoke and ash that once formed the two tallest buildings in the world, bizarre behavior was inevitable. Nothing around Deter was fixable. With all control lost, Deter focused on the one thing he retained power over—his airplane.

She imagined Deter, pulling her employment file out of his desk, asking one of the assistants to copy it and send it in his *I don't want to be bothered with this bullshit* tone. Maybe he didn't give the contents a second thought.

Maybe he really *didn't* know what was in that file.

A voice whispered in her ear. "It's not your fault."

Bron? Danny?

"I'll be there as soon as I can." Tris rang off and started to dress. A pair of jeans got halfway up her legs when she realized that she'd have to put her uniform on. Pilots, flight attendants, crew members, had been killed.

She represented them now.

She'd be a target. She didn't care. She stroked the arm of her captain's jacket. Tris even pulled her hat from the place in her overnight bag where she'd shoved it a long time ago, knowing how rarely she'd ever have to wear it.

She straightened her misshapen, crushed captain's hat with care, and secured it on her head before she walked into the hallway where people could see her, proudly displaying the identity of those who'd sacrificed their lives, and those who were still suffering.

Like Deter.

Tris wasn't a hijacker. She wasn't a victim. She was the Captain of an airplane, and today, there were the lives of comrades to honor.

Not all the fallen were dead.

Thirty-Five

THE NOW-FAMILIAR Scottish countryside rolled by Tris on her way to the airport. Diana paced outside the entrance to Signature. She'd donned her captain's hat too.

As Tris walked toward her, Diana smiled and pulled out a pack of ESSE Super Slims. She tapped it until the filter end of a cigarette poked out far enough for Tris to grab it. Tris put it between her lips and leaned toward the flame that licked atop Diana's Zippo lighter.

"How is he?" Tris asked.

"Freaked out. It's scary."

"We're all freaked out."

"You think it's the attacks? That's what this is about?"

Tris took a deep drag. "Not sure what 'this' is yet. How did he get you to come here?"

"Said he wanted to check on the airplane. He was worried that someone had planted a bomb on board. Then he started behaving like we were going to launch—asking for fuel, asking about catering. I let him go grab some snacks from the plane, trying to let him wear himself out, and have time to come to his senses. Deter grabbed a full-size garbage bag and filled it with every snack we had aboard. He completely cleaned the plane out. He walked off, the bag hefted over his shoulder and then . . ." Diana stomped on her cigarette butt and pointed at the ground. "He bent over, right there. I thought he was sick, maybe having a stroke. He wasn't hyperventilating. After a minute, he got up and walked away." Diana immediately lit another cigarette and took a deep drag.

A grin was all Tris could muster. It was possible Diana was being played.

"Look, I know you're pissed at him. I'm pissed at him for what he did, and for not purging those lies from your files. Maybe he can take it back. Maybe he can fix it."

"He doesn't want to."

Diana nodded. "Probably not."

"What do you want me to do here?"

Diana reached out and took Tris's hand in hers and squeezed. In all the years she'd known this former military pilot, Diana had never done anything so intimate. Her soft, pleading touch presaged an unreasonable request.

"Forgive him."

"No."

Diana's shoulders sagged. Her voice, usually so self-assured, became imploring.

"Tris, all those people who died. I can't stop thinking about them. How many of them left their homes angry about something that, in the end, didn't mean shit? And here's what's haunting me, Tris—how many people left behind wished they'd done or said something differently to someone they loved on their last morning on earth. I mean, *come on*."

"I don't love Deter."

"Don't you love yourself? Tris, you need to stop being bitter. Say what you have to say to him but forgive him."

Tris took a moment, then nodded. Finally, she understood. She was the mystery person in her dream, the fourth person who took that precarious route, the one that couldn't be seen through to the end. That fourth path, it was for her. The path to loving *herself*, to doing the things that served her heart, not her logbook or the employment section of her resume.

Her actual self. Who she was when the uniform came off. Could she be someone who loved herself enough to forgive?

Diana seemed to understand. "Look, I'm not asking you to like him. I'm sure as hell not asking you to respect him. Who are you, Tris? Do you have it in your heart to help him? Please?"

As a co-pilot or First Officer, Tris could always punt the answers to someone else. Now, as the pilot-in-command of the heart in question, *she* was the final authority.

There had been a moment, long ago, when Tris saw compassion in Deter. She wanted to match it with some of her own. After all, this wasn't about flying, a career, or professional respect.

This was about being human.

"I'll do it on one condition."

"Which is?"

Tris took a deep breath. "He must apologize. For Legacy. For all of it. For Tetrix, for the way he treated me. It's time."

✈

"What do you mean, who am I? I'm the captain of November 4WC. On the ramp. The Falcon 50." A guard at the entrance to the Executive Terminal eyed her skeptically.

"Not likely," he finally said, looking as though he wasn't quite sure of himself.

"Excuse me?" Agitated, she waited while the confused man checked with the people at reception. When they saw it was Tris standing at the door, they waved her in frantically.

"Captain Miles, we're so sorry. It's been an odd day. Bruno, it's fine. Let her by."

"I have to check *this lady's* bag," the man called Bruno said. "It's required now."

Tris brought her flight bag along without thinking about it. Habit. Bruno opened it and pulled out everything inside. Tris was treated to the sight of old gum wrappers, empty pretzel bags and a crushed box of Tampax.

"Go in then," he finally said, leaving her charts, paperwork, headset, and personal items laying on the table where he'd tossed them.

Is this what it's going to be like now? Am I going to be treated like the criminals who hurt us?

Tris threw everything back into her bag. Diana stood behind her the whole time, watching and not saying a word.

"He's out there?" Tris thumbed toward the ramp.

Diana nodded and was subjected to the same frisk Tris had endured. Reception unlocked the doors leading to the airplanes. They slid open and Tris entered the ramp. First, she headed toward the Falcon to confirm that it was secure, ready to fly as soon as they could leave.

The three-engine beauty sat quietly; a sky animal forced to the ground and looking none too happy about it. Tris leaned her back against its nose, her arm automatically reaching to cradle the tip.

Airplanes left the ground and returned through a series of tacit agreements between the machine and its pilots. This understanding did not include being interrupted by terrorists. Sophisticated airplane systems recognized when things were not right and alerted the pilots. Which systems screamed out during the hijackings? How loud did the crash avoidance sensors holler, "TERRAIN!" as Flight 93 sped toward the ground? Did the passengers hear it wail, "PULL UP! PULL UP!" all the way to impact?

How many times did the warning, "TOO LOW FLAPS," repeat on AA 11. Did Danny hear it? Did he try to save them? Was he scared?

"Tris." Lost in thought, she hadn't noticed Deter walk up beside her. Far from being frazzled, he was composed, stood erect, and wore his stern resting expression. The only difference she noticed was his face: the pasty color of his deeply concave wrinkled cheeks made his beak-like nose even more pronounced.

Same glasses. Same piercing blue eyes. Same Deter.

Tris donned a neutral mask—protection against any hurtful, ignorant comments. She searched Deter for evidence of the crazed man Diana described. There wasn't any.

Deter looked ancient. And small.

Both her father and grandfather often spoke of moments that defined who a person has become. Her dad made eye contact with every homeless person who stuck their hand out for money, smiling as he dug in his pocket for change or a dollar bill. Grandpa never turned away any stray dog that followed him home, no matter how dirty or mangy.

"Who you are," Grandpa reminded her, "is not what you say, Princess. It's what you do. Your actions show the world who you are— they speak to the people who can't hear you."

"Tris." Deter, this pilot who'd served his country during war time, tugged at her mercy.

"Ed. Diana is worried about you. Are you all right?"

"I've damn sure been better," Deter said. "Everything that's going on, and now I've got to deal with *this.*"

"Meaning the attacks?"

"Meaning *you.*"

"Hey, I didn't ask to talk to you." Tris searched the ramp in vain for Diana.

The old scars from injuries this man had inflicted ripped open as he stood opposite her, the glossy Tetrix Gulfstream behind him. His voice brought back echoes of the insults, the bullying, and the ultimate disgrace of the trip that set the end of her career at Tetrix, Inc. in motion. They competed in her head with the sounds of terrified passengers, the airplane crying, "DON'T SINK. DON'T SINK." And the sound of an explosion as the airplane hit the towers.

Deter didn't seem inclined to speak, so she continued. "I understand from Diana that there were some trumped up records that Zorn created in the package you sent Legacy. They pulled my class date. You know that, right?"

"I do."

"How could you send them? How could you not review documents you're sending out that have someone's future in the balance? How?"

Deter's shoulders squared, and his eyes bore into hers. "I did review them. I saw the fake reports Zorn had written. I left them in. I wanted you to know that. I wanted to tell you face-to-face."

"You knew they were lies, and you left them in. Why would you send them to Legacy?"

"Because you don't deserve that job."

Sirens blared as she turned and ran, past Diana and into the terminal.

All the emergency vehicles in range were shut down and parked.

The noise was in her head.

Thirty-Six

"HOLY FUCK. You were on that flight. How . . . ?" Randy Eller was a white boy's white boy, but Danny had never seen him so pale as when he walked through the crash pad door at 3:30 a.m. on Wednesday morning.

Eller threw his arms around Danny and hugged him like he'd risen from the dead. Which, in a way, he had.

"I was in the jetway. I was almost on board, on that flight. Crew scheduling called me right before I was supposed to board. Said my schedule had changed. I was no longer deadheading to LAX."

Eller looked like he might faint. Danny felt his own legs soften. He leaned back against a kitchen cabinet for support.

"Yup. Flight 11. Another thirty seconds, I'd have been in the cabin. My mobile woulda been off." A macabre snort followed. "They diverted me to Grand Cayman. Wait two years to get a decent trip, and it so happened to be yesterday."

The attempt at levity fell flat. All Eller could do was stare.

"I will never, ever complain about a schedule change again."

That made Eller smile.

Danny tried to loop his jacket over the back of a wobbly metal chair. Again and again, it slid down. It took him all day and well into the night to get out of the terminal, with all the amped-up security and thousands of panicked travelers. His hands wouldn't stop shaking. Maybe because he almost got hit by several cars trying to make his way to the crash pad.

Maybe because his unborn child almost lost their father.

Maybe because he was terrified.

He'd avoided certain death by seconds. Not a possible, or even likely death. Certain. Absolute. No other ending. What if his mobile didn't ring? That happened in the airport all the time. What if the crew scheduler who called him decided to stop in the men's room before he picked up the phone? Who was that scheduler who called? Danny needed to know his name, the name of the man who saved his life.

If he'd missed that call, could he have overcome the hijackers? Flown the plane? Guided them to safety?

Hero dreams.

Survivor's guilt.

He lowered his head toward his legs, hands grasping the sides of his calves. He thought he might vomit.

The outline of his mobile phone pushed against his leg. The force with which he reached into his pocket to pull it out flipped it open. From the hallway of the building, he could hear people shouting, and another sound—a man was crying and repeating, "They're all dead."

Eller thumbed toward the hallway. "Tits, this has been going on all night. Every time a flight crew member gets to their pad, they lose it. Are we next, you think?" Eller's pallor increased. "We're in Boston. Scene of the crime."

Emily. The baby.

Clutching his mobile, he punched the number he'd been dialing for hours. He got the same fast busy signal. His fingers were stuck in a continuous loop. Redial, end, redial. He wouldn't stop until she answered.

When she did, he'd lay it all out. He'd tell her that she was the only one for him, the only person he really, truly ever loved. That he'd do anything to prove to her that he was right for her. They'd been through so much but had the rest of their lives ahead of them. "I almost died," he'd say. "And all I could think about was you. How I loved you."

He had to reach the woman he truly loved. He had to find Tris.

Thirty-Seven

RAYS OF SUNLIGHT broke through the patchy Edinburgh clouds, playing hide and seek against the brocade wallpaper in Jannat's hotel room. There was no sound, no commotion in the hallway, no TVs blaring from the rooms that bordered her own.

Osama, son of Mohammed bin Awad bin Laden. Billionaire. Spoiled brat with too much time on his hands.

Her parents always talked about how Americans drew hard distinctions between different religious and ethnic groups, eschewing the fact that their core beliefs were the same. In medical school, it was assumed from her looks that her mother was smarter than everyone else. "Those Indians," her mother heard them say. "They're so damn smart."

Maman would say nothing. Correcting them, saying she was Iranian wouldn't get the reaction she'd hoped for. Americans had heard of the Ayatollah. "The Ayatollah Khomeini," people would say, "he's a bad guy." Why he was bad, what he'd done to Maman's family, to Baba's family, the grandparents she'd never known—no one cared.

"Bad guy." His reign of terror distilled into two words.

Jannat experimented with Muslim traditions when she was younger. She wore a hijab for about a year in high school. Neither of her parents encouraged her, although her mother had maintained the tradition when she first came to the U.S. After years of integrating with other Iranian immigrant families, Laleh slowly adopted modern American ways. She implored her only child to do the same, to foster her own beliefs. "*Noore cheshm-am,* be who you are," she always said, using her favorite endearment. "You are American. You were born here. Yes, you are Muslim, as you are our child. Be proud of your culture but be who *you wish*."

Jannat found the hijab hot and uncomfortable, and she derived little meaning from wearing it. Which was lucky, as it would have ended her career in aviation. Being a dark-skinned female already created roadblocks: there was no need to add a religious headdress that Jannat wasn't even sure held any meaning for her. Yet, she carried a traditional headscarf in her flight bag, to honor her parents and their past. She fingered it absent-mindedly.

Back in high school, she'd replaced her hijab with the hair clip Maman had given her, gold with a ceramic poppy attached to the clasp, passed down from her grandmother. Jannat wore it every day, even under her pilot hat on those rare occasions she'd had to don it. Tradition was never far away for Jannat.

She touched her face. She'd been told all her life she was beyond beautiful. Jannat had grown accustomed to men and women staring at her when she walked through the mall with Maman, at dinner with Randy, even when she had on sweatpants at the local Starbucks.

Her looks were now a magnet for the hate, and loss, and pain that so many people were feeling, even so very far away.

Jannat sighed. Someone had to bear the standard of her culture, show the world that Muslims only wanted peace. Slowly, she slid the nondescript piece of fabric over her head and tucked her hair behind and inside of it, so it framed her face. The beloved poppy clip, her only symbol of Maman's own mother, who she'd never met, was gently placed atop her suitcase.

It was late afternoon in Scotland, and Jannat was still in the t-shirt she'd slept in. She threw on sweatpants and slid into her running shoes. On her way to the elevator, she heard a door open behind her.

Within seconds, the peace of the hallway was broken by a man mumbling obscenities. Jannat turned to see who he was talking to. The man glared in her direction. Jannat looked around. There was no one else but her in the hall.

Ignoring the stares she attracted in the hotel lobby, Jannat darted into an empty phone booth.

She punched in the endless codes of her international calling card, then 0-1-1 and her parents' number into the phone for the thousandth time.

Maman picked up on the first ring.

"Yes? Jannat?"

"Maman. Maman. Is everything all right?"

Her mother whispered what sounded like a prayer in Farsi. "Jannat joon, finally. We have been out of our minds here. How are you? Are you safe?" Maman's first thought was about her.

"I'm still in Edinburgh, Maman. They're telling us we'll be on the ground at least another day. I'm . . . I'm worried about you and Baba."

"Us? Ah, *azizam*, always thinking of us. I am fine. We are fine. It is awful. I must see your face. You are so far away, with all this craziness. Will you be safe? In the skies?"

How could she tell her mother that it wasn't the sky she was worried about? She was a target on the ground. As a pilot and a person. Here and at home. As were her parents. How could she warn them without scaring them?

"Maman, look. I know it's still early there. But you and Baba. Can you stay home today? Can you stay inside the house?"

"Jannat, that's ridiculous. I have data to analyze. Your father has patients. No no. We will go to the hospital, as we do every day."

"I'm begging you. Stay home. I think people… I am concerned …" She simply did not know how to tell her parents that they might not be safe in their own community, their own workplace.

"What is troubling you, Jannat?" In the background, she could hear Baba say, "What's wrong? Is she okay?"

"Quiet Ali. Jannat, what is wrong?"

"Yesterday, here in Edinburgh, a woman—a stranger, someone I never saw before—accused me of being part of the group that claimed responsibility for the attacks. She called me …" She could not repeat the horrible things the woman said. "She was hysterical. Her brother died in the towers. Maman, I fear that people will turn their hate on us. For our background. Because of our culture. Be careful. Stay at home. Please. I'm begging you."

Maman was silent for a long time. Then she spoke to her husband in Farsi. Her father softly said, "Oh my." They exchanged another few sentences in their native tongue, which their daughter never learned. She could make out some of it. It sounded like they were talking about a gathering of many people.

"Jannat, of course we know this. It is a sad reality, the anger of frightened people who have nowhere to put their hate. Baba and I will be careful. We promise, Jannat."

Jannat closed her eyes. *"Moazeb bash!"* She said, which she thought was Farsi for, "Watch out!"

"Yes. Yes. Jannat, of course."

Jannat remembered the last words she'd spoken to Maman before leaving. She choked out the next words. "I love you, Maman. I will tell Randy as soon as I get home. Because it's the right thing to do. Because I am your daughter."

"*Manam dôset dâram*, Jannat. My heart."

Jannat sat quietly in the privacy of the booth, thinking.

Noore cheshm-am.

She fingered the calling card, her hand shaking as she kept missing the correct keys. The number finally entered, Jannat waited. The phone rang and rang.

"Hello? Who is this?"

"I am tired of hiding," Jannat blurted out.

"Jannat. You're safe." Suzette exhaled slowly in relief.

"I am fine. I'm fine. I'll do it Suz. What Maman said, it's true. I'll tell Randy before the wedding. He deserves to know."

"He might leave you. Have you thought of that?"

Her voice caught. "Yes. He'd be right to do it. How could I have kept this from him? I love him, you know. And I love you."

The line was quiet but for the breath of two best friends.

"Jannat joon, I love you, too. So does Randy. If the life you wish to continue is right, he will understand. If you are supposed to marry this man, he will understand."

Thirty-Eight

"WHERE HAVE YOU BEEN? Are you all right?" Rex demanded in a tone that signaled only relief. His pen clicked nonstop in the background.

"Hey Rex. I'm stuck in Edinburgh. I've been trying to get through to you, but the phone lines are crammed. You can't imagine what's going on here. What's happening there?"

"It's a cluster. We closed the airspace with planes in flight. They ended up all over the place, but we had to get them down in case of the worst, in case more planes were at risk. We'd lost four jets already." Rex's voice trailed off. "It's gonna get worse. Flying as we know it, that's over."

"What are you talking about? I don't understand."

"You wouldn't believe the conversations that we're having around here. Locking cockpit doors for entire flights—with no ability to get out and use the lav. Tris, they're throwing around the idea of *arming* pilots. Giving them *guns*. Can you imagine?"

Rex stopped to take a breath. "We're trying to find out when we can get everything moving. So many federal agencies involved. The decision to re-open the skies, along with the national security folks in DC, it's our decision." In the background was the din of office activities on steroids, phone ringing, people shouting over other's voices to be heard.

"Sounds like a madhouse already. What is it, 6 a.m. there?"

"Are you all right?" He asked again.

"Rex, I—I'm not sure. I had a friend that may have been on AA 11. I haven't been able to confirm it." Schedules changed all the time. Mike hadn't worked at Legacy for years. Who was his source anyway? They had to be wrong. It was her only hope.

"Oh my God. Tris, I'm so sorry. Someone you flew with?"

"Do you have the manifest? Do you know for sure who was aboard?"

He hesitated. "The FAA knows, yes. I suppose I could locate it. But . . ."

"But?"

"It would cost me. It can't be the FAA asking, you understand that, right? It would have to be a favor I called in. Given how crazy things are, it would be a big one."

Tris didn't have the strength—of character, or anything else— to pretend this didn't matter.

"It's important, Rex. Daniel Terry. That's his name. He was deadheading on AA 11. You know him, I'm sure. He's from Exeter. He's my best friend, Rex. He's the . . ."

She stopped, swallowed. She wasn't prepared to begin the larger conversation that she needed to have with Rex, the one that would send them their separate ways. It would have to be in person. Right now, she needed him.

Rex hesitated. "Nothing official, Tris. Okay?"

"Of course. I swear. I won't tell a soul. I have to know. Rex, I'm begging you."

"I'll do what I can. And you didn't ask, but it should be tomorrow. Thursday. We should be moving by then. Hey, look, I'm so glad you're okay. But I gotta go. Be safe, Tris. Get home safe. We've got some things to talk about."

"Yes. Thanks, Rex." He'd already clicked off.

Tris looked over at the message light on her room phone. Nothing. No voice mail on the Sat phone. Tris scrolled through voice mail messages on her mobile. There was one she hadn't listened to. It must have gotten missed in all the craziness. She held the phone to her ear to listen. It was a message from Woody; from the call she didn't take in the hangar.

Tris, the way I acted about your job offer. That was outta line. Crap on a cracker, Tris, I need you here. If I've learned anything since they started holding me prisoner in this hospital room, it's that. Let's talk as soon as you get home, okay?

I have a plan. Well, an offer. For you to stay. I was gonna wait until . . . but I'm gonna do it now. Get the plane home and get the people . . . you all home. Ah, you know what I mean."

Woody. One of her constants. She couldn't wait to tell him that she'd be staying after all, at least for a while.

Then the desk phone rang.

"Tris?" Rex. That was fast.

"Hey. What do you know?"

Rex spoke as if he were ordering from a Chinese takeout menu. Crisp, decisive, without any emotion. "Daniel Terry was on the passenger manifest to LAX on American Airlines Flight 11 leaving Logan yesterday morning. He checked in. He had a First-Class boarding pass, which was collected at the jetway. Tris . . . Oh Tris—" His voice broke.

She gasped, then choked back a sob. "Okay. Okay."

She dropped the phone on the floor.

Danny.

She grasped her pillow so tightly she could feel the threads of the cotton case separate under her fingernails.

I'm as alone as anyone could ever be. I'm all alone.

Thirty-Nine

"TRIS? HEY, IT'S CHUCK. You ready? You said four o'clock, right?"

He rapped on her door, rat-a-tat, rat-a-tat, like he was keeping time in a drum line. He had no idea.

Dead. Confirmed. They were right. Mike. Rex. Danny's unanswered mobile.

How would she tell people? How would she form the words?

A friend of mine was on AA 11. He died. Well, of course he died. Everyone died . . .

My best friend was on AA 11. Company had him deadheading to LAX.

Danny, you know, my friend from my old commuter flying days. I've talked about him, right? Well, he was on AA 11 . . . What? No, I'm good to go. I can fly, no problem.

What had she done, what horrible crime had she perpetrated to lose Danny?

Mike had called her mobile four times. The message light on her room phone flashed. It could be the office. Mike. Rex. Her crew. Housekeeping.

She didn't care.

"Tris! I hear you in there. What's wrong? What's happening?"

Tris dug her elbow in the mattress to support her body, tried to rise and fell back onto the pillow. "In a second. I'm coming." It sounded like a whisper to her, but Chuck heard it.

"Okay," he said, and stopped banging on the door.

It wasn't until she saw the surprise on Chuck's face that she realized she had on a bathrobe.

"What the fu—?" Chuck's voice sounded impatient, but there was fear in his eyes. "Tris?" She stumbled, and he reached out and grabbed her arm to steady her.

"AA 11," she whispered. "I knew someone on that flight . . ."

Chuck's shoulders dropped and he looked away. "Uh, okay. Okay. I'll . . . we'll get started. Meet us downstairs," he said. He wiped his eyes as he walked toward the elevator.

It was the pilot's way.

By herself, in the dark empty hotel room, on a foreign continent, Tris leaned against the door and cried.

The crew had commandeered a section of the august hotel lobby for their meeting, safely tucked away amid carved wood paneling and upholstered chairs. One small round table was all they had for paperwork, but each pilot would carry the ubiquitous clipboard they'd packed away in their flight bags since they were student pilots, back when they balanced charts on their knees, flashlights in their mouths, and held the yoke between sweaty palms in an airplane that barely flew at eighty knots.

Tris found Chuck sitting in his usual spot, on a backless ottoman. She smiled in response to his questioning gaze and sat in the high-backed Queen Anne chair he'd left for his boss.

Seconds later, the elevator door opened. Every single pair of eyes in the lobby were on Jannat as she walked over. Her hair was hidden behind a dark blue hijab, which fell below her shoulders. None of the other people in the lobby bothered to whisper. "Osama-ette." "Terrorist." "Fucking criminal." One man waved his fist.

The hotel staff did their best to intercede. Someone at the Concierge desk greeted Jannat. "Good morning, Madam," he said, and nodded at her with understanding and compassion.

"She's gonna blow you guys up!" someone shouted as she turned toward the corner where her crew mates waited. Hopefully, their presence, and the lack of fear they displayed as she approached, would dampen the slurs.

This Jannat walked with purpose, head held high, the way she'd often appear when addressing passengers on a flight she commanded. She sat on the edge of an armchair, posture erect, slightly bent toward her crew mates.

"Shall we get started?" she asked, with a look that said she was ready to get on with the business at hand.

"Hope you're bomb-proof," someone called from across the lobby. Both Tris and Chuck looked at Jannat. Her expression didn't change at all—not a twitch.

Tris rose from her chair, but Chuck was already up and moving toward the heckler.

"What was that, sir?" he asked in a solicitous tone. Tris came up behind him. Normally, he'd back away and let her handle whatever situation arose. This time, he held out his arm, as though he'd stopped short at a traffic light. Behind the two of them stood Jannat.

Chuck took another step toward the tall, slender man with slicked-back hair and a mustache that looked like a smear of dirt on his upper lip.

"I'm not sure I heard you, sir. Can you please repeat that?"

The stranger's face reddened, but he gestured to Jannat. "That woman. She's one of them, right? Those murderers?" His accent was hard to place.

"That *woman's* name is *Captain* Jannat Madden. She's a professional pilot, my friend, and she didn't hurt anyone. So shut the fuck *up*!"

"Watch your back," the man said as he turned away.

"*Sir.*"

The startled man faced Chuck, this time with far less bravado than he'd had before.

Chuck scowled, gave the man a dismissive wave. "You're not worth the energy it would take to punch you," he said, and rejoined the two women, both of whom were wide-eyed.

He winked at Tris and nodded at Jannat.

On the road, pilots left their real selves at home, in some box, for when it was safe to come out. Tris had listened to Chuck's quips and one-liners, often dismissed him as never having an original thought. A high-school graduate, Chuck was a man's man, a good old boy. He respected her title and was loyal to it.

This man was not just the cliché-spouting country cousin she'd judged him to be. This man had convictions, and the courage to speak to them aloud.

Chuck was a true leader.

PART III:
THE BEGINNING

September 13, 2001–September 11, 2002

Forty

LIGHT SHONE ON *the four men sitting around the table, but it was too bright. She couldn't see their faces.*

They were playing cards. Always playing cards. Was it the uncertainty, the randomness of the deal that always had them in what looked like a tense game of poker?

She finally recognized them.

Deter had the most chips. Bron was drinking his favorite green tea from Starbucks, in the biggest cup they had—she always forgot the names. Venti? Blondie? Biggie? For Mike, it looked like whiskey in his glass, that amber color, three ice cubes. Or Diet Coke?

One man wore a hoodie, and she couldn't tell who he was from the back. The light was strongest on him, but not because he was in it.

It came from him. He was the light.

Bron, Mike, and Deter threw down their cards.

"You win. You're the best of us."

She couldn't tell who spoke the words, or who they were directed to.

The light emanating from the man in the hoodie grew stronger. It brought her peace, a comfort she hadn't felt since the days of running out to meet her father when he came home from work. It was that kind of happiness, the pure joy of a child.

The man turned and smiled at her. The glow around his face was so bright, it obscured his features, but she stared into the light, desperate to know who it was.

"Papa?"

"It's me Tris. It's me."

Danny?

"You say something, Tris?" Chuck asked.

"Nope. Just thinking."

After a tense and mostly silent ride to the airport, the crew of the Westin Charter Falcon 50 walked side-by-side toward the small brick building that housed Signature Flight Support's Business Aviation Centre at Edinburgh.

Tris had warned the other pilots to expect a thorough search. Chuck's bag check resulted in him losing a pair of toe-nail clippers and a razor blade. Tris had already winnowed out a metal nail file and tweezer—more casualties of the attack. Jannat came through last, by design, so Tris and Chuck could make sure she was treated respectfully.

Jannat hadn't said much at breakfast and responded to inquiries in monosyllables.

For a split second, Tris considered benching Jannat on the trip home, and flying both legs with Chuck. Immediately, she dismissed the idea.

Then they've won. We cannot *let them win.*

After the extended security check, Tris strode toward the exit to the ramp.

"Excuse me. Ma'am?"

A tall dark-haired man in a uniform with a nightstick hanging from his belt called after her. "Have to search you. Regulations."

"Again?"

"Aye. Once when you enter the building, and again before you approach the airplanes. For weapons, ma'am."

Would this be the lives of pilots now? Would their bags be emptied before every trip, every leg at a new airport?

"Roderick, not *her*. She's our customer."

"I've got to check every single passenger," Roderick replied, hands on his hips.

Exasperated, the agent at the reception desk called to him. "She's not a passenger, Rod. She's the Captain of one of these airplanes."

This was obvious, as Tris wore her jacket, hat, pilot shirt, pants, and shoes.

"It's all right . . . Evelyn," Tris said, quickly reading the woman's name tag. Roderick's head spun between Tris and Evelyn.

"But she's a lass!" He shook his head but gestured for her to pass.

Tris shot a look at Chuck and Jannat behind her.

"You two head out to the Falcon. I'll grab the paperwork."

Evelyn led the way. "We got a fax with your updated flight planning." She pushed a thick stack of paper at Tris.

Tris considered the room. Same couch. Same magazines, perfectly arranged in a semi-circle on the same wood coffee table. Two flight planning rooms off in the back.

It was the same, exactly the same.

Nothing was ever going to be the same.

Roderick did a thorough search of Chuck's and Jannat's bags. He removed a small scissor from Chuck's, missed by the first sentry, held it with his fingertips, arm fully extended, and carried it to a trash bin. He placed it gently inside, as if it might explode. Jannat didn't get anything confiscated, but Roderick's withering gaze never left her.

Jannat's captain's hat was perched neatly above her hijab.

Moments later, the three pilots strode to the airplane.

The sky was now clear. Pouring rain fell that morning, and an hour before they left for the airport abruptly stopped.

Did you do that, Danny? Was it Bron?

They were pilots, the best she'd ever known. They were still watching out for her.

Chuck gathered the catering and took Jannat's fuel order out to the ramp to supervise the fueler. He seemed different to her somehow, and Tris realized her own perception had changed. She'd found the one glimmer of light in the blackness of the terrorist attacks.

"Madam, hello." A heavy Scottish accent sounded behind her.

"Yes?" Tris didn't turn around.

"Madam, I believe your passengers are here."

Tris turned and greeted the three people they'd brought to Edinburgh what seemed like a million years ago, but was, in fact, just a few days before.

"We'll get the airplane ready to go quickly. Let me show you aboard."

Chuck was waiting at the top of the air stairs and greeted each of the men by name. He'd always had the best rapport and demeanor with the passengers, occasionally rivaling Tris's own. Jannat was already up in the left seat. Tris stepped in to get a better look. Jannat was triple checking all the pre-flight items.

A strong aviator. A natural leader. A Chief Pilot?

Tris closed and locked the aircraft door. After distributing bottles of water to their paying customers, she took the right seat. She and Jannat would fly to Reykjavik to refuel, and Jannat and Chuck would carry the Westin Charter colors on the final leg home.

Loud voices caused her to turn around.

"Are you kidding?" One of the passengers squirmed in his seat, his arms rising and falling in protest. The lead passenger, a company Executive VP, tried to calm him down. "I'll talk to the Chief Pilot," he said to the red-faced traveler.

He shuffled toward Tris, shoulders hunched. Tris got up from the right seat to talk to him.

"Jannat, continue the checklists with Chuck." Then to the passenger, "May I help you sir?"

"I'm so sorry Captain Miles. That, uh, other pilot. I mean, that woman in the pilot suit. Is she . . . well, is she the same person who flew us here?"

"She is."

He licked his lips several times, either embarrassed or completely surprised by what he was about to say next. "Well, I don't remember . . . given what's happened, and who's responsible . . . well, does she have to wear *that scarf thing?*"

"Let me out!" The uptight passenger rose from his seat, his face a deep shade of crimson.

Tris held up a hand to calm them both. "The events of the last few days have shaken all of us. The very best thing we can all do, is to be who we've always been, who we say we are. People who value those who are different from us. Captain Madden is one of the good guys."

Tris stood for Jannat. For Danny. For the dead. They couldn't have died for nothing. Their lives—*his life*—had meaning, and defending her crew honored them all.

The lead passenger, now beyond embarrassed, nodded. Red face sat back down but continued to plead his case. Perhaps he wanted Jannat to sit in the back, maybe wear a blindfold, and stay strapped in her passenger seat so she couldn't kill anyone. He couldn't see beyond his anger, his complete lack of understanding.

Why did those terrorists attack us? Where did *their* hate come from? The freedoms people sought by coming to the U.S., the freedoms every single citizen took for granted each day—that's what caused the disaster. Hate stoked by jealousy for what we have, and they don't.

"Captain Madden," Tris called toward the cockpit, looking directly into the angry man's eyes. "Please proceed with engine start." The blotchy red spots had not faded from the distraught passenger's face.

Tris mixed him a drink, pulling out the good scotch that Woody liked to say was for passenger emergencies. She poured a healthy shot into a crystal glass.

"Ice?"

"Yes." He croaked, then muttered, "We're all gonna die." He downed the whiskey in one gulp.

It was time to go. They were finally flying home.

Forty-One

DANNY SAT BY HIMSELF at the dining room table. Emily stood in the kitchen. Her belly had started to protrude.

The house reminded him of a ghost town he'd once visited. Like the staged rooms at the tourist attraction, it contained furniture, kitchen utensils, pillows on the couch. He and Emily resembled a normal couple, like the wax replicas of people posed in everyday positions.

He half expected a tumbleweed to roll down the bedroom hallway. Emily had stopped putting photos back on the walls. Whatever made a house a home had long since disappeared.

They needed to talk, but neither spoke. Emily moved things around, picked up a clean vase and rinsed it out in the sink. Danny sipped on the Pepsi he'd picked up in the Exeter terminal.

He was lucky to make it home. The trip, normally a ninety-minute leg from Boston to Exeter, turned into a twelve-hour ordeal. The entire Boston terminal was on high alert. He'd never had his bag searched so thoroughly, or so many times, while in full uniform. They took his toothpaste, deodorant spray, and razor. He wanted to shake the security guards and remind them that pilots—that he—was a victim too, that *he* had been seconds away from certain death. He kept quiet, afraid if he protested, he'd be arrested.

Danny wore his pilot hat while walking through the deserted passenger terminal. Something about what had happened—and what had *almost* happened to him—made him want to be in full uniform. The hat was mostly an annoyance, something he had to carry when he was working to put on before the passengers boarded and which was always flung back into his flight bag once the cockpit door closed. Today it meant something.

I'm here. I'm still alive. I'm not afraid of you.

Danny quietly repeated the names he'd memorized. The names of the pilots who had flown AA11, and who died before they left the east coast.

Captain John Ogonowski and First Officer Thomas McGuinness.

John Ogonowski. Thomas McGuinness.

JohnOgonowskiThomasMcGuinness.

JohnOgonowskiThomasMcGuinnessJohnOgonowskyThomasMc Guinness.

Danny never got to meet them. Never had the chance to make the obligatory courtesy stop by the cockpit, let the captain know he was aboard. John and Thomas would have welcomed him, maybe shared a joke.

Time would pass, and while the attacks themselves would be remembered, the names of the pilots would surely be forgotten.

Not by me. No way.

"John Ogonowski. Thomas McGuinness," he whispered.

As soon as he could get through the crazy phone lines at Legacy's dispatch, he'd locate the crew scheduler that called him seconds before he boarded that flight. The man who saved his life.

He couldn't believe his luck. Against all odds, he was home. He was alive.

Emily walked into the laundry room to check the clothes in the dryer. Satisfied, she came back and sat across from him at the table. She still didn't look at him. Emily was many things, but she was no fool. She knew when she was bested.

"Em. I have something to tell you."

"Danny. You want to tell me it's not working, right? Between us?"

He twisted the top back on the liter bottle of Pepsi. "It's not."

"No. I wish it was … Oh, Danny, I wish." At last. The Emily he'd loved. The one he married. The one who understood.

His heart pounded. "Are you going to keep it, Emily? Our child? Will you still have it? The whole time I was stuck in Boston, I thought about our baby, what would have happened if I'd been on that plane. He—or she—wasn't even born and would lose their father."

Emily drew a circle through the dust on the wooden table with her finger. Round and round, making sure that she got it right. Her thumb rubbed out any mark that didn't fit. That was his wife. Nothing outside the lines.

"Can we make it as divorced parents?"

"Danny." She said his name matter-of-factly, and looked past him, out the bay window in the living room, at the overgrown hedges that separated their property from the identical one next door. She shook her head.

"If we're not together, not a family … I don't know."

"So, you'd … ?" He couldn't bring himself to say it. The four Twinkies he'd stuffed down moments before he got home started to rise in his throat. "Don't you want our child?"

Emily looked at her hands. "Of course."

"I want the baby, too. I'll do anything." He reached over and touched her stomach. "I already love it, Em. You can't tell me you don't."

Crying, Emily reached out and took his hand. "Danny, I don't know if I can do this. If *we* can. Of course I love him."

Danny laughed. "You're sure it's a him?"

Emily sighed. "It's still early. We don't have to go through with it."

"Baby. Please." He swallowed back bile.

"Especially after these last few days, what could have—" she choked on the words, "what could have happened to you. I'm afraid. What if . . . ?"

Her hesitation wasn't at all what he'd thought. "Em, you think I'm gonna die? In an airplane? Leave you and the baby alone?"

Tears slipped silently down her cheeks. "It could happen," she whispered. "It *did* happen."

Emily understood that eight pilots perished on 9/11, eight pilots who showed up on a normal Tuesday to fly their trips. She was right. If it could happen to them, it could happen to him.

JohnOgonowskiThomasMcGuinnessJohnOgonowskyThomas McGuinness.

"I will be here for our child. If I think for one minute that my career . . . my job . . . would harm him—or her—in any way, I'll quit. I swear it, Em."

She smiled. "I know. *You're* the kind, big-hearted one. You're the one who feels things others don't. I fell in love with you because of it. But I'm not the one you want, am I?"

Danny looked at his feet.

"I love you, Danny. But I will not be the girl who makes you stay." Emily's eyes held the anguish of unmatched love.

"I do love you, Emily. I truly do. I always will."

Maybe it was the attack, the realization that their lives would never be the same, that they'd experienced real tragedy, and lived through it.

The couple stood and hugged each other, their doomed union falling away in favor of a bond they'd never had while they were together. They'd doubted each other from time to time, but in this moment, their embrace had not a shred of uncertainty, distrust, or disbelief. In a way, they'd never loved each other more.

"We'll take it day by day, Em. I'll be there for you. For our child. You know I will. It'll be loved. *We'll* love it."

Emily hugged him tighter than she had in a long time.

"I'll always love you," he whispered in her ear.

"I know."

He'd be a father. They would be parents.

Danny stepped back from Emily and slowly put on his jacket. His overnight bag was still packed. He'd get a hotel room, and tomorrow, first thing, he'd find her. He wouldn't wait.

He and Bron used to talk about "the one." It set them apart from a lot of their colleagues, whose main goal in life seemed to be flying fast and screwing as many girls as they could. Maybe that's why the two became best friends.

Bron knew that Tris was the one, even back then. As Danny did today.

There was only one woman for him.

He'd apologize to Tris for his stupidity, for thinking he could ever have stayed with Emily, for sneaking away like a criminal the morning after, not leaving a note, being too afraid to break the spell.

For telling her that lie. For saying that he didn't love her.

He'd find her, tell her that even if she didn't know it, they were a team. A couple. Two people who could go the distance. To make her see, once and for all. Every minute they spent apart was wasted, thrown away, when who knew how many moments they'd each have left.

Those three thousand people.

Gone.

Not over years, aging, naturally moving toward their eventual end, but in seconds. The ones in those towers, they knew they were going to die. It wasn't quick, it wasn't sudden. They desperately tried to escape. They couldn't get out. The first responders, the ones that rushed in to save them, with the confidence that they'd be successful, and walk out heroes. They died too.

John Ogonowski. Thomas McGuinness.

JohnOgonowskiThomasMcGuinnessJohnOgonowskyThomasMc Guinness.

Life had begun again for him.

If it took a lifetime of trying, he'd be with Tris.

Danny pecked his wife on the cheek. "Thank you, Emily. I've gotta go."

Danny started the Jeep, whirled it out of the driveway, and pointed it toward the one place where he always would belong—the airport.

Forty-Two

"FALCON FOUR Whiskey Charlie, Exeter tower. Wind one-four-zero at three knots. Runway One-Four Left, cleared to land. Welcome home."

The Westin Charter Falcon 50 slid down the final approach course onto the runway at Exeter International Airport at 7:00 p.m. on September 13th. Familiar buildings that marked the last five miles to touchdown passed underneath them. Chuck and Jannat had the approach well in hand, giving Tris the chance to focus on the darkening blue sky, highlighted by twisting, rope-like contrails from another jet passing high above.

Chuck landed the Falcon with practiced ease and turned it toward the Westin Charter ramp. A small group of people stood outside to welcome them, but not nearly the amount Tris expected. She could make out Phyll and Ip, a couple of the other Westin pilots. A woman with long dark hair carrying an oversized tote stood slightly apart from the group. Lurking in the distance was Mike.

"Shutdown checklist please," Chuck commanded. The serial

clicks of their passengers' seatbelts followed. Chuck pressed buttons, lowered levers, and threw switches expertly, then blew out a huge breath.

"It's done," Jannat said softly. "We're home." She looked directly at Tris when she spoke. Nothing further was said. The three pilots all wore the same expression—one of relief and gratitude for performance above and beyond.

The changes in their world had already begun. Communications on the radio with Air Traffic Control were all different today. Crisp and professional, no jokes or the usual slang. Tris recognized compassion and understanding in every anonymous voice. Every call sign was repeated with an emphasis that announced, "This is *my* airplane," and every clearance was relayed with a hint of urgency.

The passengers quickly exited and rushed into the waiting area as soon as rampers retrieved their bags. Chuck and Jannat waited for Tris to walk with them and greet their welcoming committee together.

"You coming Tris?" Chuck's brow furrowed.

Tris did a slow reconnaissance of the inside of the airplane. From nose to tail, she took in every inch of the cabin and the cockpit. More change would come, that was certain. How? When? That was up for grabs. Instinct told her that her crew, and this airport, would never be the same again.

"Hey baby." Mike walked up the air stairs and reached his hand out to guide her down the path she'd traversed hundreds of times. She smiled at him but didn't take the offering.

"Mike. It's nice to be home. What are you doing here?"

His eyes clouded with concern. "I couldn't let you land after these last few days with no one here to meet you." He pulled her close to him and whispered, "I'm so sorry. So sorry for your loss."

"You mean Danny?" Her mobile phone had been buzzing non-stop since they landed. She had at least twelve voice mails, mostly from Diana and Rex. But there were several with a Denver exchange.

"Mike, give me a second?" she said, not sure how he thought he'd be able to console her. Her grief was tucked securely in its own compartment, where it had to stay in order for her to get back home. She'd take it out again when she was alone and free to feel it fully. She'd go to the cemetery and tell Bron herself. Though of course he already knew. Danny was with him. They all were.

Her phone buzzed in her hand. The Denver number. She gently pushed Mike away.

"Tris Miles."

A sigh of relief came from the other end of the line. "Tris. I've been trying to reach you. This is Jennifer Prince."

Tris didn't respond.

"I am sorry. There was a, well, a misunderstanding on our end. We didn't quite have all the context for your records. Luckily, we had some internal intelligence. Of course, all new hire classes are canceled until further notice, and under current circumstances, we can't say when we'll be hiring again. Right now, we're discussing furloughs, unfortunately. I wanted you to hear it from me. You're in the hiring pool. We'll get you in here as fast as we can."

Tris held the phone away from her ear and stared at it.

"How?" She couldn't form a sentence.

"An internal connection. Let me check the name."

"Mike Marshall?" Tris looked over at him and smiled.

Papers fluttered on the other end of the line. "That's not the name I have. Do you know a Daniel Terry?"

Tris headed toward the Westin offices like someone trapped in darkness, running her hands against the hangar walls to guide and steady herself. The small crowd had dispersed. Where had everyone gone?

Mike appeared in front of her again and put both hands on her shoulders. Pain in his face.

"You'll want to talk to Phyll."

"What's up?"

"Go talk to her."

Phyllida and Ip were standing close together in the dispatch room inside the hangar. They were finishing up a conversation.

"Phyll?"

The British woman wore a black headband around her fire-engine-red hair, teased into a beehive. She looked like she hadn't slept. Her heavy eyeliner, an homage to her 60s style, was askew. Had she only put mascara on one set of lashes?

"How awful this all must have been for you, Phyll. Woody and I, we'll make it up to you."

Phyll looked bereft.

"Come sit. Come sit with me, Tris."

The older woman took the Chief Pilot's hand in both of hers. "He's gone. Woody's left us. It was the stress, Tris. The stress of the attack. It was too much for his heart."

"He retired? In the middle of all this? That's nuts. It's so Woody—"

Phyll held up her hand to stop Tris's monologue.

"Stop. No. We've lost him, Tris. Woody's passed."

Tris screamed. Then she screamed again. People came running, and the security guard Westin put in place in the last twenty-four hours dashed into the room with his taser drawn.

"It's fine. It's fine. I've got it." Phyll said, as she put her arms around the Chief Pilot of Westin Charter.

Mike walked toward the two women, but Ip grabbed his arm and shook his head. The two men waited for Tris to calm down. She and Phyll exchanged some words neither could hear.

Eventually, Phyll gave Tris a kiss on the cheek and moved away. Mike sat down next to her and put his arm around her shoulder.

"Did you hear, Mike? Woody's gone. Danny's gone. And all those people, they're all gone. They're all gone," she kept repeating. Every time she said it, he squeezed her tighter, until she could barely catch her breath to speak.

"Shh, shh. I'm so sorry. I'm here. You'll be all right," Mike whispered as she buried her face in his crisp white pilot shirt.

Forty-Three

"YOU MADE IT."

"Welcome back, Chief. I'm so sorry."

"These last few days . . ."

"That must have been something. Yeah, something . . ."

A cadre of people walked by Tris, every one part of the team at Westin Charter, each making a point of saying how glad they were that she was home, despite the horrible personal and immediate loss they'd suffered on top of the disastrous news of two days ago.

Mike said something about heading back to WhisperJet, that he'd call her later. Rex appeared at some point; Tris couldn't remember when. She'd hugged him as he whispered condolences in her ear that she barely heard. It was the tone she was getting used to. "I'm sorry," was spoken so differently when there had been an actual loss, as opposed to a flippant apology someone didn't really want to make.

"This is like a fucking nightmare," one of the senior mechanics at Westin said, as he sucked one cigarette after the other. The Westin hangar was a no smoking area—of course—but today no one said a word or told him to put it out.

Tris wasn't sure how much time had passed. Phyll had moved back to her desk after depositing a box of tissues next to Tris.

Rex was now on the other side of the hangar, talking to one of the airport supervisors who'd stopped by to welcome the Falcon 50 home.

Tris looked around, saw the grief in all the faces of her peers and realized that she'd been a victim of the attacks—and that everyone in that hangar, everyone in aviation had as well.

It was all about the airplane, all the pieces assembled as a workday exercise, a flying bomb which required only ignition to make it explode. She was one of those few specially trained who could make it fly. A pilot. Pilots unwittingly put the bombs in the terrorist's hands. Rampers, fuelers, mechanics, the FAA—they were all co-conspirators.

All had offered Tris their greetings, fist bumps, handshakes, back slaps, and congratulations for flying home—a job well done.

Was it? Terrorists learned to fly at a flight school exactly like the one she'd learned and taught at. They'd taken flight lessons like any other student, logged their flight time, had their training aircraft fueled.

Wasn't everyone who made an airplane ready to fly responsible in some small way?

People moved, amoeba-like, between her, Jannat and Chuck. Jannat still wore her hijab. No one in the Westin hangar looked at Jannat with anything but compassion. Here in this place, she was one of theirs. That was all anyone needed to know.

She stood apart from everyone else, hugging the dark-haired woman in high heels. The two had their cheeks pressed together, and the woman was whispering in Jannat's ear. They held each other in an embrace that was well beyond friendly.

That's it. What Rex meant. She'd almost forgotten Rex's clumsy reference to Jannat's 'lifestyle.' Tris stopped short of drawing any conclusions, but felt she understood her stoic young captain much better than she ever had.

These people around her, who worked long hours, mostly for pay that was well beneath their intelligence and skill, and as in her case, their level of education, to move an airplane from one place to another. Her people.

No. We are not to blame. Those terrorists, they may have taken enough flight instruction to learn how to hit something so big it could not possibly be missed, but they are not part of our family—they are murderers. They are not pilots.

The moment of tragedy that was heaped on more tragedy had passed. Tally the losses, welcome home the bedraggled, put-upon travelers, and return to normal life.

It needs to be done. Take the first step.

It was harder for Tris.

Her losses had names.

Rex sat next to her. He was about to speak, but she held up her hand.

"Rex, I can't."

"Hey Tris?"

"Yes."

"Someday, when the shock of this passes, I'd like to know what it was like being in the air, away from home, while all this happened. What it looked and felt like to be a crew member who left the country before it happened and came back after. Can we talk about that some day?" Rex needed to know, to place himself in it, to connect with the tragedy as experienced by others like himself—to hear her story so he'd be able to tell his own.

"Sure. Some day." She kissed him on the cheek. "I'm so sorry, Rex. I never asked you . . . that day. How hard it must have hit you too. So much loss . . ."

He flashed a quick smile and took her hand. "It brought a lot of pain, but some happiness too. The night of September 11th, I was just out of my mind. It was too late in Edinburgh and, well . . . I called Cali, you know, my ex-wife. We ended up spending the night. All the emotion we were feeling that day made us realize that maybe we weren't done after all. We're giving it another try, Tris. Look, I know what I said . . ."

"I'm happy for you," she said, still sniffling. Rex had found beauty in the ashes and had saved her the emotional effort of ending their relationship.

"Do you think we can stay friends?" he asked, an odd request, since they'd never actually been friends. They'd skipped that part and went straight to benefits.

"Sure Rex. I'd like that."

"Bye Tris," he said, and he was gone.

The crew's welcomers had thinned out and only a few still buzzed around her. She stared at the Westin Charter Company logo above the reception desk.

How in the world would this business go on without Woody?

Ip sidled up to her.

"What can I do for you?"

Her invitation unleashed a torrent. "Well, first of all, your mobile phone is ringing off the hook. Don't you hear it? I mean, it's ringing, like, every ten seconds. Also, well, Jimbo ... he asked me if he could speak to you, like, right now. I know, I know, you want to take a few hours. He says," and Ip, in his best shit-kicking-Texan imitation, drawled, "Why, tell that young lady I need a sit-down with her but fast. We all got some things to talk about."

A sound escaped her, not a laugh, not a cry. Something in between. Jimbo had no idea how to run Westin Charter. "Phyll put us on the calendar for first thing tomorrow. I'll grab a few hours' sleep if I can, but I don't hold out a lot of hope. Ip, what are the ... arrangements for Woody? When? Where?"

He shrugged. "There aren't any. No viewing. He's getting cremated tomorrow. Giselle and the kids are going to have a memorial service for him in a month or so. She'll place his remains in the family niche. She said Woody'd always told her to stuff his ashes in a Hefty bag and dump them on the ramp."

Tris laughed for the first time in days. "Sounds like Woody. I'm going home. Unless there's an emergency ..." She stopped. "Ip, if you need me, call me. Anytime."

"Yes, get some rest."

"Rest? I've got two memorials to plan for."

Forty-Four

"MAMAN, I AM FINE. Fine. Honestly. And Baba?" Her mother's *fesenjan* simmered on the stove and filled the huge home with the smell of pomegranate molasses. Jannat wished she were hungry, but her appetite had not yet returned.

A sad sigh escaped before her mother spoke again. "He's resting. He's fine. A few scratches. Mostly his pride."

"*His* pride? After being attacked? Have you called the police? Has the Imam?"

"Of course not. Why?"

The local police had never wrapped the Muslim community in their warm embrace. In Exeter, minorities were as geographically segregated as they were culturally separate. Shocking when compared to places like New York and Los Angeles. Exeter was home to three million people, all kinds of people. And yet. And still.

How could anyone want to hurt the sweet man who went to his holy place to pray for the dead? The Imam, a family friend, someone Jannat had known her whole life, had walked her father home after the assault. Poor Baba, who every day grieved the death of his family at the hands of a tyrant in a land thousands of miles away; the same man gently brushed aside the tangled hair of his only child when she fell off her bike, making her feel safe, loved, and part of something bigger.

Jannat wondered, not for the first time, when it would ever be enough. When would her family, her friends, the community she grew up in ever have given enough to be thought of as Americans? When would the rest of her country realize that she hurt right along with them?

The mosque had sustained minor fire damage from the Molotov cocktail. According to the Imam, three white men in a pickup truck drove by and threw it in a window. Such a cliché. And then she thought of Chuck. Cliché.

There was no doubt in her mind. Chuck would be the new Chief Pilot of Westin Charter. He was ready. She was not. She'd withdraw from consideration.

"I want to see Baba before I leave."

"Jannat joon, don't wake him. You're going home to Randy. You're going to tell him?"

"Yes, Maman. He has a right to know."

Maman smiled ruefully. "What will become of the big wedding both of your mothers are dreaming about?"

"I don't know, Maman. One step at a time."

***

After readjusting the couch pillows for the third time, Jannat plopped down and waited. Randy was on his way. They'd talked several times in the last twenty-four hours. He was safe, tucked away in the crash pad in Boston.

It was time to be clear, come clean.

She heard the familiar sounds of Randy letting himself into their place. He was home.

How long would it be their home? Would he move out? Would she?

By the time she reached the door, Randy had completed the habitual motions of turning the deadbolt, and then tapping twice on the wood trim that surrounded it. She'd asked him where he'd picked this habit up, and he couldn't recall. Another pilot ritual.

The look in his eyes combined sadness, resignation, and relief. The same set of emotions she was feeling when she put her arms around him. So much taller than she was, Randy rested his chin on the top of her head. There was a picture of them somewhere embracing like this. In it, his expression was unmistakably one of love. She imagined that look on his face now, eyes closed, lips meeting but relaxed, as he hugged her tightly.

"You made it." He said this three times, while moving his hand up and down her back. She didn't doubt that he loved her. She never had.

"You too. We're here."

Finally, he pulled away. "Baby, I'm so sorry about how you were treated by those people. I wish I could have been there to stand by you."

"My crew stood with me," she said proudly.

"How's your father?"

Jannat looked up at the eyes of her fiancé, filled with genuine concern.

Such a good, decent man. So like Baba. He deserves more.

"He has a few scratches. They'll heal. He's not afraid. 'I survived the Ayatollah, I'll survive this,' he said."

Randy's expression turned from concern to disgust. "Those people. Those terrorists.

Jannat headed off that part of the conversation. "Did you get through to your parents?"

"My mother's crazy upset that we didn't get together this week."

"Surely she understands."

Randy shook his head. "I'm not so sure." Then, "Maybe."

"Randy, sit down. Let me get you some tea."

"Sure, baby. Tea."

Jannat stood first at the sink, then the stove, and finally the pantry, and rehearsed the words that would end their relationship. She'd staunched any feelings about it. It was too much. The terrorist attacks. The hatred in people's eyes. Baba. And this.

The two settled into the couch, each sipping from their favorite mugs.

Jannat leaned into Randy's chest, and he held her tightly. A loving and familiar motion that she craved in this moment. She'd hate to lose it, but she'd sacrifice it for the truth.

"Randy." After his name, she couldn't say anything more. He didn't move, adjust himself on the couch or speak. Luckily, he couldn't see her face.

"Randy," she said again. "These last few days, the horror of it all, the magnitude. You saw it. I mean, you know it could have been . . ."

"Us. Yes. It could have been us on any of those airplanes. Repositioning, jump seating . . . any of us."

"I have something to tell you." Slowly, she straightened up, slipped off her engagement ring and placed it on the coffee table's glass top.

"Jannat?"

"Randy, you know we can't get married."

"Yes, we can."

"You don't understand."

"But I do. Jannat, how can you think that I'd ask you to marry me, and not know you?"

"There are things you couldn't possibly know."

He didn't hesitate. "I can't think of anything you'd tell me that would make me love you less. Make me believe that we aren't a great pair. Especially after all of this. Hey, you want to be Chief Pilot, I'm behind you. Whatever you want, Jan. I just want you."

Jannat squeezed his hand.

"I love you. But I . . . You know I'm close to Suzette. She and I have been so close for so long, it was bound to . . ."

Randy looked at his beloved with genuine concern. The way he put his hand on her shoulder made her burst into tears.

"Baby, what is wrong? You're scaring me!" He moved closer. Jannat pulled away and wiped her face on her sleeve.

"I can't do this to you. Suzette is, we're . . . we're involved. We've been intimate. Many times. We're . . ."

Jannat searched Randy's face for some reaction. Shock. Repulsion. Sadness.

Nothing. There was nothing but the practiced non-reaction of the professional pilot.

"You and Suzette?"

She whispered. "Yes."

He nodded. "Are you attracted to me at all?"

"Randy, of course I am. I want to be with you. I want to be your wife. It's not fair, though. I didn't . . . I haven't . . . I've kept this . . ."

Tears welled up in his eyes. "Do you love me?"

She took a deep breath. "I do love you, Randy. I want to be with you. I can't pretend I am one thing, though, when I am . . . more. Aren't we asking to be ridiculed? If people found out?"

"Anyone who'd ridicule you for being who you are, well, they're not a whole lot different from the men who attacked your father, or the terrorists that took down the towers. They hate people for who they are, not what they do, or say. If this week taught me anything, it's that we never know when . . . we have to live the lives we want. I *know* who you are. I'm certain of it. I love you, Jannat."

Randy put his mug down on the oval silver and glass coffee table.

"I guess I assumed that's why we'd chosen each other," he said. "To be ourselves, together. I believed in that. I *still* believe in it." Randy took her hand, the one that no longer wore his ring, and laced his fingers through hers.

"Suzette must stay in my life, Randy. As she has been. Don't you see?"

They sat in silence, eyes closed, breathing synchronized. Eventually, Randy stirred, and Jannat's body took the cue and straightened up.

"Baby, who says we can't live exactly the way we want to? Whatever that is?"

Jannat stammered. "You'd consider . . . you'd still . . . we could . . . ?"

"Yes. Because we love each other. All this talk about 'alternative lifestyles.' Let's make our own, shall we?"

Jannat watched his smile beam with a happiness that mirrored her own. He took the marquis-shaped diamond ring and slid it back on the ring finger of her left hand.

Forty-Five

JIMBO TRIED TO CATCH the quarter he'd been flipping in the air. It popped out of his hand and rolled across Woody's enormous desk.

"Damn. What did Woody need such a big desk for?" The quarter hopped off the desktop and landed on the navy-blue carpeting. Jimbo hated the color. He said so every time he visited. "It hides the dirt," Woody would say to the snickers and head shakes of everyone else. When you own the company, when you've grown it from one airplane and an office the size of a janitor's closet into the largest charter operation at Exeter, you get the carpet you want.

"What a week," Jimbo said again, and Tris could only nod. Exhausted, emotionally spent, aching to be alone with her losses, Tris wished he'd tell her whatever it was he needed to say.

"Jimbo, like you said, it's been a week. You know that I lost someone. On AA 11."

"I heard. I'm so sorry. So. Someone close? Or . . . ?"

How to describe Danny. A good friend. The man who told her

Bron had died. Who grieved with her. Who wanted her, then walked away. Who saved her career—twice. Who made her love him.

He was each and all of those things. One thing was certain: *he* knew her. He'd seen her at her best, stood by her at her worst. Every high, every low.

She'd loved him, this way and that, all along. Now his memory formed yet another chasm in her overburdened heart.

"Yes. A very good friend."

"I'm so sorry. I know it's personal to you, but we all lost something that day."

She could only nod. "You wanted to see me?"

He cleared his throat, noisily. Before he opened his mouth to speak, he cleared it again. "I know you're planning on leaving."

Aviation was a small community. Woody would have had to tell his partner that their Chief Pilot had accepted another job.

"Well, actually," Tris began, but he cut her off.

"All right, young lady. You need to hear this." He cleared his throat again. "Woody had a will. Did you know he had, uh, quite a bit of money?"

"Woody? No. I mean, he dressed like a . . ." She wanted to say bum, but he looked way more disheveled than the guys who slept outside at the airport. "It never showed. He was a modest guy."

Jimbo nodded. "Yeah. He made sure Giselle and the kids were well protected. His share of the business, though . . . he left that outside the family."

"Oh no. To who?"

Jimbo took another quarter out of his pocket and began flipping it through his fingers expertly.

"To you."

"Jimbo, that's . . . unbelievable. Why?"

"He always said, 'Tris, she's not just the brains of this place. She's its beating heart.' Kinda put me off a bit, that talk. I mean, what sorta *guy* says that? Woody did. More than once. Those exact words were in his will. 'Beating heart.' He wanted you to have his share. He couldn't think of anyone else who could run this company." Jimbo cleared his throat. "I sure as hell can't. I'll stay in it if you're in. We have a winning combination, Tris. You and me. Let's air it out and see what this baby can do."

Jimbo spoke in the language of business, which Tris would learn, and she'd teach him how to speak flying.

"What an honor. I don't know what to say."

In the background, she heard shouting. It didn't have that faraway sound, like it was coming from the ramp. Ip's voice was unmistakable.

"She's in a meeting. You can't go back there."

"Tris. *Tris!*" Someone yelled her name.

She jumped up and jerked open the door to Woody's office.

There in the hallway, legs spread, breathing heavily, arms reaching toward her, was a ghost.

Danny.

"Tris." He tried to catch his breath. His chest heaved.

"Danny. How are you here?"

He stood before her and took both of her hands in his. "It doesn't matter. I'm here. And I'm staying. I'm staying right here until you choose me." He looked her in the eye. "I love you. I always have. If you don't feel the same, I'll keep coming back until you do."

The tears that flowed down her cheeks dripped onto her pilot shirt, making little marks in the thick cotton. With both hands she held his face and let her kiss do the talking.

September 11, 2002

Exeter Memorial Park

"*DO YOU LOVE HIM, Flygirl?*"

I'm not surprised by your question. You always know what's on my mind, don't you? You always have.

I was meant to know you, Bron. I'm so grateful for your wisdom. I realize that it was you all along. My dreams. The men I'd loved. The four pathways, the chambers. The final one, for me. It wasn't only about who loved me. It was about loving myself.

It's beautiful today, cool and breezy, your favorite weather. Danny and I paid our respects to Woody, whose remains are a few yards away. It seemed right on the anniversary of his death, and of so many others, to be somewhere we could mourn.

There's a quote below his name, and the date of his death:

"The pain of grief is just as much a part of life as the joy of love; it is, perhaps, the price we pay for love, the cost of commitment."

At the entrance to the garden, right by the fountain, Danny whispered the names of the pilots of AA11, the flying bomb he didn't board. He says their names every day. Every day. He still carries survivor's guilt, and probably always will.

He threw a quarter in the murky water and made a wish. He didn't tell me what he wished for. He didn't have to.

Danny got furloughed from Legacy within a month of the attacks. Who knows when—or if—they'll ever call him back. In the meantime, Mike got him a job at WhisperJet. Mike stepped up for him, for us.

"Your people are your people. They stay your people."

You're right. Mike's one of mine. One of ours.

Danny's daughter is five months old now. Did he tell you? A little girl named Ella. His ex-wife Emily picked the name. Danny got to choose her middle name—Bronwyn. That's how much he loved you.

I hadn't realized that Danny also came to visit you here. I should have guessed.

Danny and I wanted you to be with us, to mourn the dead together. All of them. The first responders, the people in the towers, from top executives to the guy that sold coffee in the lobby. Those men, women, all races and origins. Woody. There simply is not enough sorrow in the world to honor them all.

A year later and I still ask myself if people understand what was lost? Can they process it? Do they care? How can you differentiate someone who does from someone who doesn't? Bron, can you tell me?

The ones who died. Watch over them, Bron.

It took a long time before I could see beyond the tragedy of that day and feel happiness again. My place, where I was meant to be, is Westin Charter. Things work out the way they're supposed to, every time. I had it in my head that I'd steer the careers of so many pilots, so many *women*, who needed to learn how to carry themselves, how to express their ability to command, how to *be* who they really were inside and be pilots too. How much it would mean to other female pilots for me to sit in the cockpit of a major airline, a captain flying the largest jets ever made all over the world.

Success looks different for me now. Every day, running Westin Charter safely, assuring the lives and careers of the team of pilots I've chosen to surround myself with, that's enough.

It's more than enough.

I was able to keep my promise. Now that I'm in charge of the business, I elevated Chuck to Chief Pilot. Jannat is his Assistant. It was an easy choice—she took herself out of the running. She wasn't ready. She will be, though. I'll get her there.

Bron, there will never be a day that I don't wish I could change history, keep you from leaving my apartment that night. I've never stopped loving you. I never will.

As Danny and I stand by your grave with my hand in his, all I can think about is you. What it was that made me love you; why it was that we could not be together. And why you have stayed with me, guided me, long after death.

Danny's eyes are closed, his lips moving silently. I don't want to interrupt him in case he might be praying. Or maybe the two of you are deep in conversation.

I've asked Danny to spend the rest of his life with me. We came to get your blessing.

My love for Danny is different from my love for you. I'm my best, most perfect imperfect self with him; safe, but not in the way that means I've given up, or that I don't want a big career, or a significant life. It's knowing that he will be there when I need him, and he will support me in all my life choices. He loves me that much.

Danny's eyes open when I squeeze his hand.

His voice is soft. "Tris, do you really want to marry me?"

The wind picks up. In a swift gust, you ask me again. *Flygirl, do you love him?"*

Thank you for this second chance. Thank you for guiding my heart, for giving me the strength to finally say the right words.

"Yes. Yes, I do."

Author's Notes & Acknowledgments

I ALWAYS KNEW that I would write about the impact 9/11 had on me and my fellow pilots, but revisiting the event was unthinkable for a very long time. It took me over two years to complete a first draft of this book primarily because I knew I'd have to face head on the memories that haunted me. I'm glad I did, I'm glad I wrote this book, and I'm glad I could finally look those demons in the eye. I only hope I've satisfactorily honored both the people who lost their lives that day, and those whose lives, like my own, were forever changed.

During the worst of the COVID restrictions, my writing sanctuary, San Diego Writers, Ink., held online read & critique groups. I was fortunate to share early versions of this book with author Mark A. Clements and other participants. I'd like to thank Jennifer Karp, poet extraordinaire, for her early critique. I trust this book appropriately honors the memory of Phyllis Young, a group member whose comments were particularly salient, but who passed away before the book was finished.

There are no more important contributors to a published book than its editors. For their efforts, I'm deeply indebted to Alexandra Shelley and Jennifer Silva Redmond. Alexandra studied early outlines of the book, and her suggestions were both motivating and transcendent. Jennifer was the first to read an early version, and her feedback encouraged me to keep going. She performed both developmental and line edits, the most important and exacting of reviews, and truly helped me get my prose to hum.

I am honored that Beverly Weintraub, Dr. Jacqueline Boyd, Gene Desrochers, Dennis K. Crosby, Laura L. Engel, David Reed and Julie Tizard, agreed to read non-final versions of this book, and provide cover quotes.

Bev is a Pulitzer Prize winning journalist, winning that august award for editorial work she did at the *New York Daily News,* a constant presence during my youth. Dr. Boyd has been a tireless advocate for women in the flying world through her work with the 99's and the Amelia Earhart Scholarship Fund. Thank you both for your contributions to this project.

Jessica Therrien and Holly Kammier of Acorn Publishing Ltd. have once again hit a grand slam with this book's cover. I'm grateful for their insight and support throughout the publication of all three of my books.

One day, I discovered a Facebook group called "Aviatrix Book Club," started by a retired Coast Guard helicopter pilot who was writing her first book. The founder, Elizabeth "Liz" Booker, has been a constant presence in my writing life ever since, and through her tireless efforts to highlight women writing about women in aviation, inspires me every day. Her support of my work has truly lifted me, as has the community she created.

No author can get to the finish line without the contributions of friends and family. For that, thanks to Mitchell Kardon, who did a close read of an early draft and pointed out errors no one else caught; Barbara Shaw, who has been my biggest cheerleader since *Flygirl* was published; and Jennifer Coburn, who encourages me in ways she doesn't even realize. I'm extremely grateful to Negin Mirmirani and Laleh Mohseni for helping me understand Persian culture. Thank you, Amy Reder, Mimi Loucks and Robyn Frank for your continued interest in my work.

The *Flygirl* Trilogy is finished, but I'm not. Until we meet again . . .

About the Author

Studio Bijou Photography

ROBIN D. "R.D." KARDON is a native New Yorker, educated in the New York City Public school system. She attended New York University where she earned a B.A. in Journalism and Sociology, magna cum laude, and was a member of Phi Beta Kappa. Robin graduated with a J.D. from the American University, Washington College of Law.

After ten years as a litigator, Robin began her professional flying career. She holds an FAA Airline Transport Pilot certificate with three captain qualifications and has flown all over the world in everything from single-engine Cessnas to the Boeing 737.

She currently resides in San Diego where she volunteers with local animal rescue organizations and dotes on her beloved rescue pets.

Follow Robin at
rdkardonauthor.com
@rdkardonauthor

Praise for **The Flygirl Trilogy**
*by **R. D. Kardon***

"Kardon's narrative is both thoughtful and gripping. She vividly portrays the fine line between respect and familiarity that women in nontraditional roles must walk to do their jobs well in the face of sexual harassment on one hand and antagonistic resistance on the other. Tris is an appealing and relatable character who struggles to keep both her self-respect and her ambition intact while negotiating the slippery morality of the corporate world." —**Kirkus Reviews**

"[This] exciting, spirited debut [Flygirl] follows a new female pilot as she vies to move up to the captain's seat . . . This soaring testament to the value of following one's dreams delivers the goods." —**Publishers Weekly**

"Kardon creates a relatable heroine in Tris, a character who, along with her grit and determination to succeed, displays a range of authentic emotions and vulnerabilities . . .[I]interpersonal conflicts and the heroine's clear aspirations result in a satisfying narrative arc." —**The Booklife Prize**

*"[**Flygirl** is] a wonderful piece of writing with a bit of history and real-world issues laced throughout."* —**The Indie Express**

"Well written and interesting, [Kardon] tells the truth about those times." —**Texas Book Nook**

"R. D. Kardon is such an imaginative and descriptive storyteller." —**On a Reading Bender**

*"**Angel Flight** is a fabulous piece of writing about important issues."* —**Novel News Network**

*"**Angel Flight** is one-part adventure, one-part romance and two parts nail-biter. Shake it all up, pour and sit yourself down to a satisfying read that will stay with you and leave you clamoring for more."* —**Robyn F., Goodreads Reviewer**

*"**Angel Flight** launches the reader out of the hangar and into the

fascinating world of commercial aviation on the wings of Tris Miles, a powerful and inspiring character. R. D. Kardon uses the drama and intensity of flight as the perfect stage for this exciting and emotional story, laced with psychological tension." —**Gene Desrochers**, author of **Dark Paradise** and **Sweet Paradise**

*"Readers will love **Angel Flight** with its masterful subplot and five-star suspense! R. D. Kardon's sequel to her acclaimed novel Flygirl follows Tris Miles as she continues her quest to break aviation's gender barriers. **Angel Flight** is a fascinating look at the psychological burdens borne by professionals whose most sacred responsibility is the safety of their passengers. Tris walks a tightrope as she juggles love, loyalty, and her own mental well-being."* —**Mike Murphey**, author of **Section Roads** and **The Conman, a Baseball Odyssey**

*"One of my tests for the legitimacy of a character in a novel is that I must have yelled at them before I finish. Did I yell at Tris Miles in Book 1: **Flygirl**? I certainly did. And again, in Book 2: **Angel Flight**, yes, I yelled at her. In the third of the series, **Flying Home**, Kardon's writing sucked me so far into the continuing story that I yelled at the entire crew. The situations that Kardon creates . . . are tremendously realistic, not sugar-coated or overly dramatic—simply real . . . I don't want this series to end."* —**Jacqueline Boyd, PhD, Chair Amelia Earhart Memorial Scholarship Fund**

*"**Flying Home** by R. D. Kardon is a gripping story, haunted by echoes of the past and overlaid with a sense of foreboding as the clock ticks down to the one of the darkest days in the nation's history. Kardon brings the reader inside the mind of an accomplished pilot as she struggles to make the toughest decisions of her professional and personal lives"* —**Beverly Weintraub, Winner of The Pulitzer Prize** and author of **Wings of Gold: The Story of the First Women Naval Aviators**

*"Spellbinding! R. D. Kardon had me hooked on page one of **Flying Home,** the final installment of The **Flygirl** Trilogy. I was captured in a gripping, methodically woven story web, a turbulent ride centered around compelling characters, where everything changes on one fateful day. A real page turner: I couldn't put it down."* —**David W. Reed**, author of **Uphill And Into The Wind**

*"I loved reading **Flying Home**. R.D. Kardon captures the drama, action, and joy of flying as only a professional pilot can. I can't wait for her next book!"* —**Col. Julie Tizard, USAFR (ret.),** author of **The Road to Wings** and **Free Fall at Angel Creek**